Montana ★ MAVERICKS™

Welcome to Whitehorn, Montana—the home of bold men and daring women. A place where rich tales of passion and adventure are unfolding under the Big Sky. Seems that this charming little town has some mighty big secrets. And everybody's talking about...

Suzanne Paxton: This mystery woman showed up in Whitehorn with no warning, and she's taken the Kincaid ranch by storm. She was supposed to stay just a few days, but Ms. Paxton shows no signs of leaving....

Rand Harding: Where did this lonesome cowboy find this pretty little houseguest? Everyone thought ol' Rand was a confirmed bachelor. Maybe everyone was wrong!

J. D. Cade: Another mysterious drifter. What drew him to Whitehorn? And why does he seem to know so much about the town?

Montana
★ MAVERICKS™

JACKIE MERRITT
Letter to a Lonesome Cowboy

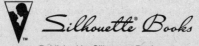

Silhouette® Books

Published by Silhouette Books

America's Publisher of Contemporary Romance

Special thanks and acknowledgment to Jackie Merritt for her contribution to the Montana Mavericks series.

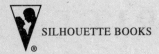

SILHOUETTE BOOKS

ISBN-13: 978-0-373-36207-3

Recycling programs
for this product may
not exist in your area.

LETTER TO A LONESOME COWBOY

Visit Silhouette Books at www.eHarlequin.com

Printed in U.S.A.

JACKIE MERRITT

is still writing, just not with the speed and constancy of years past. She and her husband are living in southern Nevada again, falling back on old habits of loving the long, warm or slightly cool winters and trying almost desperately to head north for the months of July and August, when the fiery sun bakes people and cacti alike.

One

In a small apartment in Baltimore, Maryland, Suzanne Paxton, a pretty, dark-haired young woman, wept quietly in her bedroom. She'd lost her job two weeks before, not because she was an incompetent accountant, but because the company had become so computerized employees were no longer necessary. Well, some were necessary, but she wasn't. Downsizing, they called it. Suzanne had a few other words in mind when she thought of it, but they were words she rarely spoke out loud and certainly not in anyone's hearing.

But she'd already wept because of that; her tears tonight were because she hadn't been able to find another job, and she'd been trying so hard. What was going to become of her and her fourteen-year-old brother, Mack? She'd taken Mack in two years ago when their parents were killed in a car accident. She'd been married then, but six months of Mack had been enough to destroy her marriage. Oh, the breakup hadn't been *all* Mack's fault. Suzanne wasn't dense, and she'd known for a long time before Mack moved in that her husband, Les, had been falling out of love with her. In fact, she believed wholeheartedly that Les had used Mack's intrusion into their life as an excuse for him to walk out of it.

Well, she was over her failure of a marriage but she was definitely not over losing her job. She was the sole support of Mack and herself. Les hadn't stuck around Baltimore long enough to see the final divorce papers, but even if he lived right next door he was a slippery devil, and Suzanne knew she would never receive a dime of the alimony the judge had ordered Les to pay her.

Every time Suzanne wept these days, for whatever reason, some of her tears were because she couldn't control Mack. At fourteen, he knew it all. He skipped school whenever he felt like it, he was a slob around the house, he picked fights with other kids and he stayed out till all hours of the night. Whenever Suzanne tried to talk to him about his behavior, he told her, "Leave me alone, you're not my mother."

It was true, of course, and she knew Mack was still grieving their parents' deaths. But so was she, and a boy of Mack's nature was darned hard to handle for a twenty-four-year-old sister.

Life was the pits, Suzanne thought while choking out another sob. She had a modest savings account, but how long would that last? There was rent and utilities to pay, and food to buy. Insurance, gas and maintenance for her six-year-old car were crucial, and Mack was growing at such a rapid pace he always needed new clothes.

Hearing the apartment's front door slam loudly, Suzanne quickly wiped the tears from her face. Mack was home, and she hoped he was in a good mood, because she simply could not deal with one more problem tonight.

"Mack, is that you?" Suzanne called out. She heard sneakered feet approaching the bedroom and quickly dried her eyes and nose with a tissue.

"Of course it's me. Who else is it going to be?" Mack greeted her in his usual tone, a mixture of boredom and surliness.

He stood in her bedroom doorway, his lanky arms crossed over his chest. He was dressed in his usual outfit—baggy jeans, a gray hooded sweatshirt and a battered Baltimore Orioles baseball cap, with a blue knapsack hanging off his shoulders. Suzanne could never figure out what he carried around in it. She doubted it was filled with schoolbooks since he rarely, if ever, did homework. Being totally honest with herself, she realized that she didn't want to know.

"Did you have anything to eat yet? There's some chicken in the fridge. I could make you a sandwich," Suzanne offered.

"I ate at Kip's," Mack replied. He studied her face, and Suzanne self-consciously wiped her fingers over her damp eyes.

"My allergies went haywire today. Guess spring is really here."

"Yeah, allergies. Bad news," Mack replied. His expression told her that he didn't believe her excuse. Yet, neither did he ask why she'd been crying. "I'm going to watch TV in my room," he said, and turned down the hall. "Good night."

"Good night," Suzanne called after him. She heard his bedroom door shut and then the sound of the small portable set filtered through the thin wall that separated their rooms. Suzanne closed her own bedroom door and sighed. Well, at least there hadn't been any heavy scenes between them tonight.

Mack flopped down on his bed and stared blankly at the TV screen. His thoughts wandered.

Sometimes Mack felt bad about the disagreements with his sister, but she was constantly on his back about something. He was fourteen, for hell's sake, not four!

At least she hadn't tortured him with some dumb lecture about cleaning up his room or getting better grades. He'd probably go crazy living around here if not for his friend Kip Dingle. Kip was the only real friend Mack had made in the two years he'd lived with Suzanne. They'd become friends after a terrible fistfight because Mack had made fun of Kip's name. "Are you sure you ain't related to Kriss Kringle?" Mack had taunted. Kip had come at him with balled fists, and Mack had been ready. They'd fought themselves into exhaustion, bloodying each other's noses and slamming teeth into cheeks and lips, and finally, too tired to throw one more punch, they'd lain flat out on the ground to catch their breaths.

After that they'd started talking and ended up buddies, but even Kip didn't know everything there was to know about Mack. Some things were just too private to talk about, Mack believed. This evening, however, that attitude had changed, although even Mack himself didn't realize it until it happened.

Tonight at Kip's house, after they were in Kip's bedroom, away from his parents' eyes, Mack had pulled a magazine from under his jacket.

"What's that?" Kip asked.

Mack looked a bit sheepish. "A western magazine. I filched it from the newsstand. There's something in it I want you to hear."

Kip made a face. "A western magazine? When'd you start reading those things?"

"Do you wanna hear it or don't 'cha?" Mack demanded belligerently.

"Well, sure, you don't have to come unglued. What is it?"

Mack flipped to the back pages of the magazines and sat on the edge of Kip's bed. "Listen to this. 'If you're a single lady between twenty-five and thirty, honest, clean, a non-smoker and reasonably attractive, write to this Lonesome Cowboy. Kincaid Ranch, Box 16, Whitehorn, Montana.'"

"So?" Kip said.

"What d'ya mean, so? This guy's looking for a wife."

Kip chortled. "I don't think you're what he's got in mind, Paxton."

"You moron, I'm thinking of my sister."

"Your sister! You're the moron if you think Suzanne would write to a jerk who calls himself a lonesome cowboy."

"I know." Mack suddenly grinned. "That's why I'm gonna answer this ad for her. Wanna help?"

Kip stared for a minute, then laughed. "Sure, why not?"

And so the two boys composed a letter they both rated "excellent," and increased Suzanne's chances of receiving an answer by enclosing a snapshot of a scantily clad pinup girl.

Mack read the last paragraph out loud. "I am enclosing a picture of myself so you will know what I look like. Please answer right away. I'm dying to know your name, Lonesome Cowboy, and if it's at all possible, please send a picture of yourself. Hugs and kisses from a lonesome lady in Baltimore, Suzanne Paxton."

Kip collapsed on the bed in a spasm of giggles. "That guy will fall over when he reads that letter and sees that picture."

"That's the whole idea," Mack said, extremely proud of their effort. "Got an envelope?"

"Suzanne's gonna kill you."

"Nope, she won't. She's all alone, except for me, she's out of a job and can't find another one, and I'm solving all her problems with this letter. She won't kill me, she'll thank me."

"Well, I guess you know your own sister," Kip said.

"Yep, guess I do. Now, I'm gonna let you in on a little secret, but first you have to swear you won't tell another living soul."

"Jeez, Paxton, what'd you do now?"

"Can it, Dingle. Do you wanna hear my secret or not?"

"Okay, I swear it will never pass my lips."

"Good enough. Okay, here it is. I've always wanted to go west and live on a ranch. A *big* ranch, with cows and horses and real cowboys. Once my folks took us on a vacation out west and we stayed over at a real ranch for almost a week. It was way cool."

Kip's mouth dropped open. "You'd really leave Baltimore?"

"Kip," Mack said earnestly, "I have to leave Baltimore. Either that or I'm gonna end up in jail. I know it, you know it, Suzanne knows it. She'll jump at the chance to get us out of here."

Nothing was said for a long moment, then Kip nodded his acceptance of Mack's attitude. "You're probably right, Mack, you're probably right."

This year, spring was as raw and rough as chapped hands. Bundled up against the cold wind, Rand Harding, foreman of the Kincaid Ranch, scowled down at the mutilated heifer lying in a shallow ditch about a quarter mile from the compound. The two men who had run across the animal and then notified Rand nervously shifted from foot to foot and mumbled to each other about devil worshipers and UFOs.

Rand gritted his teeth and glanced at the two men with open disgust. Every weird incident on the ranch—and the events *were* starting to add up—incited the ranch hands' imaginations. They came up with the most ridiculous reasons—in Rand's opinion—for accidents and dead animals, including ghosts, of all things.

"The person or persons who did this are as human as the three of us," Rand said flatly. He walked to his horse. "Bury it."

Both men backed away, refusing to touch the carcass. Rand knew what was coming next, and his gut knotted. He was right, because they both quit on the spot.

Rand turned to face the men. He'd been losing cowhands left and right, and it was getting harder all the time to replace them. Word was getting around the area, people were talking: something strange was happening on the Kincaid Ranch.

Well, the gossips weren't wrong. Something strange *was* going on, but the incidents were not caused by aliens or ghosts, and every time Rand heard someone express such a ludicrous explanation, he saw red.

"Didn't think you two were cowards," he said, looking each man in the eye. They flushed and stared off into the distance, but they each bore a stubborn expression that Rand had come to recognize. They wanted to get off the Kincaid Ranch as fast as possible, and nothing he could say would change their minds.

"Forget it," he said gruffly, turning to pick up the reins of his horse. "I'll tell George to draw up your final checks." George Davenport was the ranch's bookkeeper, and he lived in the large, two-story bunkhouse that everyone else on the place called home.

Mounted, Rand pointed his horse toward the compound. From behind he could hear the men scrambling to get on their own horses. Another two down, Rand thought with worry gnawing at his vitals. He'd already been operating with a short crew, and now this. Someone was definitely up to no good, but he sure wasn't a ghost and he wasn't swooping down onto Kincaid land from a flying saucer, either.

Rand puzzled over it all the way back to the compound, exactly as he'd done many times in the past few months. Who was that "someone," and what was his reason for causing so much trouble?

Tethering his horse near the bunkhouse, Rand dismounted and went inside.

The cook, Handy Olsen, the bookkeeper, George Davenport, and Rand used three of the downstairs bedrooms, the crew all slept upstairs. There were too damned many empty bedrooms in the bunkhouse, one on the first level and a good half dozen on the second. Now there would be two more. Rand's expression was grim when he walked into the office and addressed George.

"Joe and Russ quit. Make up their final checks. They'll be in to get them in a few minutes."

George laid his pipe in the ashtray on his desk and gave a brief, wry nod of his head. He was pushing sixty, a lifetime bachelor and shared Rand's disdainful attitude toward ghosts and mysterious beings from outer space. Handy, the cook, was also an older man, and in Handy's own words, "No danged ghost is gonna chase me off this ranch." Rand honestly wished he could find enough older men with good old-fashioned common sense to man his entire crew.

"What happened to send Joe and Russ packin'?" George asked.

"It's the same old story, George. We found another dead heifer. Joe and Russ seem to think there's something supernatural about it. They want to leave, so let 'em. I'm tired of half-wits. Get their checks ready right away."

"Will do," George said.

Rand was getting too warm in his outdoor gear. "See you later." He went back outside and breathed in the stingingly cold air. Winter wasn't letting go this year. It was April, and while Montana weather could be unpredictable, one could usually count on warmer temperatures by this time of year.

Rand's gaze fell on the old Kincaid mansion, vacant since the day he came to work on the ranch. All the Kincaids were dead, except for one tiny girl that had been adopted by Sterling and Jessica McCallum. Sterling and a lawyer named Wendell Hargrove managed the child's estate, and Rand had been hired by Sterling. He reported ranch business to both men, who were as concerned about the accidents, or whatever they were, occurring on the ranch as Rand. Standing outside the bunkhouse, Rand wondered if he should call one of them now and relate the latest incident.

He released a heavy sigh. There was nothing Wendell or Sterling could do about the dead heifer. Hell, there was nothing *he* could do beyond burying it. As a matter of fact, if he was going to call anyone, it should be Reed Austin, the deputy sheriff who'd come out to the ranch a few times to investigate some of the incidents. Maybe he'd do that later, Rand thought while mounting his horse. But first things first. Right now, getting that carcass underground so it wouldn't attract hungry predators took priority over anything else.

Riding away from the buildings, Rand headed for the southernmost range, where the rest of his crew was moving cattle. His lips set tightly as he wondered how many more men would quit before this was over.

The ranch settled down early at night. While the other men snored in their beds, Rand walked the floor. He had called Reed Austin before supper, and they'd had a lengthy conversation, which kept running through Rand's mind.

"I'll drive out there if you want me to," Reed had offered after Rand told him about the latest strange event.

"Reed, I appreciate your offer, but what good would it do? I'll tell you, man, I'm mad as hell about this. Someone is deliberately trying to undermine this operation, and for what reason? What possible gain would anyone receive from ruining this ranch?"

"Stay cool, Rand," Reed had advised. "Even if you discover who's doing it, don't take the law into your own hands."

Rand had grimaced. He was not a violent man, never had been. But there were moments when he'd just love to get his big hands on the bastard killing valuable animals and wrecking ranch equipment. And there'd been a couple of fires, as well—one in the middle of a pasture and the other right behind the barn. If someone hadn't spotted the one so close to the barn before the flames had gone wild, the entire compound could have burned to the ground.

But Reed was right. If this were Rand's own ranch, he might do things differently. As it was, Sterling McCallum was a high-ranking officer in the Whitehorn Police Department, and at the very first sign of trouble on the ranch, Sterling had told Rand to notify the sheriff's department, as this was county business.

Reed Austin had been assigned the case. He was a smart young officer, and Rand had liked him on sight. Unquestionably the fires had been set, but as Reed had said more than once, there wasn't a shred of evidence pointing to any specific person.

On the phone this afternoon Reed had said it again, but this time had added, "I've done a lot of thinking about the matter, Rand. My belief is that our perpetrator is someone who is living right under your nose."

"One of my men?" Instantly everyone on the ranch flashed through Rand's mind. Besides himself, there were a half-dozen men who'd been on the ranch from the very first incident. Plus Handy and George, of course, but Rand would trust either of them with his life. The rest of the crew were too new to come under suspicion. "I've considered that possibility before, Reed, but I could never bring myself to believe that any of the hands who've stayed throughout this mess could be causing it."

"It *could* be someone else," Reed agreed. "Just keep your eyes and ears open."

Rand thanked the deputy and promised to call if anything else happened. Weary of mulling the whole miserable mess over and over again, he went in search of something to read. The first floor of the building contained a modern kitchen and laundry, a large dining room, an office, three bathrooms and four bedrooms. The upper level was all single-size bedrooms and full-size bathrooms, except for one larger room where the men could play cards, watch television or just sit around and talk or read in their off time. He'd read all the books and magazines in his bedroom, so he climbed the stairs to the second floor and walked into the great room, where he thumbed through the variety of magazines lying around.

Ignoring the girlie mags, he took one with a western theme. He noticed from the cover it was a brand-new issue. Downstairs in his room, he undressed to his briefs and undershirt, then crawled into bed. He adjusted the lamp for reading, stacked his pillows and opened the magazine.

He read an interesting article about the history of branding irons, then yawned and desultorily flipped through the remaining pages of the magazine. At the very back of the publication were three pages of ads. He scanned quickly until he found the one he was looking for—his own.

Although he'd heard of mail-order brides before, he'd had no idea the custom was still alive and apparently thriving until two weeks ago, when he'd first seen these ads. Imagine all those lonely cowboys advertising for wives!

But what kind of man would settle for a loveless union just because he was lonely? he'd thought at first.

Rand had frowned. What kind of man *wouldn't* prefer a loveless marriage over living alone? In fact, the men who had placed these ads could be very much like himself. Two years ago, a good year before he'd come to the Whitehorn area to look for work, he'd been in love, engaged and deliriously happy. His job then had been on a ranch, too, a ranch that lay sixty miles from the nearest town. Sherry, his fiancée, had known from their first meeting that ranching was his career, but she hadn't said one word about it until three days before their wedding date. Then she'd hit him with a bomb.

"Rand, darling, I've found the cutest house to rent, and Larry Miller is looking for a man to oversee his feedlot. I've already talked to him, and he's very anxious to interview you."

Rand stared at his beloved as though struck from behind.

"Sherry, we're going to live on the ranch. The owner has even given me permission to move into one of the little houses reserved for married men. Honey, I've taken you out there. I thought you liked the ranch."

"Well, I don't, and I'm not going to live sixty miles from my friends and family. What on earth would I do way out there all day, every day? Be realistic, Rand."

Yeah, Rand thought wryly, be realistic. If he hadn't been before that evening, he sure as hell had been afterward. When he hadn't caved in and agreed to move to town and take that job in Miller's Feedlot, Sherry had angrily called off their wedding. About three months later he'd heard through the grapevine that she had gotten married. So much for love.

Truth was, he didn't want to fall in love ever again.

But neither did he want to live out his life all alone.

The more he thought about it, the better those ads sounded. In fact, they seemed downright sensible. Any woman answering these ads would have the same attitude toward love and marriage as the men who had written them. She would be a down-to-earth person, a woman with commonsense values and enough brains to know that companionship was far more important than romance.

It had taken Rand about ten minutes to decide. The first thing he thought of was what *he* had to offer a potential wife. Number one, he was a hard worker and would always have a steady job, if not on the Kincaid Ranch, then on another. Secondly, he was young, only thirty-two, and pretty darned good-looking, if he had to say so himself. He was tall and lean, with thick, almost black hair and deep blue eyes. He couldn't call himself a ladies' man, but women didn't daunt him. He'd never had any trouble in talking to them, or in getting a date back in the days when he'd wanted a girlfriend.

He was honest and only cussed once in a while, unlike some of the ranch hands who couldn't complete an entire sentence without substituting obscenities for every adjective, adverb and a lot of the nouns. He didn't smoke or drink—well, maybe a beer now and then—and while he wasn't a churchgoer, he believed in the Almighty and lived accordingly. Actually, Rand decided, he would be a darned good catch for some lonely gal.

Yep, two weeks ago it had seemed like a great idea. But now that he'd seen his ad in black-and-white, somehow he wasn't so sure....

Two

Rand took the handful of mail from the mailbox and quickly thumbed through it. He'd been watching the incoming mail very closely, thinking one minute that no one would answer his ad and certain the next that someone would.

At last, Rand thought with a quickening of his pulse. Today's mail included an envelope that he knew was an answer to his ad. He read the return address: Suzanne Paxton, Baltimore, MD. *Suzanne* suddenly seemed like the loveliest of feminine names, and, sitting in his pickup, he rolled up the window and slid his finger under the sealed flap of the envelope.

A photo fell to his lap as he extracted a folded sheet of paper. Rand picked it up and could hardly believe his eyes. This sexy, beautiful girl was Suzanne? "Holy smoke," he mumbled, thinking that he'd hit the jackpot for sure. After reading Suzanne's letter, he felt almost light-headed. The lady was *more* than interested, she was eager!

Turning the truck around so fast its tires spun, he headed back to the compound. Before he did one other thing he was going to answer Suzanne's letter. And he wasn't going to wait for tomorrow's mail delivery to send it off, either. He would drive to town and take it to the post office. He might even send it one-day delivery service so the luscious Ms. Paxton would get it tomorrow.

Parking near the bunkhouse, Rand was out of the truck before the engine had completely quit running. Dashing inside, he dropped the other mail on George's desk, mumbled something about being in a hurry and all but ran to his bedroom, where he closed the door, shrugged out of his jacket and sat at his small desk to begin his letter.

Dear Suzanne,
Your letter is a dream come true. You sound, and look, exactly like the type of woman I've been hoping to meet. I can't thank you enough for answering my ad.

Let me tell you a little about myself. I've always worked in ranching, and presently I'm the foreman of the Kincaid Ranch. It's a beautiful place, with breathtaking scenery in every direction. You said you've been longing for the wide open spaces, and you would certainly find them here.

You've probably been wondering why I felt the need to advertise for a wife. There are single women in the area—many of them—but I'm not looking for romance, Suzanne. I'm looking for a woman with both feet firmly planted on the ground, a woman with pragmatic views on marriage, a woman with old-fashioned ideals and one major desire—to marry for companionship, a good home and a husband who will always support her. I would like to have children someday and hope you feel the same on that point.

I have enclosed a snapshot of myself. I'm thirty-two years old, six-feet-one-inch tall and weigh one-ninety. From your photo, you are obviously a very beautiful woman. I hope my photo measures up to yours in your eyes.

Please answer right away. I will be watching the mail every day for your letter. One thing more. If traveling money is a problem, let me know. I would be honored to send you enough to cover airfare and incidentals.
Sincerely yours,
Rand Harding

Rand read his letter twice, then folded it, and inserted it and his snapshot into an envelope, which he sealed and addressed.

Yanking on his jacket, he stuffed the envelope into a pocket, then hurried away to tell George he had to go to town. "I'll be back in a few hours."

George merely nodded, and Rand quickly left the bunkhouse to climb into his truck. He hadn't felt this excited in a very long time, and he drove to Whitehorn with his eyes on the road and his thoughts on Suzanne Paxton. Good fortune was smiling on him today, that was certain.

Rand wasn't back at the ranch five minutes when a four-wheel-drive vehicle pulled into the compound. The vehicle was unfamiliar, though it bore Montana plates. Rand strolled over to the truck. Its driver, a stranger, got out just as Rand approached.

"Hello," the man said.

Rand nodded. "Hello."

The stranger was as tall as himself and had a lean, wiry build. He was dressed like Rand, in jeans, boots, hat and heavy jacket. Although the hat covered most of the man's hair, what showed below it was a pale, silvery color. Rand judged this unexpected visitor to be several years past forty.

The man smiled slightly. "I think I'm lost."

"Where are you heading?"

"A little town called Whitehorn."

"Oh, well, you're not far from your destination." As Rand recited directions to town, he noticed the man's gaze sweeping the compound, as though he was trying to take in everything at once.

He seemed to be staring at the big, empty house. "Nice place you've got here."

"I only work here. I'm the foreman. This is the Kincaid Ranch, but there are no Kincaids living on it. The house is vacant. All the hands and such live in the bunkhouse." Rand figured it was time they introduced themselves, and he offered his hand. "Rand Harding."

The man noticeably hesitated, and Rand felt a little silly standing there with his hand out. But then the stranger shook it and stammered, "Uh, J.D., uh, J. D. Cade."

"Nice meeting you, J.D. By any chance, you wouldn't be looking for work, would you?"

J.D.'s gaze returned to the house. Rand suddenly got the strangest sensation, almost a premonition. "Have you been here before?"

J.D.'s head snapped around. "Never been in this part of Montana at all till today. You got a job to fill?"

Rand snorted out a short laugh. "More than one, J.D. I'm going to be honest with you. There've been some mighty strange happenings out here, and I've been losing men over it. Have you ever worked on a ranch?"

"Yeah, I have."

"Well, you don't look to me like a man who'd run from trouble. Are you interested in that job?"

"What kind of trouble are you talking about?" J.D. asked.

The intensity with which J.D. looked into his eyes startled Rand, although he maintained an impassive expression. There was something different about J. D. Cade, something Rand couldn't get a handle on. He had no choice but to believe J.D. hadn't been in this area before, and yet there remained the question of how a Montana man, even a stranger to these parts, could get lost looking for Whitehorn and end up at the Kincaid Ranch.

Putting that niggling doubt aside for the time being, Rand braced himself to answer J.D.'s question. He hadn't yet lied to any man about the unexplainable events on the ranch and he wasn't going to start now. He related the strange events, then added, "Been quiet for a couple of weeks now, and I keep hoping it's over, but I can't guarantee it, J.D."

"Why do you think this particular ranch was targeted for sabotage?" J.D. asked. "Or have other places been bothered, too?"

"None that I know of, just this place. I like your word *sabotage.* It's logical, at least. A lot hasn't been in the past few months. Some of the hands that quit thought we were being invaded by UFOs, others laid the incidents on ghosts."

"Ghosts! Good Lord," J.D. muttered. "*Whose* ghosts?"

"The Kincaid family had some troubled times," Rand explained. "Some people say…" Rand abruptly stopped himself from repeating the silly gossip. J. D. Cade stared at him intensely, but said nothing.

"Listen, I have no idea why this particular ranch is targeted, and neither does anyone else," Rand continued. "Frankly, we're getting quite a reputation in the area, which I'm sure you'll hear in great detail if you're going to be in Whitehorn very long."

"Well," J.D. drawled with another look around the compound, "I intend hanging around awhile, but maybe it'll be out here instead of in town."

"You'll take the job?"

"Don't know for how long, Rand, but yes, I'll take the job."

"Great! I'll take you to meet the bookkeeper, and he'll get the payroll data out of the way. You can move your things into any empty bedroom on the second floor and start work in the morning. That okay with you?"

"It's okay with me," J.D. said.

At supper that evening Rand introduced his new hand. "Everyone, this is J. D. Cade. He's starting work in the morning."

Some of the men said hello and then started eating. Rand pulled out a chair next to his for J.D. "Dive in, J.D. Handy's a pretty good cook."

"Thanks," J.D. said.

Dale Carson sat across the table. Dale had worked on the ranch almost as long as Rand had. Rand considered the young man a good hand, although he wasn't overly bright. But he had a strong back, a willingness to work hard, an open, honest face and had been raised on a ranch. The Carson family had lost their land years ago, and from what Rand had heard from Dale himself, Dale wanted to earn enough money to one day buy his own ranch. Rand thought the young man's goal to be admirable, very much like his own. Someday Rand, too, would like to be the proud possessor of his own land and cattle operation.

Dale started asking J.D. questions. "Where do you hail from, J.D.?"

J.D. glanced at the younger man. "Here and there," he replied calmly.

To Rand, that sort of answer to a question was a signal to drop the subject. But Dale proved again that he was a little light in the upper story by pressing on. "You've got Montana plates. Where'd you live before coming here?"

J.D. merely sent Dale a noncommittal look. Regardless, Dale continued his interrogation. "What does J.D. stand for? What's your real name?"

Apparently J.D. had had enough. "Listen, fella, if I wanted everyone to know my business I'd put it in the newspaper."

No one at the table said a word, not even Dale. Rand continued eating, but chuckled inwardly. He liked J.D.'s ways, even if J.D. did seem to possess an air of mystery. Obviously the man was intelligent, and if he wanted to keep his affairs to himself, it was fine with Rand. He suspected, gleefully, that he'd hired a darned good man today. Only time would tell, of course, but right now Rand would bet anything that J. D. Cade knew his way around a cattle ranch as well as he did.

The following morning Mack left the apartment for school, hid behind a long line of garages and waited until his sister drove away in her ongoing quest for a job. Then he returned to the apartment and let himself in. He liked being home alone. Turning on the television set, he made an enormous, triple-decker sandwich, poured a huge glass of cola and settled down in the most comfortable chair in the living room.

He was still watching TV two hours later when the doorbell rang. "Yipes," he muttered. Should he answer the door? Maybe a nosy neighbor had heard the TV and was coming by to check up. He'd been caught doing this before and Suzanne had thrown a fit.

Mack tiptoed to the door and peered through the peephole. The postman! Hastily he undid the locks and yanked the door open.

"Delivery for Suzanne Paxton," the uniformed postal worker said.

"She's my sister. I'll take it."

"Sign here, please."

Mack scrawled his signature and took possession of a large express-mail envelope. "Thanks, man," he said, and shut the door. He nearly shouted with glee when he saw the return address: Rand Harding, Kincaid Ranch, Whitehorn, Montana.

Sitting down again, he tore the mailing envelope open. Inside was a smaller envelope, hand-addressed to Suzanne Paxton by Rand Harding. For a few moments Mack just sat there and grinned. Even the guy's name sounded western. This was so great he could hardly believe it was happening.

Unconcerned that the envelope really belonged to his sister, he slid his finger under the flap. Inside was a letter and a snapshot. Mack studied the picture. Hey, he thought, Harding's a good-looking guy! All the better. Unfolding the letter, he pored over every word.

Now he could hardly wait for Suzanne to get home, although he couldn't help being a little nervous over how she would take his news.

But, heck, he thought, why wouldn't she be thrilled to hear a man in Montana wanted to marry her? There sure wasn't anything going on here to keep her in Baltimore.

She'd be thrilled, Mack decided. *Darned* thrilled.

"You what?" Suzanne asked, her pretty face registering shock and disbelief.

"I answered an ad in a magazine. This here letter came today. Suzanne, the guy wants to marry you."

"You answered an ad using *my* name? Mack, have you lost your mind?"

"At least read the letter, okay?" Mack held it out. "This guy is legit, Suzanne. He really wants a wife."

Suzanne was momentarily speechless. Mack had always been a handful, no two ways about it, but this went far beyond anything he'd pulled before. Weakly, feeling utterly helpless, she sank to the sofa. "I can't believe you did such a thing, Mack."

Mack frowned. Was she on the verge of tears? Heck, he hadn't gone to so much trouble to make his sister cry.

"I thought you'd be thrilled," he mumbled, lowering himself to the chair he'd used most of the day.

"Well, I'm not," Suzanne retorted.

"Aren't you gonna read Rand's letter?"

"Rand? That's his name? Mack, do you realize that you might have put us in contact with…with some kind of pervert?"

"I don't think he's a pervert," Mack said with a laugh. His expression sobered. "Read his letter, sis. He's foreman of a big cattle ranch in Montana. He's *somebody!*"

"Well, do you think a pervert or a criminal would admit it in a letter? Use your head, Mack. Men don't advertise for wives these days. Not men with anything going for them, for heaven's sake."

Mack frowned down at the letter in his hand. After a minute he said, "Well, I believe every word Rand wrote. He even said he'd send you the money to get to Montana."

"So he could do what when I got there? Mack, this whole thing is absurd. Can't you see that?"

Mack was wearing his stubborn expression. "You don't trust anybody."

"That's not true, and you know it. But I certainly have no reason to trust a man I've never met."

"Well, how're you gonna meet him if you won't even read his letter?" Mack shouted.

"Don't yell at me, Mack. What you did is abhorrent, and I will not—let me repeat—I will *not* be a part of it."

Mack got up, tossed Rand's letter on the sofa next to his sister and stormed out of the room. Suzanne sighed heavily as his bedroom door slammed shut. She knew Mack hated living in an apartment; she knew he hated his school and this section of Baltimore. Their parents had left a very small estate, and she could not afford any better life-style than what they already had. For that matter, without a job she couldn't really even afford that, and if she didn't find a job very soon, she and Mack were in for some very bumpy times.

But he was still only a boy, and she knew he didn't fully grasp what she was going through. He actually believed that marrying her off to some idiot in Montana was a solution to their problems. How very, very sad.

Desultorily she picked up the envelope and looked at it. Maybe she should turn it over to the police. Wasn't it illegal to cross state lines with letters of a dubious nature? Sighing again, she shook out the contents of the envelope onto her lap. The snapshot was the first thing she picked up. Her eyes widened in surprise as she studied the handsome man in the photo. Dark hair, blue eyes, it looked like, and rugged, manly features. Clean-cut, though—really a very attractive man.

But dare she believe this was a genuine photo of the letter writer?

Curious in spite of her misgivings, she unfolded the letter and read it. "Oh, my God," she whispered when she came to the part about her being a beautiful woman. *What* photo had Mack sent him? She wasn't a troll, by any means, but beautiful?

In his room Mack was whispering into the telephone to Kip. "She won't even read Rand's letter. I'm going, Kip. With or without Suzanne, I'm going to Montana."

Suzanne did not sleep well anymore. Her daytime worries went to bed with her, and too many times she woke up in a sweat, struggling to pull herself out of some awful nightmare. Again tonight, breathing as though she'd just run a footrace, she sat up in bed and battled tears. What was she going to do? She *had* to find a job that paid enough to live on. So far all she'd run across were minimum-wage clerical positions, and she was an accountant, a *good* accountant.

Her digital clock read 3:23 a.m. She needed more sleep, but the thought of another nightmare made her shudder. Getting out of bed, she pulled on a robe and slippers and left her room. Passing Mack's room, she stopped at the door to listen. All was quiet and she continued on to the kitchen, where she switched on the ceiling light and put the teakettle on the stove to heat water for a cup of instant cocoa.

When the cocoa was ready, she sat at the table, sipped the hot drink and worried. How much longer could she go on without a job? Not financially speaking. Financially she knew almost to the day how long that small savings account would last. But on an emotional scale, how much longer could she bear living like this? Mack was one problem after another. His latest prank was as ridiculous as it was dangerous, and he was too immature to realize it.

Her lips pursed. She would not forget what Mack had done until she let Rand Harding know that *she* was appalled by the whole idea of advertising for a wife.

Getting up, she went to the living room, took Harding's— if that was really his name, she thought disdainfully—letter from the top of her small desk where she had tossed it last night, found a pad of paper and a pen and returned to the kitchen table. It didn't take her long to write her thoughts.

Mr. Harding,
First of all, I did not answer your ad, my teenage brother did. Secondly, I don't know whose photo he sent you, but it certainly wasn't mine. Let me make myself very clear, Mr. Harding. I am not now nor ever could be interested in an advertisement such as yours. I find the entire idea of advertising for a wife repugnant and disgusting. As for your letter, I can only say that I have never read such drivel in my life. If you're lonesome, it's your own doing. I could not care less. Please do not contact me again, and don't attempt to contact my foolish young brother, either. If you do I will turn this whole ridiculous matter over to the police. That is not a threat, Mr. Harding, it's a promise.
Suzanne Paxton

Suzanne addressed an envelope, inserted her letter, put a stamp on it and left her apartment to walk to the mail drop at the end of the hall. The hallway was chilly and she hurried back to her warm kitchen to drink the rest of her cocoa.

After swallowing the last of it, she rinsed the cup and left it in the sink. She had to try to get some more sleep tonight, because she had to rise early, wake Mack to get ready for school and then prepare herself for another day of job-hunting.

Sighing heavily, she returned to her room and bed.

Suzanne's alarm clock awakened her at 6:00 a.m. Yawning, she got up, put on her robe, went into the bathroom, washed the sleep out of her eyes and brushed her teeth. On her way to the kitchen to put on a pot of coffee, she rapped on Mack's door. "Time to get up," she called. No sound reached her ears. "Mack? Wake up."

Still no sound. No groans of protest or the blast of music from Mack's radio, which he always turned on the minute he came to every morning.

She tried again, this time knocking louder. "Mack?" Anger suddenly gripped her—Mack was so darned inconsiderate sometimes—and she turned the knob and pushed the door open. His bedding had not been disturbed, and Suzanne's first thought was that he'd snuck out in the night and hadn't bothered to come home again. Her lips pursed tightly. Didn't she have enough on her mind without this?

Honest to God, she thought, if she didn't love Mack so much she would hate him. How dare he stay out all night? How dare he cause her unnecessary worry on top of what she already had to bear? Had he no understanding at all of their situation?

She was about to yank his door closed when she noticed the vacant spot on his nightstand where his radio ordinarily sat. Her heart skipped a beat as her anger evolved into fear.

That radio meant the world to Mack, and she couldn't see him taking it to a friend's house or hauling it around while he wandered the streets. Was anything else missing?

A quick examination of his closet and bureau made Suzanne's knees go weak. Mack's favorite clothes were gone! She swayed, and grabbed the corner of the bureau for support. That was when she saw the piece of yellow paper taped to the mirror over the dresser. Letting go of the bureau she tore the paper loose. It was a message from Mack.

Sis, I don't want you getting all hot and bothered about this, but I went to Montana. Don't worry about me, I can take care of myself. I'll say hello to Rand Harding for you. Love, Mack.

"Oh, no," Suzanne moaned. In the next instant she was running for the kitchen and that letter from Rand Harding. What if Mack had taken it with him? Although she'd written Harding's address only a few hours ago, she didn't remember any part of it except for *Montana*. She only breathed again when she had it in her hands.

When her bank opened its doors that morning, Suzanne was its first customer. She went to a teller and closed out her savings account. Her heart sank when she realized that Mack had helped himself to a good half of their money. Although the money belonged to both of them, the account was in Suzanne's name. He must have forged her name on the withdrawal slip, she realized. He'd done it before. It would take every penny they had left now to find her brother and bring him home.

But that was exactly what she was going to do.

Three

J. D. Cade was as good as Rand had predicted. The man was a natural, one of those people born to ranching. He seemed to love animals and could gentle the orneriest horse with a few soft words.

Humans, now, were a different matter for J.D., Rand noted. It wasn't that J.D. was unfriendly, he just wasn't talkative. He eluded questions about himself, usually tactfully, but if tact failed he used other methods to ward off curiosity, such as he'd done with Dale at the supper table.

It surprised Rand that Dale hadn't been put off by J.D.'s challenging snub that evening. To the contrary, the younger man seemed to follow J.D. like a shadow. Rand couldn't figure out what was going on in Dale's head, but the arrival of J. D. Cade had definitely changed Dale's disposition from sunny to brooding. And anytime Rand spotted J.D. on a horse, he knew Dale wouldn't be far behind.

But Rand couldn't concern himself with the relationships of every cowboy he hired. There was too much variance in personalities for all of them to be friends, and he'd learned long ago to stay out of disagreements that didn't involve the ranch. Rand was certain that if and when J.D. got tired of Dale shadowing his every move, he would handle it.

Frankly, Rand wished he had a dozen men like J. D. Cade in his crew. But he knew that men of J.D.'s ilk might stay on a job for years or take the notion to leave after a week. J.D. himself had said he didn't know how long he'd hang around when he'd taken the job, and in Rand's opinion it was the God's truth: J.D. simply didn't know.

Rand's habit was to discuss chores for the day at the breakfast table. Most of the time he broke up his crew, sending three or four men to do one thing, three or four to do another, and so on. The experienced men knew what had to be done each day almost as well as Rand did, but the greener hands always waited for their daily instructions.

This morning Rand announced that the whole crew would be working together. "I want the trees and brush scoured on Granite Mountain for stray cows and calves. We're going to start branding the new crop in about a week, and I've seen some Kincaid cattle on the mountain with my own eyes. Bring them in."

When breakfast was over, the men left and Rand headed for the office. His own chore for the day was one for which he had little affection: paperwork. He plopped down behind the second desk in the room, upon which George had already placed a stack of unpaid invoices. They would remain unpaid until Rand initialed them, signifying approval. Rand sighed, considering the boring day's work ahead. He wondered if the mail would bring another letter from Suzanne. That event would surely brighten his day.

A few minutes later George wandered in with a mug of coffee and sat at his own desk. The older man chuckled under his breath at the frown of concentration on Rand's face.

George liked paperwork and accounting. He always felt a little thrill of satisfaction when his books balanced on the first try. He was an old-school bookkeeper—everything was done by hand. No computers for him, no sirree.

Rand worked with a red pencil, writing notes on the invoices, muttering in undertones, looking as though he was in great pain. George lit his pipe, puffed on it a couple of times and chuckled again. Rand was a man of the outdoors, and the four or five days a month he spent in the office were obviously agonizing for him. But ranching was a business like any other, and it required paperwork.

Rand looked up suddenly. "George, this invoice is for two cases of dynamite. I only ordered one." His frown went deeper. "And we only received and used one." They'd been blowing granite boulders out of a pasture a few weeks back, and had used the entire case of dynamite.

George got up and went over to Rand's desk. "Let me see that invoice." He studied it for a moment, then went back to his own desk and dialed the company's phone number.

Rand overheard him checking on the invoice. George finished the phone call and turned to Rand, a puzzled expression on his face.

"The records show that there were two calls, Rand, each for one case. Two were delivered. One for the ninth and the other for the tenth. The bookkeeper over there says both receipts were signed by Rand Harding."

"I signed for one case, and only one," Rand insisted. "Call them back, George, and ask for a copy of those delivery receipts. Do you realize what damage someone could do to this ranch with a case of dynamite?"

"Damned right I do," George said, dialing the phone number again.

Rand sat back, angry and frustrated. Now someone was forging his name? As frustrating as that knowledge was, however, it proved that the person responsible for all the dirty tricks on the ranch *was* living on it.

Once again Rand mentally ran through the faces and names of his men. Damn, he couldn't believe any of them were so devious. It was a darned good thing *he* went over the bills before George paid them, or they might not have caught this blatant deception.

Well, the dynamite might be hidden somewhere on the place, but where? Rand shook his head, feeling almost dazed. He wouldn't even know where to *start* looking for it. And when would the creep use it? On which part of the ranch? The buildings? The bunkhouse? God, if someone blew up the bunkhouse in the middle of some dark night, a dozen people would die. This was a hell of a lot more serious than a mutilated heifer.

Rand reached for his phone. "I'm going to call Sterling and Wendell about this. They should know what's going on."

He was told that Sterling was out of town, but Wendell's secretary put him through at once.

"Rand," Wendell exclaimed, sounding genuinely glad to hear from him. "How are you? How's everything at the ranch?"

"We've got a problem, Wendell, a *major* problem." Rand explained about the case of unauthorized dynamite, expecting Wendell to explode himself.

But the attorney only said calmly, "It appears as though we have a thief on our hands."

"A thief! Hell's bells, Wendell, I'm not concerned about a damned thief!"

"Well, surely you're not thinking that someone's going to blow up the place?"

The snicker in Wendell's voice made Rand's spine get ramrod stiff. Since when was a case of dynamite in the wrong hands a laughing matter?

Rand's voice turned cold as ice. "Sorry I bothered you, Wendell. I thought you'd want to know. Goodbye."

"Rand, hold on a minute! I'm sorry I didn't react as you thought I should. It's just that the idea of anyone blowing up an entire ranch is a bit preposterous. Things like that don't happen around Whitehorn."

"Wendell, from what I've heard about this area, anything's possible. I'm going to call Reed Austin. You might not think a case of dynamite in some fool's hands is serious business, but I do. Goodbye."

Rand slammed down the phone, dialed the sheriff's office and asked for Reed Austin.

"Reed, I need some advice," Rand greeted him. Again Rand explained about that second case of dynamite. "I think it's still on the ranch. Got any ideas?"

"This is getting serious, Rand."

"Yes, it is," Rand agreed.

Reed suggested a night watch and thought Rand could trust the new men who'd recently been hired.

"They couldn't possibly be responsible for things that happened two and three months ago," Reed stated. "Use them."

Rand took a relieved breath. "You're right."

"And do a little looking around. This guy is clever, but maybe he's a little too clever. Could be he stored that case of dynamite in plain sight. You know, Rand, sometimes criminals outsmart themselves. He's gotten away with so much already, he might be feeling a little cocky. Have you talked to Sterling about this? I'm sure he'd want to know."

"Sterling's out of town for a few days."

"Well, stay in touch," Reed said. "And if you want me to come out there, just let me know."

"Will do, Reed. Thanks."

As Rand put the phone down he happened to glance out one of the office windows. A young boy with a backpack was wandering around the compound. He motioned for George to take a look out the window. George looked back at Rand and shrugged; he didn't know the boy, either.

Rand frowned when the boy started hiking toward the big house. He jumped up, grabbed his jacket and hat and hurried out of the office and bunkhouse.

"Hey, kid," he yelled while heading for the big house and that strange boy.

The boy turned, hesitated a moment, then started walking toward Rand. Rand watched a large, goofy grin develop on the boy's face as he got closer.

"Hi, Rand," he said.

"Do I know you?"

"Nope, but I know you. You're Rand Harding, foreman of this ranch. I'm Mack Paxton. Suzanne's my sister."

Rand gaped at the boy. It took a minute, but he finally got his bearings. "Is Suzanne with you? How'd you get out here? I don't see a car anywhere."

"I hitched rides clear from the airport in Billings."

Rand frowned and cleared his throat. "Suzanne hitched rides?"

"She didn't come. She's still in Baltimore."

"*Is* she coming?"

Mack knew the jig was up. Rand Harding looked like his picture. He was a cowboy through and through, which thrilled Mack no end. But from the expression on this cowboy's face, Mack knew that he had the same weird ideas about what kids should and shouldn't do that Suzanne had. He decided he had no choice but to lie.

"She couldn't get away right now," he mumbled. "But she's coming."

Rand studied the boy, who couldn't be more than fourteen or fifteen years old. If Suzanne was the sort of woman who would permit her little brother to come to a completely strange place by himself, maybe he *didn't* want to know her. His face hardened.

"I think you and I should go into the bunkhouse and call your sister," he said sternly. "Come on."

"The bunkhouse?" The very word excited Mack. "Which one's the bunkhouse?"

"You'll find out," Rand said through tensely set lips. He started away.

Mack followed on Rand's heels, suddenly scared spitless. This wasn't turning out quite as he'd planned, and he wasn't getting any great ideas about how to get things on the track he wanted. Maybe getting Rand to talk would help, he thought in a flash of inspiration.

"This is really a great ranch," he said to Rand's broad back. No answer. "Uh, do you live in that big house?"

"Nope." Rand kept going, his long legs keeping him well ahead of Mack.

"Is your horse one of the ones in that corral over there?"

"The black one with the white blaze on his chest."

"He's beautiful. What's his name?"

"Jack."

"Jack? That's a funny name for a horse."

Rand nearly laughed at the boy's disappointment. Obviously Mack's knowledge of the west was heavily biased by shoot-'em-up cowboy films, in which the hero's horse was his best friend and always bore some glamorous and completely unrealistic name.

"Here we go," Rand announced while opening a door into the bunkhouse. The boy seemed to be hanging back. "Come on, Mack, I haven't got all day." Mack's eyes darted around, as though seeking escape. "Mack," Rand said with more firmness. "Get your butt in here!"

The boy shuffled into the bunkhouse with his eyes down. "We'll use the office," Rand told him, and, taking Mack by the arm, led him into the room.

George smiled. "And who might you be, young fellow?"

"Mack Paxton," Mack mumbled.

George looked questioningly at Rand, who suddenly realized the embarrassing and awkward position this kid's un-invited presence had put him in. Everyone on the place would probably fall on the ground laughing when they heard he'd advertised for a wife! God Almighty, he thought as panic nearly choked him. He should have thought of this before dragging Mack into the office.

"Uh, Mack's the brother of a friend, George," Rand stammered, garnering a look of youthful suspicion from Mack. But he was a bright kid, and it wasn't three seconds before he caught on. Mr. Lonesome Cowboy hadn't told his pals on the ranch about that ad!

"Yeah," Mack said to George a bit cockily. "Rand's friend is my sister."

"Really," George said with one eyebrow raised.

"Yeah, and Rand invited me for a visit, didn't you, Rand?"

Rand swallowed hard. It was either 'fess up now or forever hold his tongue. He gave Mack Paxton a glare that would bring much older men to their knees, but Mack merely grinned that goofy grin of his and looked smug.

"Just wanted you to meet him," Rand mumbled to George, and he quickly steered Mack Paxton out of the office, down the hall, up the stairs leading to the second story and finally into an empty bedroom. Closing the door, he backed Mack into a corner. "If one more lie comes out of your mouth, you'll wish you'd never set one toe out of Baltimore. Understand?"

Mack believed him and mutely nodded.

"Good. Does your sister know you came here?"

"I left her a note."

"You didn't talk to her about it, you just wrote a note and

came. Why? What in hell made you think I wanted *you* out here?"

"You wanted my sister, didn't you?"

"I wanted to *meet* your sister. Are you capable of comprehending the difference?"

"You wanted to do more than meet her," Mack said sullenly. "I read your letter."

Rand was stunned. "She let *you* read it?"

"Uh…" Mack was thinking fast. This guy was apt to haul him back to Billings and put him on a plane if he learned what had actually taken place over that letter. "She didn't *let* me read it. I read it when she wasn't looking."

"But she told you about my ad."

Mack was really getting into his story now. "Why wouldn't she? She was really thrilled about it, Rand." Seeing the doubt on Rand's face, he added, "You gotta believe me, man. After she got your letter she started talking about the two of us going to Montana to meet you in person. I just jumped the gun a little. I've always wanted to see a real cattle ranch, so—" his voice weakened considerably "—here I am."

Rand left Mack where he was and paced a circle around the small room. He didn't know what to believe, and he rubbed his jaw with the palm of his hand in abject frustration.

Mack watched Rand's every step. Clearly this lonesome cowboy was confused. Excellent, Mack thought. At least he'd get to hang around for as long as it took Rand to figure out what to do with him.

Rand turned abruptly and pulled a little pad and a pen out of his shirt pocket. "What's your sister's telephone number?"

Mack's face fell. "You're gonna call her?"

"Yes, sir, I am." The look on Mack's face touched a years-old note in Rand's system, something about himself at Mack's age. Rand's hard-nosed attitude softened some. "Mack, she's probably worried sick about you. At least I can tell her you're all right. Give me the number."

Mack heaved a long-suffering sigh. "Okay." He recited the phone number at the apartment and Rand wrote it down, then shoved the notebook and pen back into his shirt pocket.

"You can use this room while you're here. There's more than one bathroom on this floor and they're not hard to find. Take clean sheets, pillowcases, two towels and two wash-cloths from the hall linen closet. It's not hard to find, either. There's a laundry room on the first floor. You'll wash your own clothes *and* the bed linen and towels you use. Stay out of the men's rooms. No one goes into another man's room without an invitation. At the end of the hall is a room with a TV, which you may use, but not exclusively. The men have favorite programs, and if they're different than yours, tough. If you've got a radio or tape player in that backpack, don't play it before five in the morning or after eight at night. And don't *ever* play it at a volume that disturbs anyone else. Think you can remember all that?"

"I'm not stupid," Mack mumbled.

"At this specific moment, that's a debatable point. I'm going downstairs now." Rand stopped at the door. "Supper's at six. Just follow your nose to the dining room." He left.

Mack hurriedly shucked off his backpack, dropped it on the bed and followed Rand down the stairs. "Is it okay if I look around?"

"Outside, you mean? Yes, it's okay. The men are out on Granite Mountain today, but if some of them happen to come in early, don't get in their way. And be careful around the horses. Some of them spook real easy." He breathed a sigh of relief when Mack raced through the door to get outside. When submitting that ad, he sure hadn't bargained on a teenage brother-in-law who apparently did as he damn well pleased.

Shaking his head, Rand continued on to the privacy of his bedroom and closed the door behind himself. He went immediately to the phone, listened for a moment to make sure it wasn't already in use, then dialed the number Mack had given him. He let it ring ten times, but no one answered.

Suzanne Paxton deplaned in Billings, collected her luggage and went to the car rental area of the terminal, where she obtained not only a car but directions for the best route to White-horn.

"Are you familiar with the Whitehorn area?" she inquired of the agent.

"No, ma'am, sorry."

Suzanne managed a weak smile. "I figured my chances were slim on that score, but I had to ask."

"Are you looking for a particular place near Whitehorn?"

"The Kincaid Ranch."

"I've heard of that ranch. There were a couple of murders out there, if I remember right."

Suzanne felt herself go pale. "Murders? Are you sure?"

"Pretty sure." The young man shrugged. "Whitehorn was in the newspapers a lot about a year or so back."

"Because someone was murdering people?" Suzanne asked in a thin little voice.

"Yes, a woman. She was killing Kincaids. I think she's dead, too."

Suzanne's hand rose to her throat. "That's horrible!"

She left the agent's counter feeling dazed and frightened. What in God's name had Mack gotten them into?

By the time Suzanne reached Whitehorn, asked directions to the Kincaid Ranch and started the drive toward it, darkness had fallen. She wasn't used to empty country roads, and her heart pounded unmercifully as she crept along at about thirty miles per hour. Other than what her headlights fell upon, the countryside was a blur. There were hills in the road, and curves, and each mile that brought her closer to the Kincaid

Ranch was pure torture. Was Mack there? Was he safe? My Lord, was it safe for *her* to drive up to such a place after dark?

When it started snowing, Suzanne really went into shock. She'd known it was cold out, but snow at this time of year? What kind of hell was Montana?

Meanwhile, there was bedlam at the ranch. Handy came rushing into Rand's room yelling, "My only sister had a stroke! I have to go to her. I already packed a few things and I'm leaving right now!"

Rand stood. "Handy, calm down. Didn't you tell me your sister lives in Seattle? Have you called for a plane reservation?"

"I'll get one at the airport. I'm leaving right now!" That was it. In the blink of an eye, Handy was gone.

Rand went to an outside door and watched him driving away much too fast. Feeling helpless—how on earth were they going to get by without a cook?—and worrying about Handy driving too fast, Rand looked up at the night sky. It was snowing!

"Oh, no, not that, too," he groaned. But surely it wouldn't last, he told himself. Not in April.

"Rand," George called from inside. "What's going on?"

"For starters, it's snowing. And we just lost our cook. Handy's sister had a stroke and he's on his way to Seattle."

Rand went to the kitchen and poured himself a mug of coffee, sitting on a stool at the counter to drink it and worry. It seemed that things were going from bad to worse. He still could hardly believe Suzanne's kid brother was on the ranch. Had she found Mack's note, or was it possible Mack hadn't left one and lied about it? Maybe Suzanne had no idea *where* her brother was.

The worries started going around in a circle in Rand's mind—that case of dynamite, the snow, Mack Paxton, Handy's departure—until he got tired of the whole damned thing. Hell, he'd do the cooking himself, if he had to, and a little snow was no tragedy. They'd get by. As for Mack, he'd eventually manage some kind of contact with Suzanne and get *that* straightened out. The worst problem, by far, was the dynamite. He'd followed Reed Austin's advice and put J.D. and another new man on night watch, which made good sense to him.

As if on cue, J.D. and the other man on night duty came walking in. They were dressed in heavy winter clothing, with only their faces exposed. "We're heading out, Rand," J.D. said. "Did you know it's snowing?"

The other man added, "And it ain't just a skiff, Rand. I heard on the radio that we're in for a blizzard."

"In April?" Rand looked dubious.

"That's what the weatherman said."

"Great," Rand groaned. "Well, stick close to the buildings and come in every so often and warm up."

"Okay. See ya later." The two men filed out.

Rand heaved a sigh. It was quiet upstairs; most of the men must have gone to bed. It was also quiet downstairs, Rand realized, so George, too, must have retired for the night. It was then that he heard the sound of a car approaching the bunkhouse.

"Handy!" he exclaimed, jumping to his feet. Now, if the old guy would just slow down long enough so he could talk to him…

Rand yanked open the outside door, fully expecting to see the old cook. But it wasn't Handy climbing out of a small blue sedan, it was a woman. She saw him in the doorway at the same time he saw her, and they both froze for a second.

Then she reached into the car for her purse, closed the door and slipped and slid on the new-fallen snow to reach the bunkhouse and Rand.

Her chin was high, he noticed, as though she was all set for battle. Who was she and why in hell was she out here looking for a fight?

She stopped directly in front of him. "My name is Suzanne Paxton, and I'm looking for my brother, Mack. Is he here?"

Four

Rand stood in the doorway with inside lights behind him and Suzanne stood outside with those same lights reflecting on her face and clothing. All she could make out was the large, dark form of a man blocking the entrance to the building. But Rand could see her quite clearly and he was truly in shock.

This was Suzanne Paxton? She was pretty—quite pretty, actually. Tall, slender and nicely dressed in a long, blue wool coat, hose, mid-heel pumps, black leather gloves and shoulder bag. But she was definitely not the woman in the photograph. This woman had dark hair and his dream lady in that photo was a blonde!

"Uh, are you sure you're Suzanne Paxton?" he asked, and instantly wished he could bite off his tongue. What a stupid thing to say!

Stunned by such a moronic question, Suzanne squinted her eyes in an attempt to see the dark form better. In a reflexive reaction to such obvious simplemindedness, she took a step back, putting herself beyond the protection of the small roof over the stoop. Her feet were freezing in their hosiery and city pumps, and new-falling snow stacked upon her shoulders and hair on top of what had already gathered during her walk from car to building. It was coming down harder by the minute, she realized, although the half-wit she was attempting conversation with didn't seem to notice.

"I think I know my own name," she said, keeping her voice as even as she could manage. She was, after all, in the most frightening situation of her life—miles from civilization, standing in a blizzard and trying to talk to a dark, shadowy figure with very broad shoulders and a very low IQ.

She fought to keep her teeth from chattering, although the low temperature mingling with pure fear made it difficult to do so.

"My brother is fourteen years old, just a teenager. His name is Mack, and I have good reason to believe he came to this ranch. Could you please tell me if he's here?"

Rand tried desperately to grasp what was happening. If this woman was Suzanne Paxton, who was the woman in the photo? And why had she sent *that* photo to him instead of one of herself?

Still, despite the uneasy machinations of his mind, other factors began seeping through. It was snowing hard, and he was keeping a woman standing outside!

"Uh, come on in," he stammered.

Suzanne's heart skipped an extremely nervous beat. She would like to get out of the snow and cold, of course, but enter that building with this…this person that she still couldn't see clearly? No way, she thought, lifting her chin again.

"Look, all I want is an answer to a very simple question," she said. "Is my brother here? Did a young man you didn't know show up on this ranch sometime today? He may have given you a different name. He might be calling himself something other than Mack, but I assure you Mack is his name and he's my brother."

"He's here," Rand said. "Sleeping, probably."

"At eight-thirty?" The idea of Mack, who never went to bed before midnight in spite of her repeated objections, already in bed and sleeping was preposterous.

"Everyone's sleeping, except for me," Rand said.

"And exactly who do you mean by *everyone?*"

Rand was beginning to feel the cold himself. "My men," he said with some impatience. "Are you coming in or not? The whole bunkhouse will turn into an icebox if I leave this door open much longer."

"This building is the bunkhouse?" For some reason that made her feel a little less afraid. At least if she went inside she wouldn't be alone with this peculiar person. And maybe he was telling her the truth. Maybe Mack *was* in there, although she still doubted that he was in bed and asleep at this early hour.

Inspiration struck her. "Would you please wake Mack and tell him his sister is here? I'll wait in the car."

Rand frowned. "Why not wait inside?"

Try as she might, she couldn't come up with an answer that wouldn't give away her fear, and she didn't want him knowing how truly frightened she was of this horrid place. And maybe of him.

"I...I really don't want to impose," she finally said.

"Is going into someone's home an imposition in Baltimore?" Rand's initial shock was receding. Now his struggle was in trying to understand this woman's reluctance to get out of the storm.

Suzanne stared as a horrifying picture began developing in her mind. But it couldn't be true. This man *couldn't* be the handsome man in the snapshot that resided in her purse this very second. "Did...did Mack tell you that's where we live?" she asked, praying that was the case. She had hoped to pick up Mack and get off this ranch without even seeing Rand

Harding, a doubtful prospect to be sure, but still she had hoped, ardently.

"You told me yourself."

Her spirit dropped to a record low. "Then you're Rand Harding."

"One and the same. Suzanne, I can't leave this door open any longer. Are you coming in or not?"

She knew now why he had asked that inane question about who she was. An urge to explain the ridiculous fiasco Mack had created for all of them overwhelmed her fears, and she nodded. "Yes, thank you."

Despite Rand's complaints about the cold coming through the open door, it seemed warm inside to Suzanne. The very first thing she felt compelled to do, once inside, was to take a good look at Mr. Harding. Apparently he had the same goal, because when she raised her gaze to his face, he was staring at hers.

Well, why wouldn't he be curious? she thought with an inward sigh. Whatever photo Mack had sent him probably didn't resemble her in the least. At the same time she was a bit stunned that Rand Harding was even better looking than his snapshot depicted. But "tall, dark and handsome" was merely a thumbnail sketch of this man. His vivid blue eyes exuded intelligence, a strength of character and a macho sexuality that any woman would recognize. There was nothing wrong with his IQ, Suzanne thought weakly. Actually, one would be hard-pressed to find anything wrong with any part of him, tangible or *in*tangible.

This was a terribly awkward moment for both Suzanne and Rand. Their thoughts, although similarly focused on the photograph Rand had received, were still vastly different. Suzanne knew what she had to do—explain what her recalcitrant younger brother had done—but Rand didn't. How did a man ask a woman why she would do something so devious as to pass someone else's picture off as her own?

"Um, how about a cup of coffee to warm up?" Rand asked.

Suzanne thought about it. She should get back to White-horn tonight, so she and Mack could begin the return trip to Baltimore early tomorrow morning. She couldn't discount the weather, either. At the rate it was snowing, the roads would probably be impassable in a very few hours.

But she was chilled through and through, and a cup of hot coffee was hard to pass up. Besides, she still had to relate Mack's disgusting behavior to Rand Harding. Certainly she didn't want him to continue believing what he now thought was true.

"Thank you, I would really like a cup of coffee," she said. The hall they were standing in ran both ways, Suzanne saw. Three doors were visible on her right. To her left the hall faded into darkness.

"Follow me," Rand told her, and began walking to the left. "The kitchen's this way."

Suzanne followed, praying that she wasn't doing something rash. Rand switched on lights as he went, which made her feel slightly better, but her inner self remained nervously alert. When she passed the stairs leading to the second floor, she hesitated and asked, "Is my brother sleeping upstairs?"

Rand stopped and turned. "All the men sleep upstairs." He raised an eyebrow. "Would you like a tour of the bunkhouse?"

Why, he was making fun of her! She almost told him to shove his coffee up his nose, but common sense prevailed and she drew a breath to pacify her injured pride.

But she couldn't speak to him with any degree of friend-liness. "No, thank you," she said coolly.

Smirking slightly, Rand resumed his walk to the kitchen. If there was anything he hated more than lies, he couldn't think of what it was at the moment. Suzanne might be pretty and he might be lonely, but he would live alone for the rest of his life before settling for a liar.

The kitchen surprised Suzanne. It was large, brightly

lighted—once Rand snapped on the ceiling lights—and equipped far better than her own. Everything was of a commercial size, the stove, three ovens and two grills, the dishwasher, the huge refrigerator, even the counters and wood-block island. And it was spick-and-span, the stainless steel gleaming, the floor clean enough to eat off. She was impressed by this, at least, however uncomfortable she was with everything else.

Rand immediately busied himself with the coffeepot. There was a whole cupboard of coffeepots, and he chose the smallest. "Take off your coat, if you want," he said over his shoulder. "This will take a few minutes. You can sit on one of those stools at the counter."

In the next heartbeat he remembered the two men on night duty, and exchanged the small pot for one much larger. He would let them know there was hot coffee in the kitchen, he told himself. It was something he should have thought of before this. Handy would have.

Keeping an eye on Rand, Suzanne removed the leather gloves from her hands and unbuttoned her coat. But she left it on, just in case. After all, was there any reason why she should trust Rand Harding? What kind of man advertised for a wife, for pity's sake?

Perching on a stool, she pondered that question. There *had* to be something wrong with him. A man with his looks shouldn't have any trouble at all in attracting women.

With the coffeepot prepared and immediately gurgling, Rand turned around. Leaning his hips against the counter, he looked at Suzanne. The snow she'd brought in with her had melted, and water droplets glistened in the dark sheen of her hair. No doubt about it, he thought, she was darned pretty. Why wasn't a picture of herself good enough? Why had she sent him another woman's photo?

Suzanne darted him little glances, finding herself uneasy

about looking him directly in the eyes. But he kept staring, silently, and finally she had no choice. Besides, she thought, she might as well explain everything right now and get it over with.

She cleared her throat. "Whatever you're thinking right now, it's wrong," she said.

"Oh? How would you know what I'm thinking?"

"Trust me, I know."

Rand folded his arms across his chest. "Is this a preamble to some sort of discussion?"

"You could say that. Mr. Harding, I have never written to you. No, wait, that's not true. I *did* write a letter, but you couldn't possibly have received it yet."

"You didn't write but you did write. Is that supposed to make sense?"

She wasn't doing this well, Suzanne realized, probably because the part of her that loved Mack didn't like putting him in a bad light. Not that he didn't deserve it, the little brat, but he was still her brother, her only family, and blood was thicker than water. She drew a breath, preparing herself to begin again.

Before she could say a word, however, an enormous gust of wind hit the side of the bunkhouse, startling her, and in the very next instant a man wearing a heavy coat with a hood walked in.

"Rand…" George noticed Suzanne and immediately produced a truly warm smile. "Hello, ma'am."

"Suzanne Paxton, George Davenport," Rand said by way of an introduction. To Suzanne he added, "George is the ranch's bookkeeper."

A bookkeeper. Her very own trade. And what a pleasant man George Davenport appeared to be. Suzanne felt most of the stiffness vanish from her spine.

"Very nice meeting you, Mr. Davenport," she said.

"Now, now, none of that mister stuff. We're quite informal around here, Suzanne."

She smiled. "Very well, it's nice meeting you, George. I'm a bookkeeper, too."

"Is that a fact, now. Well, isn't that interesting. We'll have to compare notes." George looked at Rand. "Right now, though, I'm going to go out to the barn and check on Daisy and her pups."

Daisy had appeared out of nowhere about a month ago, scraggly, hungry and obviously expecting pups. She was an outside dog and wouldn't come into the bunkhouse no matter how much she was coaxed. Nevertheless, George had named her Daisy and had taken it upon himself to see that her food and water bowls were kept full. Daisy's litter was about two weeks old now, five adorable fat puppies that lived in the barn.

"Be careful," Rand said. "It's slippery out there, George."

"I'm sure it is," George agreed. He smiled at Suzanne again, and went through a door opposite to the one she had used to enter the kitchen. She could tell it wasn't an outside door, because George's footsteps on hard flooring were audible.

"Where does that door lead?" she asked Rand, unable to allay her curiosity.

"The dining room. It has an outside door."

Suzanne nodded. "I see." This building totally destroyed her former idea of what a bunkhouse was like. Obviously the men on this ranch lived in comfort. There was central heating—apparent from the wall vents blowing warm air—plumbing, electricity, phone service, and it had the most impressive kitchen she'd ever seen. It was certainly a far cry from the bunkhouses she'd noticed in western movies.

Suzanne had only been on a ranch once, years before, during a family vacation. It had been a guest ranch actually, with no cattle, a very small operation compared to this one, she realized. This bunkhouse made her extremely curious about the rest of the place. The big house she'd caught sight of in the sweep of her headlights when she'd driven into the compound, for example. Did anyone live in it? And was that terrible story the car agent had told her about the Kincaids having been murdered out here true?

She wanted to ask, but stopped herself. She wasn't here to learn the history of the Kincaid Ranch; she was here to get her brother, and the sooner the better. She would have that cup of coffee, explain to Rand Harding how this whole fiasco had come about, wake Mack and get them both back to White-horn. It shouldn't take more than another fifteen minutes before they could leave.

The coffeepot quit gurgling and Rand filled two mugs. "Cream or sugar?" he asked.

"Just black, please."

Rand brought the two mugs to the counter at which Suzanne was sitting and placed one in front of her.

"Thank you," she murmured, and picked up the mug for a sip. The coffee was strong and hot, and it tasted delicious. Rand remained on the other side of the counter, sipping his own coffee, but he was much closer to her than he'd been, which increased her discomfort level again.

Regardless, she forced herself back to the topic they'd been discussing when George came in. "I believe we were talking about letters," she said with as much calmness as she could manage. Internally she was a mass of nerves, but she was doing a good job of not showing it.

"Yes, I believe we were," Rand said, not even trying to conceal his disdainful attitude.

A spot of pink appeared in each of Suzanne's cheeks. She could easily get angry right now, but how would anger help her situation? She wasn't guilty of anything, Mack was, but until Rand Harding heard the whole story, he had every right to blame her.

After another sip of coffee, Suzanne set the mug down and forced herself to look Rand in the eye. "I didn't answer your ad, Mack did."

For the longest time Rand just stared at her. She gave him time to digest what she'd told him, and apparently he finally did, because he said, "You're telling me your kid brother wrote that letter?"

Oh, God, what was in that letter? Suzanne thought with a silent groan. What had Mack written in her name? She should go upstairs this very minute, wake him up and… and…

Well, she didn't know what kind of punishment Mack should have to endure, but it should be something he would remember for the rest of his days. She had never once laid a hand on him, although there had been plenty of times when she'd thought a good spanking was what he'd needed, even *before* their parents' demise. Of course, he had never received a spanking, just as she hadn't as a youngster. Their parents had both been gentle, mild-mannered people, and they had been appalled over the people they'd known who had actually spanked their children.

"Do you still have that letter, and…and the photo Mack sent with it?" she asked Rand with a weary note in her voice.

"You know about the photo?"

"I figured it out from your letter."

"And that's the letter you answered."

"Yes."

"I tried to call you when Mack got here," Rand said. "You must have already been on your way to Montana."

"I really didn't know how many hours ahead of me he was. I didn't discover he was gone until I tried to get him up for school this morning." Was it really only this morning? Suzanne thought with an exhausted sigh. This morning she'd been in Baltimore, tonight she was in Montana. It didn't seem possible. More accurately, it didn't seem *real!*

But here she was, seated on a stool in a strange kitchen,

talking to a man she didn't know nor ever would know. God forbid that she ever fell in love again—one bad marriage was enough—but she wouldn't be human if she didn't appreciate Rand Harding's good looks.

That was neither here nor there, though. The mere thought of mail-order marriages made her nauseous. What did Rand Harding think marriage was, a game? He'd find out if and when he accomplished his goal of finding a woman moronic enough to marry a man she didn't know.

The sound of someone bursting through a door and yelling, "Harding!" broke into her thoughts.

Rand went around the counter at top speed. "What's going on?"

J.D., covered with snow and carrying a rifle, ran into the kitchen. "George took a fall down by the barn. I think he's hurt bad."

Rand muttered an oath and took off with J.D. right behind him. Suzanne heard the slam of the dining room door, sat there dazed for a moment, then got up to cross through the dining room to open the door again and peer outside.

"Oh, my God," she whispered when she saw how much snow had piled up just since she'd been inside the bunkhouse. And it was coming down in sheets, mountains of snow tossed around by a hard, driving wind.

She'd seen blizzards before, but none to compare with this one. She tried desperately to see through it, to see in which direction Rand and the other man had gone.

She couldn't do it. There was nothing but swirling white out there, and the bitter cold penetrated her clothes in seconds. Stepping back, she closed the door with a shiver that racked her entire body.

Returning to the kitchen, she took a swallow of her coffee and shivered again. Then she remembered that Rand had gone outside without a jacket!

"He'll freeze," she whispered. "George will freeze." Oh, what a horrible place! Blizzards, murders, isolation. A noise from upstairs, just over her head, had her jumping out of her skin. She wanted to bawl. This totally unnecessary trip—and Mack's—had taken most of her savings. When they returned to Baltimore, they would be on very short rations for God knew how long. She would never forgive Mack for putting her through this, never!

The door burst open again and Rand ran through the kitchen without even glancing her way. He looked like a snowman, but he didn't stop to shiver and drink coffee.

Suzanne couldn't prevent herself from following him. He went through a door off the long hall, and she reached it and stood watching him as he quickly dialed a number and waited impatiently for someone to answer.

Apparently someone finally did, because Rand said into the phone, "This is Rand Harding at the Kincaid Ranch. A man fell and seems to be seriously injured. I'm afraid to move him. Send an ambulance at once."

Suzanne brought her fingertips to her lips in horror. That nice man, George, was injured that badly?

"I know how bad the storm is, but George needs immediate medical attention," Rand said. After a moment he said, "Okay, I'll do what I can, but get here as fast as *you* can." He hung up.

Again he passed Suzanne without a word, this time running down the hall to the last door. Tense as a coiled spring, she waited for his next move. In seconds he appeared again, wearing a hat, jacket and gloves and carrying an armload of blankets.

"Rand?" she said as he ran past her.

"I don't have time to answer questions," he responded to her over his shoulder, and disappeared into the storm again.

Suzanne wilted against a wall. She heard someone coming down the stairs and prayed it was Mack. It wasn't. A grizzled, bearded man wearing trousers over long underwear and nothing else stopped at the bottom of the stairs and yelled, "What in hell's going on down here? Don't you know we're trying to sleep up there?"

Gulping in fright, Suzanne stepped into the office and shut the door very quietly. If it wasn't storming so horribly she would brave that stairway, wake up Mack and leave. But she knew she couldn't maneuver that little rental car through so much snow.

She was stuck in this awful place, and so was Mack.

Falling into the chair at one of the desks, she laid her head on the desktop and wept.

As though from a great distance Suzanne heard a voice. "Miss?" And again, "Miss, wake up."

Suzanne opened her eyes, saw the tall man towering over her and raised her head from the desk so fast she nearly blacked out. "What?" she asked frantically. "What do you want?"

J.D. looked disgusted. "Don't get hysterical on me. Rand said to tell you to go to bed. I'll show you the room."

"Oh." She felt very foolish and tried hard to smile. "I—I guess I fell asleep. Where's Rand now?"

"He followed the ambulance to town. Come on and I'll show you that room."

"You mean the roads are passable?" Suzanne got up from the chair.

"They are if you've got four-wheel-drive and chains."

"I...don't."

"Then they're not passable."

Suzanne followed him from the office and down the hall. He opened a door. "Rand said you could use this room. Good night."

"Uh, wait. Could...could you get my luggage from my car?"

"Yes, I can do that. Is it locked?"

"No, but my suitcases are in the trunk." Suzanne fumbled in her purse for a moment and came out with the car keys. "I appreciate this, thank you."

J.D. grunted something unintelligible and left. Suzanne stepped into the room and saw that it was small, contained a bed—unmade but there was a stack of bedding and two pillows on it—one dresser and a door that she assumed was a closet. She opened it and discovered a bathroom instead. It, too, was small, but there was a shower stall and another door that opened into a tiny closet.

It struck her that she'd been given the guest room. All of the men slept upstairs, Rand had said, so she was probably the only person on this floor. Frankly, she was so tired, the thought merely flashed through her mind with no lasting effect.

J.D. carried in her two suitcases and set them on the floor. One was a cosmetic case, and Suzanne had packed several changes of clothes in the other since she hadn't been a hundred percent certain about Mack's destination. Yes, he'd written in his goodbye note that he would say hello to Rand Harding for her, but as sad as it was to face, she really didn't believe much of anything Mack said anymore.

"Thank you," she said. Nodding, J.D. started to go. "Wait! What about George? Do you know how badly he was injured?"

"The paramedics said his right leg is broken and there's something wrong with his back. That's all I know."

"All right, thank you."

The man left. Suzanne bit down hard on her lower lip. She would like to let Mack know she was here, but she had no idea of the sleeping arrangements upstairs, and looking for her brother among a bunch of strange men could prove to be extremely embarrassing, to say nothing of their reactions to getting disturbed.

No, she would wait and see Mack in the morning. Sleepy-eyed and yawning, Suzanne made the bed with the clean sheets and blankets. All she had the strength to do was wash her face and brush her teeth; she would shower in the morning. Her last ounce of energy was used to get out of her clothes and into a pair of pajamas. Once in bed, however, the fury of the storm outside kept her awake for some time.

It was a logical reason to worry, she realized uneasily. After all, if it snowed all night, would she be *able* to leave in the morning?

Five

Rand waited at the hospital with George through X rays and examinations from several different doctors. Finally Rand got a diagnosis out of them. George had a broken leg and a severely sprained back. He would be in the hospital for at least a week, possibly longer.

Rand talked to him before he left. "George, I don't want you worrying about things at the ranch while you're here. Just take it easy, obey the doctors' orders and get well."

George had just been given a sedative for the pain—at long last—and it hadn't yet taken effect. "That's easy to say, Rand, but there's a payroll to get out and bills to pay."

"I'll write checks for the men, so put that out of your mind."

George closed his eyes. His leg had been set but not yet cast. His face was pasty because of the pain he'd been suffering, but the doctors had been firm about no sedatives until they'd reached a diagnosis on his injuries.

"I feel like a dolt," he mumbled thickly, indicating to Rand that the sedative was beginning to dull his senses. "Falling down like a kid and causing everyone so much trouble. And I was trying to be careful, too. I must be getting old."

"Younger men than you have taken a serious tumble, George."

"Daisy," George mumbled.

"I'll see that she's fed, don't worry about that." Rand could tell that George was going under. He patted the older man's arm. "Get some rest."

Leaving the hospital, Rand stopped in his tracks. The blizzard had reached a new level of intensity. It was entirely possible that the road to the ranch was closed.

But he had to get back. With Handy, George and himself gone, there would be no one with any authority whatsoever on the ranch, and all hell could break loose.

Grimly Rand got into his rig and started the engine. It was going to be one very treacherous drive, but his vehicle was a four-wheeler and he'd put chains on the tires while the paramedics had been seeing to George.

He'd make it. He *had* to make it. Putting the shifting lever into low gear, he began the perilous drive home. He passed a snowplow before reaching the edge of town. Whitehorn would be plowed out long before the rural areas. The ranch could be completely cut off from the rest of the world for days, if this storm kept up. Even at that they would manage as long as the electricity held. If a power line snapped and the ranch was without electricity, surviving this storm wouldn't exactly be accomplished in comfort.

Rand frowned over that visual, but not for long. He was plowing snow with the front of his rig, barely creeping along, and the windshield kept fogging up no matter how high he turned up the defroster. Plus, the wipers weren't able to keep so much blowing snow from sticking to the windshield, and every so often Rand had to stop, get out of his rig and wipe the snow from the glass. This was, without a doubt, the worst blizzard he'd ever seen, and he had seen many in his thirty-two years. If the power lines did hold, it would be a miracle.

There was so much to worry about right now that his mind kept jumping from one thing to another in no apparent pattern—George's disability, Handy's absence, that box of dynamite and whoever had ordered it, the misery of having to feed the cattle and horses in this kind of weather and, last but certainly not least, the Paxtons being at the ranch.

What in hell kind of people were they? Why was Suzanne the person to come after her brother? Weren't there any men in the Paxton family? Didn't anyone care what Mack did? Imagine a kid pulling the kind of stunt he had. Rand shook his head in utter disgust. Suzanne seemed like a nice woman—pretty, too—but Mack needed a swift kick in the seat of his pants. *He* might not be the one to administer it, but make no mistake, that kid was going to behave as long as he was on Kincaid land!

Rand thought about how Mack had dogged his footsteps all afternoon, while he'd searched every building on the place for that case of dynamite. The boy had never stopped asking questions. "What 'cha looking for, Rand?" "What's this thing, Rand?" "What d'ya use this for?" "Will you teach me to ride?" "Would you show me how to use a lasso?" "Do you like western movies, Rand?" "How come your folks named you Rand? I never heard that name before."

On and on, Rand thought now. He'd answered only a few of Mack's incessant questions, because his mind had been totally focused on finding that dynamite. Then the men had started riding in, and Rand hadn't wanted them to know what he'd been doing and had stopped poking into every nook and cranny of the buildings. Mack had gotten so excited about the cowboys' return that he'd left Rand alone and hung onto the corral fence as the men unsaddled their horses.

Walking to the bunkhouse, Rand had chuckled, because Mack was now questioning the hands. "What's your horse's name?" "How long have you been a cowboy?" "Are you gonna wipe your horse down?" "What's that you're feeding him?" "Is that one a stallion?"

Just before going in, Rand heard J.D. drawl, "Hey, kid, are you any relation to Dale Carson? He's just full of questions, too."

Thinking of that now, Rand saw it from a different perspective than he had at the time. Mack was honestly curious about everything on the ranch. Was it possible he'd answered that ad in his sister's name hoping that Suzanne and Rand would click and he and his sister would move to Montana?

But if that was the case, he didn't know his sister very well, did he? Mack might be wild about the west, but Suzanne sure wasn't. At the very least she didn't understand western hospitality. Why, she wouldn't even take off her coat to drink a cup of coffee.

Still, she must have received quite a shock upon learning what Mack had done. Imagining *that* scenario caused Rand to snort out a laugh. Suzanne would probably never see the humor in it, but now that he thought of it, it seemed pretty darned funny.

A three-foot-deep snowdrift across the road took Rand's mind off everything but his driving for several minutes, and he was glad to see the other side of it. That had been the worst drift so far, and it gave him a pretty good idea of what he'd find at the ranch. If the storm blew itself out by morning, he would plow them out tomorrow and everything would get back to normal.

But, if anything, the storm seemed to be gaining fury with every passing hour, and he feared they were in for a hell of a few days.

The ranch's long driveway was the worst of all. If Rand hadn't known it so well, he never would have been able to stay on the roadway, as it was completely drifted over. Thank God for four-wheel-drive, he thought as he peered through the windshield praying to see some lights. If he didn't, that meant the electricity was out, and it wasn't as if everyone could hop into four-wheelers and get off the ranch while they still could. They had to stay to feed the animals. In this kind of weather the cattle and horses needed lots of feed to keep their body temperature up. It wasn't impossible for cattle to freeze to death in storms like this one, and they would definitely be in jeopardy without food.

An enormous sigh of relief lifted Rand's shoulders when he spotted lights ahead, blurred though they were through the heavy snow coming down. He came to a grinding halt in a bank of snow and turned off the engine. That was when he let the exhaustion he'd been fighting overcome him. It took every ounce of energy he could muster to haul himself out of his rig and trudge through the snow to the bunkhouse.

He went in and turned right in the hall, fully intending to immediately fall into bed. But a voice behind him stopped him.

"Rand?"

He turned and saw J.D. "Hi," was all he could get out of his mouth.

"You look beat."

"I am."

"Is George all right?"

"He has a broken leg and a badly sprained back." Rand couldn't keep from yawning. "Sorry. I can't even see straight anymore. The roads are damned near impassable, even with a four-wheeler."

"I'm surprised you made it back at all. Rand, I told Slim to go to bed. It's so bad out there I doubt if anyone's going to try any sabotage tonight. I plan to stay up, though, and if anyone comes down those stairs, I'll know it."

"Thanks, J.D. Appreciate it. Good night." Rand turned

away and headed for his bedroom. He passed the door to the room in which Suzanne Paxton slept, but he never even thought of her.

In truth, he wasn't thinking of anything but closing his eyes and getting some sleep as he entered his bedroom.

Even before Suzanne's eyes opened the next morning she knew where she was—the wind-driven snow hitting the bunkhouse was evidence enough. Her spirits spiraled downward; the storm was raging.

Huddled under her blankets she recalled hearing noises in the night—voices, footsteps, the closing of doors. The memory wasn't vivid or clear as she had only just barely come awake at the sounds and had immediately gone back to sleep.

But it was logical to think that Rand Harding had returned at some point during the night, and it was him coming in that she'd heard. Lying there pondering her situation, she wondered if she could make some sort of arrangement with Mr. Harding. He had obviously driven to Whitehorn and back in spite of the storm, and maybe he would agree to driving the distance again, to take her and Mack to town where she could possibly make further arrangements to be driven to Billings and the airport.

Of course there was her rental car to consider. If Rand *did* agree to take her and Mack to Whitehorn, then he would also have to see that her car was returned to the Billings airport when the storm broke. It was a lot to ask of anyone.

But, dammit, *his* stupid ad had started this whole fiasco! she thought with a sudden burst of fiery temper. It was impossible to say at this point who she was most angry with, Rand Harding or Mack. Her timidity last night while explaining herself to Rand infuriated her this morning. What did she have to be meekly apologetic for, anyhow?

Her anger propelled her out of bed and into the small, adjoining bathroom for a shower. She thought of George's injury last night—poor man. Her ardent hope that he was all right took the focus off *her* problems. But she soon felt them all again, acutely and with the added issue of the raging blizzard outside.

It took twenty-five minutes from her shower to being fully dressed and ready to face the day. She'd put on the warmest clothing she'd brought with her, a pair of navy slacks, a blue-and-white striped shirt and a navy pullover sweater.

Quickly she made the bed, put her cosmetics and blow-dryer back into her suitcase, then opened the door of the bedroom and stepped into the hall. She realized at once that there wasn't even the slightest sound coming from anywhere in the building.

Pulling the door shut, she walked toward the kitchen, peering into the office and up the stairs as she passed them. At the kitchen doorway, she stopped cold. There were dirty plates, bowls, pots and pans everywhere, frying pans with congealed grease on the stove and crumbs, spills and eggshells on the counters.

"Good heavens," she whispered, recalling the pristine condition of this room only last night. What on earth had hit it, a minitornado?

Continuing on to the dining room, she saw coffee mugs and more dirty dishes on the tables. Frowning, she noticed the windows without drapes or blinds and hurried over to them.

"Oh, no," she moaned at her first good look outside. There were mountains of snow and it was still coming down. In fact it was snowing so hard and so densely, she could just barely make out the dark shape of a building in the distance. Where were the men? Where was Mack?

"Still upstairs in bed," she muttered, turning to dash to the staircase and unhesitantly climb to the second floor. This morning and under these dire circumstances, she was not in the least concerned about propriety. If the other men were still in their beds and she disturbed them, tough!

But there wasn't a soul up there. She opened door after door and saw only empty bedrooms and bathrooms. In one of the rooms she spied Mack's royal blue backpack on top of a bureau. The bed was neatly made, the room tidy. The backpack indicated that Mack had slept here last night, but since when had he started making his bed?

Annoyed that he would tidy his room on this ranch when he was such a slob at home, Suzanne closed the door inordinately hard and returned to the first floor. Going to the kitchen in search of a cup of coffee, she tried to figure out the situation.

Who had made this awful mess and then left it? Who was going to clean it up? Didn't the ranch have a cook, or was he outside with the other men, doing only God knew what in this terrible weather?

Poking among the debris on the counter, she was thrilled to find a large, electric coffeepot filled with hot coffee. Pouring herself a cup, she took it to the stool she had used last night and sat down. Did Mack even know she was here? she wondered angrily. Had Harding bothered to tell him?

She stewed through that first cup of coffee, then got up for a refill. Realizing she was hungry, she found the bread and dropped a slice into the large toaster. Looking for some jelly, she opened the door of the refrigerator and was amazed at the amount and variety of food it contained. The side-by-side freezer was full, too. Curious suddenly, she began opening cabinet doors. There was enough food in this kitchen to feed a small army for weeks!

With her piece of toast on a small plate and second cup of coffee, she again perched on the stool. Well, damn, she thought irately. Where were the men, and what could they possibly be doing in so much snow? Mack was with them, obviously, but why? If she had the clothes to conquer the snow and cold outside, she would go looking for him. She was furious with him and ached to tell him so. A second later she began worrying about *his* clothes, and if he was dressed warmly enough to survive such bitter weather.

After a while Suzanne heaved a long-suffering sigh. She might never be able to completely forgive Mack for putting her through this, but he was still her brother and some part of her would always love him whatever shenanigans he pulled.

As for herself, she couldn't just sit there and stare at that filthy kitchen while she waited for Mack to come in. Leaving her perch, she began cleaning up. Rinsing dirty dishes from both the kitchen and dining room, she stacked them in the huge dishwasher. She put away bread and pancake mix, and she filled one of the sinks with soapy water and washed the greasy pans by hand. She even mopped the floor, as she had located a broom closet that contained mops, brooms and a vacuum cleaner.

It all took more than an hour, but finally the kitchen looked as it had last night. Maybe someone would thank her, maybe not. It didn't matter. She had killed some time and worked off some nervous energy. And although she felt absolutely no obligation to do anything that might benefit Rand Harding, she was proud of the result of her work.

Rand and the men were hauling hay with teams of horses and sleds. There was no way even a four-wheeler could get through the amount of snow covering the fields, and it was cold, miserable, backbreaking work. There was plenty of grousing among the men, but it was mostly aimed at the weather. They had put blankets on the horses before harnessing them, but the snow was soft, and the heavy animals' every step was an effort. The sleds even sank some with their loads of hay, but the cattle were belly-deep in snow and bawling for food.

Feeding in a blizzard was a form of organized chaos. Some of the men drove the teams, the others dropped hay. They went back and forth from the ricks of hay near the compound to the fields, again and again. Water was another problem. Rand put two men to work chopping through the ice covering the drinking ponds.

By noon everyone was exhausted and ravenously hungry. Remembering the mess he'd left in the kitchen after cooking breakfast, Rand's lips thinned. But he'd somehow wade through it to heat some soup, make sandwiches and more coffee. The men had to be fed as well as the animals.

They filed into the dining room and began shedding heavy jackets, caps, gloves and mufflers. "Mack, how about giving me a hand in the kitchen," Rand said.

"Sure," the boy agreed. His cheeks were red as apples. He'd done the work of a man this morning, and Rand was feeling a good deal of respect for Mack Paxton. He hadn't yet told him about his sister being on the ranch, but now was probably a good time to do so, he figured. Leaving his own outdoor gear near the door of the dining room with the other men's, he headed for the kitchen with Mack on his heels.

"Whoa," he exclaimed when he saw the clean room. There was only one person who could have done this, and he turned to face Mack. "There's something I have to tell you. Your sister is here."

Mack's face fell. "Aw, heck."

Rand couldn't help grinning. "You mean you're not thrilled?"

"She's just gonna haul me back to Baltimore," Mack mumbled unhappily.

Rand glanced around the spotless kitchen. "Obviously she doesn't like a messy kitchen."

"She doesn't like *anything* messy," Mack said gloomily.

"Well, cheer up, Mack. She might be planning to take you back to Baltimore, but it's not going to happen right away."

Suzanne had heard the men come in and had hurried from her bedroom to the kitchen. She walked in just as Rand made that comment about her and Mack's return to Baltimore not happening right away.

"Why isn't it going to happen right away?" she demanded while glaring at her brother. Mack stepped behind Rand, as though putting a barrier between himself and his sister's wrath.

"Because the roads are completely drifted over," Rand told her, feeling the strongest compulsion to laugh because of Mack hiding behind him and trying to look invisible.

"You made it to Whitehorn and back last night," Suzanne reminded him a bit sharply.

Rand couldn't suppress a smile any longer. Mack glued to his back, Suzanne looking as though she would like to strangle someone—it seemed pretty funny. "Simmer down, sweetheart," Rand drawled. "Last night and today are worlds apart." He heard Mack snicker and jabbed the boy with his elbow. *He* could laugh about this, but not Mack. Not after what he'd pulled on his sister. "Have you taken a look outside this morning?"

"Of course I looked outside! The whole bunkhouse was totally deserted when I got up, you know."

"Then you know there's about three feet more snow on the ground than there was when I drove to town," Rand retorted. "And the reason the bunkhouse was deserted when you got up was because we had to get an early start on feeding the cattle."

Mack stuck his head around Rand's arm. "We've been hauling hay with horses and sleds," he said to his sister, as proudly as if he had introduced the practice to snowed-in ranchers.

Suzanne shot Mack a dirty look, and he quickly ducked out of sight again. "Would you please stop acting as though I beat you on a regular basis?" she shrieked.

"She does, Rand," Mack whispered.

Rand laughed right out loud. "Don't kid a kidder, Mack."

"What did he say?" Suzanne snapped at Rand.

"Nothing you'd be interested in," Rand replied evenly. Even though he didn't approve of what Mack had done, he couldn't help liking the boy and his wide-eyed enthusiasm for everything on the ranch. Plus, the way Mack had worked this morning, he deserved *some* consideration in Rand's opinion. "Incidentally, thanks for cleaning the kitchen."

Suzanne's lips pursed. She was still mad as hell at both Rand Harding and her brother, and she couldn't help showing it. "I have never seen a worse mess in my life. If that's the norm around here…"

"It isn't." Rand was taking in Suzanne's fetching outfit. Her dark, shoulder-length hair was shiny clean and gleaming with auburn highlights, and her lips and cheeks had a pink, healthy sheen. Even with anger shooting from her heavily lashed dark eyes, she was one very pretty woman, and he truly enjoyed looking at her.

However, she didn't seem exactly receptive to male admiration at the moment, so he cleared his throat in an attempt to clear his mind of such personal thoughts. "Normally we have a cook. It was just starting to snow last night when Handy—that's his name—had to leave for a family emergency. Not very long before you got here, as a matter of fact. The two of you might even have passed each other on the road."

Suzanne's eyes narrowed suspiciously, which Rand didn't miss. "I did not see one single car when I drove out here," she said in a rather haughty manner.

Rand ignored the queen-for-a-day tone of her voice and shrugged. "Guess Handy could have taken a different road. Anyway, thanks for cleaning up. Mack and I are going to make some lunch for the men now, aren't we, Mack?"

Mack squirmed, then took one very small step to stand at Rand's side. "Suzanne, don't be mad," he pleaded.

"Don't be mad! Mack, do you have any realistic idea of what you've done?" She didn't want to talk about money—or their lack thereof—in front of Rand, but the subject was all but written in her eyes. Mack visibly cringed, and Suzanne knew he was fully aware to what she was referring. He had wasted their very slim savings on a foolish trip to Montana, and forced her to do the same. His was not a minor prank, not by a long shot, and it was going to be a very long time before she forgave him.

Rand broke in. "Look, if you two need to talk, go on into the office. I've got a dozen hungry men to feed before we go out again and finish today's work."

"I'm going with you again," Mack said to Rand. He dared to look at his sister. "And I'm gonna help make lunch, too."

Mack was different, Suzanne realized with no small amount of surprise. What was there about this place that had changed him from a lazy, apathetic, sullen boy into a young man not only willing but eager to help out? Her gaze moved to Rand. Was it *this* man's doing?

But Mack had only been in Harding's company a few hours longer than herself. Well, maybe a day longer, she conceded, eight or nine hours longer, but that certainly wasn't time enough for anyone to change another person's entire personality.

However, the changes she sensed in her brother were positive changes, and she had to wonder if he would revert back to his former smart-alecky self when they returned to Baltimore.

She suddenly wasn't so sure of herself. Not that she could have stayed in Baltimore and done nothing after learning her fourteen-year-old brother had run away to go to Montana. But herself arriving angry, and showing anger now, could be a mistake. There was something going on with Mack—maybe had been for a long time—that she didn't know about. Something he'd never talked about. Would he talk about it now?

No, not this minute, she decided. But later, maybe this evening.

"Would you like *me* to help with lunch, too?" she asked quietly.

Her abrupt turnabout startled Rand, but he could sure use her help. "You bet," he said enthusiastically. "Mack, go into that last cupboard and get out four large cans of soup. Any kind will do, just make sure all the cans are the same. Suzanne, you can start making sandwiches. There's ham and—"

"I know what's in the refrigerator. I took a peek," she told him.

Rand grinned. "Great. Okay, we're organized. I'm going to make fresh coffee and set out dishes and condiments."

Suzanne sighed to herself as she set to work. Never in a million years could she have imagined herself on a ranch in Montana, making sandwiches in a kitchen like this one with a raging blizzard howling outside.

Did fate have any other tricks in store for her?

"I certainly hope not," she mumbled under her breath.

Six

Lunch was ready. "Join us in the dining room?" Rand said to Suzanne.

She hesitated, thinking of eating with all those strange men, whom she could hear talking and laughing among themselves.

"Thank you, but I think I'll have my sandwich in here." They were alone in the kitchen—Mack had toted an enormous tray of sandwiches into the dining room—and as she looked into Rand Harding's deep blue eyes, she felt a flush creep into her cheeks. Obviously he was a serious man, but there was also a devilish twinkle in his eyes that told her he wasn't *all* business.

Well, she thought, maybe it took a man with a sense of humor to advertise for a mail-order bride, shocking as the whole awful idea still was to her.

Rand was thinking of something else entirely. Without the blizzard, Suzanne would have picked up her brother and immediately left. As much additional hard labor as the storm was causing everyone, he was suddenly glad it had struck.

"You don't have to eat alone," he said, thrilled with the high color in her pretty face. She obviously wasn't comfortable being alone with him, which he took as an indication of physical attraction. Well, he felt it, too. It wasn't overwhelming desire, or anything like that, more of an awareness of each other, but it was a good feeling and he wanted to explore it. The storm was going to keep Suzanne here for at least another day, and he'd be a damned fool not to make the most of the opportunity. He smiled.

Suzanne looked away from that smile, which seemed a little too friendly to her. They weren't friends—just barely acquaintances, in fact—and she didn't want him getting any funny ideas about her.

"I prefer eating alone, if you don't mind," she said with her eyes everywhere but on his face.

Rand looked at her for another few moments, most definitely enjoying the view, then shrugged. "Suit yourself."

After he'd gone, Suzanne took a deep breath and began making another sandwich. There was a nervous flutter in her stomach that she couldn't blame on hunger. All right, so he's good-looking, she conceded uneasily. But when did good looks ever pay the bills?

But Rand had a good job, didn't he? A job with loads of responsibility, a crew of men to run, valuable property to oversee. The owners of this ranch, whoever they were, must trust him implicitly.

Now, why would a man with Rand's looks and apparent—thus far—steadfastness need to advertise for a wife? There had to be *something* wrong with him, some trait or characteristic she hadn't yet seen in him. Maybe he had a violent temper, or perhaps he had gone through all of the available women in the area and had a bad reputation where women were concerned.

She knew she was reaching, but his advertising for a wife

seemed so crazy to her that she couldn't help looking for a reason for what she considered abnormal behavior.

Seating herself at the counter again, she started eating. There wasn't quite so much chatter coming from the dining room now, she realized. The men must be too busy filling their stomachs to talk.

A minute later one of those men walked into the kitchen. He was tall, lean and looked so much like a real cowboy that Suzanne gaped. He also looked vaguely familiar, although she was certain they'd never met. Maybe he merely reminded her of someone she knew in Baltimore, she thought, though she couldn't imagine who it might be.

"Hello, ma'am," he said in a soft voice. "Just came in for that coffeepot. Sorry to bother you."

"No bother at all," Suzanne responded, still wondering why he would look familiar. He was older than Rand, and she instinctively suspected that he had been born and bred on a ranch and then had worked as a cowhand all his life. She watched him pick up the huge coffeepot with one hand and suddenly wanted to delay his departure. "I'm Suzanne Paxton, Mack's sister. Do you know Mack?"

The man's mouth twitched, as though a grin was just waiting to happen. It gave Suzanne the impression that he didn't grin very much. One of those strong, silent types, she thought.

"Yes, I know Mack," he said. "I'm J. D. Cade. And I met you last night, Miss Paxton. I woke you in the office and showed you to the bedroom Rand said you should use."

"Of course," Suzanne said, finally placing him, albeit as a very faint memory. "It's nice meeting you, Mr. Cade," she added.

"Nice meeting you, Miss Paxton." Nodding, he walked out with the coffeepot.

Gosh, things are different out here, she thought with a sigh. Had anyone ever addressed her as "ma'am" in Baltimore? Certainly her ex-husband hadn't treated women with such respect. She would bet anything that J. D. Cade opened doors for women, stood when they entered a room and pulled out chairs for them.

Did Rand do those things, too? Did he think of women as the fairer sex, or as equals and let them open their own doors? Which did she prefer, equality or respect?

"Hmm," she murmured. This was not a subject she'd ever thought of before. She had carried her own weight for so long—even during her marriage—that the idea of a man actually taking care of a woman was startling. Of course, if she looked back, her father had not only financially supported her mother, he had treated her with a great deal of respect. It was only her own life that had gotten so out of hand. Marrying Les had been a dreadful mistake in judgment. If she ever married again...

No, she was not going to fantasize about something that would probably never happen. Her reality was getting back to Baltimore as fast as she could and finding a job that paid enough to support her and Mack. Granted, she hoped for more out of life than a steady paycheck, but right now she would settle for that.

But she had her dreams, make no mistake. For one, she wanted so much for Mack to look at high school as a serious step to his future. She'd even gone to his school and talked to his counselor, coming home with all sorts of information on grants and scholarships for students with high grades. Mack had refused to even look at the material, and she remembered asking him if he wanted to dig ditches for a living when he graduated high school, if he ever did.

Her eyes narrowed slightly when she recalled his answer: *I got plans, Suzanne, and I don't need any college education to make them work, either.* She had tried to get him to tell her about those plans, but he'd clammed up and that had been that.

Now he seemed so…dare she use the word *happy?* Was working on a ranch the height of his ambition? Had he been thinking about becoming a cowboy all the time he'd been living with her? If so, why hadn't he felt she should know? Did he think she wouldn't understand, or that she would attempt to undermine his boyish fantasies? And yet he didn't seem quite as boyish out here as he had in Baltimore. Yes, hiding behind Rand had been an immature reaction to seeing her, but when he finally had shown himself, she had seen something new and alive in his eyes, an excitement he hadn't expressed since their parents' deaths.

Suzanne sucked in a breath and released it slowly. This was definitely food for thought. She was Mack's only living relative and his legal guardian. He should live with her until his eighteenth birthday, but if he was determined to live in Montana, would she be able to stop him? Somehow she had to get Mack to open up with her; they *had* to have a serious discussion.

Rand came in, interrupting her ponderous reverie. He was carrying a large stack of dirty plates. Sending her a smile, he set them in the sink. "I'm going to appreciate Handy a lot more when he gets back than I did before he left," he said with a bit of a chuckle.

"I'll clean up," Suzanne said quietly.

Rand turned to look at her. "You don't have to do that."

"It will give me something to do. Go on back to work. I can hear the men getting ready to leave."

"Are you sure?"

"Very sure. I would appreciate your doing one thing for me, if you don't mind my asking."

"What is it, Suzanne?"

"Keep an eye on Mack. He might think he's as old and grown-up as the men in your crew, but he's only fourteen and he's green as a gourd around *any* kind of work. He's rarely been around large animals, either. I…I've just figured out— or I think I have—the reason he answered your ad. He wants to be a cowboy."

"And he thought if he married you off to one…" Rand let the implication dangle.

Suzanne flushed slightly, but she answered candidly. "That's what I believe, yes."

Rand shook his head in a show of amazement. "Well, you've got to give him points for having the grit to go after what he wants out of life, Suzanne. And I'll tell you something else that might make you feel better. He worked as hard as any man out there all morning. I wouldn't worry too much about him if I were you. He's a pretty good kid."

"But he *is* just a kid, which is why I would like you to keep an eye on him." She could have added that Mack hadn't been "a pretty good kid" in Baltimore, and that he had tried her patience to the breaking point nearly every day, but she didn't, firmly believing that family problems should stay in the family.

"I'll watch him, don't worry," Rand said. "I'd better get back to work now. See you later."

"Yes," Suzanne murmured. "See you later."

After the kitchen was back in order, Suzanne felt at loose ends. Wandering the first floor, she looked out every window she came to and shuddered repeatedly. This had to be a record-breaking blizzard. Hoping to hear a weather forecast, she searched for a radio. There was one in the office, and she turned it on. All she got was static, and after a few minutes she gave up.

It occurred to her then that the telephone hadn't rung all day. Picking up the receiver of one, she immediately knew why there'd been no calls: the phone was dead. Did Rand know? Goodness, they couldn't even call the hospital and check on George. Rand *must* know, she decided, because she couldn't imagine that he hadn't attempted to learn how George was faring.

Looking around the office, it struck her that there wasn't a computer. Apparently George did his bookkeeping by hand. How strange in this day and age. The ranch was a composite of opposites, she decided—an ultramodern kitchen with every possible convenience and an outdated accounting system was a very good example.

She sighed heavily. This was certainly a different world than the one she lived in. Why was Mack so enchanted with it? And how had he known before coming to Montana that he *would* be enchanted with it?

There was an awful lot she didn't know about her brother, wasn't there?

By two-thirty Suzanne was ready to tear out her own hair. The fury of the storm outside was nerve-racking. She had tried to read in her room, but the only books she'd found were not to her liking—spy novels and westerns—and the magazines were even worse.

She ended up back in the kitchen. With nothing else to do, she figured she might as well prepare something for the men's dinner. Not that she was accustomed to cooking for so many people, but it shouldn't be that hard to do when everything in the kitchen was oversize and obviously designed for very large meals.

After checking the refrigerator again, she decided on a beef stew and set to work.

After announcing that no one would have to stand night guard that night, Rand sent all but three of the men to the bunkhouse. The storm was too bad for night patrol, he told them, which was only the truth. J.D. and the other man assigned guard duty had gotten precious little sleep last night—Rand hadn't slept much, either—while the saboteur, whoever he was, had probably spent a restful night in a warm bed. It wasn't only unfair, it was downright infuriating. Looking each man in the eye while he announced no night duty, Rand had wondered if the culprit was among his crew and chuckling to himself, planning to brave the storm *this* night and use that dynamite.

But anyone sneaking down those stairs would be in for a surprise: he would run into Rand himself.

They were done feeding the cattle for today—only to have to repeat the exhausting process again tomorrow—but the horses they'd used to pull the sleds needed tending, and Rand wanted to make sure it was done right. Thinking ahead to a sleepless night with a grim expression, Rand, with the help of the three hands, unharnessed the two teams, then each of them led a horse into the barn.

"I want them wiped down till they're dry," he told the men. "And check their hooves and legs for frostbite and injuries." Rand had done that throughout the day. These were valuable animals, huge draft horses that were kept on the ranch for exactly this sort of emergency. No one had ever ridden these horses. They had never felt a saddle or a human on their backs, and they probably never would.

"Better check ourselves for frostbite," one of the men grumbled.

They looked half-frozen, Rand had to agree, with their reddened faces, watery eyes and snowpacked clothing. But any man choosing this line of work had to take the bad with the good, and there were many, many good days. And once this storm passed, the good days would start. They were, as hard as it was to believe with gale-force winds and a blinding snowfall going on outdoors, heading into summer, and the summers in Montana were glorious.

As he wiped down the horse he'd brought into the barn, Rand felt himself starting to sweat. He stopped working to take off his heavy, sheepskin-lined jacket, and spotted a pair of dark brown eyes peering at him over the short wall separating this stall from the next.

"Mack, for hell's sake," he exclaimed. "Why aren't you in the bunkhouse?"

Mack came around the end of the wall, then leaned on it. "'Cause I wanted to see what you were gonna do with the horses."

Rand frowned at the boy. He not only looked half-frozen, he looked ready to fall over from exhaustion. There was something touching in Mack's avid curiosity, but he was carrying that curiosity too far right now.

"Mack, I told everyone but these three men to go inside," Rand said gruffly. "That included you. Now get your butt out of this barn and into the bunkhouse. If you're planning to work on a ranch when you're older, you've got to learn to follow orders."

"Uh, when I'm older? How old d'ya have to be to get a job on a ranch? Wouldn't you hire me?"

"Hell, no, I wouldn't hire you." Rand went back to wiping down the huge horse.

"But I'm a good worker. Didn't I work hard enough today?"

"You're a damned good worker, but you have to take life in some kind of order, Mack. Right now you belong in school."

Mack's expression turned sullen. "I hate school."

Rand straightened up and looked at the boy. "Why?"

"Lots of reasons," Mack mumbled. "It's stupid, Rand."

"What's going to be stupid is you if you don't finish high school." Rand began drying the horse's wet hide again.

"Did you?"

"Yes, I did."

"Did you go to college?"

"No, but there are times when I wish I had."

"Why?"

"Because this is a big world, Mack, and there's an awful lot I don't know about it." He faced the boy. "Have you ever met and talked to a truly educated person? They're different than you and I, Mack."

"My teachers are educated, and they're dopes."

"I doubt that, Mack. Did you ever once stop thinking of them as teachers and try to get to know them as people?"

Mack grimaced. "Hell, no," he said disgustedly.

"Then you really don't know what you're talking about, do you?" Rand turned back to the horse. "I want you to go to the bunkhouse now. Get out of those damp clothes, take a hot shower and warm up. I'll be in to make some supper for all of us in about ten minutes."

Mack shuffled away with his head down. Taking a moment to watch him go, Rand shook his head. He was beginning to get a glimpse of Mack's and Suzanne's relationship, and it wasn't all peaches and cream. Without question Mack had a mind of his own and a stubborn streak a mile wide. It must be really tough for a young woman to deal with a brother like Mack, Rand thought as he finished the drying process and hung the towel he'd used on a hook.

Fetching some oats, Rand poured them into the horse's feed bucket, then forked the stall's trough full of hay. For about the twentieth time that day everything fled his mind but that case of dynamite. He felt that he'd searched the barn thoroughly, as he had the other outbuildings, but it had to be somewhere—maybe, as Reed had suggested, right under his nose.

Well, there was nothing he could do about it tonight. He had to get inside and scare up some supper for the men. Maybe he could get some of them to help out, maybe not. They were cowhands, not cooks, and weren't above telling him so. Then there was the cleaning up and finally what he'd planned for the long night ahead—guard duty at the foot of the stairs. The whole damned night was nothing to look forward to with anything but disgust and anger.

Shrugging into his jacket, Rand yelled, "Are you guys finished?"

He got three different responses. "Almost." "In a minute." "I'm feeding now."

"I'm going in to see about some supper," Rand called.

"Good," one man called back. "I'm hungry enough to eat this here horse." The other two men chuckled.

Trudging to the bunkhouse, Rand wondered if he should have left them alone in the barn. If one of those men was the saboteur…?

But he'd picked the three men at random from the crew, and he felt that the guilty party was doing his dirty work solo. He wasn't apt to pull anything in front of two other men.

Stamping snow from his boots, Rand opened the bunkhouse door and walked in. Instantly he smelled the wonderful aroma of hot food. His whole system went into meltdown mode for Suzanne Paxton. Not only was she pretty and intelligent, she was adaptable, considerate and, judging from the mouthwatering smells, a mighty good cook. A fine woman. Any man would be very, very fortunate to have Suzanne for a wife.

He'd come in through the laundry room door, which Handy had adamantly demanded the men use when they were dirty or wet at the end of their workday. It wasn't unusual for the men to undress in here and carry their dirty clothes to their individual rooms in their stocking feet. Each of the bedrooms was equipped with a hamper, and each man washed his own clothes. There were four washers and three large, commercial dryers in here, plus a chart on the wall on which a man could write the time and day he wanted to do his laundry.

With a woman in the building, Rand suspected the men had gone to their rooms carrying only their boots. He took off his own, his heavy jacket, hat and gloves and headed for the kitchen with the armload. The smells in the air made his stomach growl with hunger, and his face was tingling from the warmth of the building. A smile stretched his warming skin when he saw Suzanne using a long-handled spoon to stir whatever was in the huge pot on the stove.

"I didn't expect you to cook supper, but I sure do appreciate it," he said. "Thank you."

Suzanne put the lid on the pot, set down the spoon and turned to look at him. His hair was hat-flattened, his face ruddy and he was still the best-looking man she'd ever seen. Flustered suddenly, she attempted an ordinary smile, which came off pretty weak.

"I—I had…nothing…else to do," she stammered.

Why, she's embarrassed, Rand thought. Embarrassed over a simple thank-you. Didn't anyone ever thank her for what she did in Baltimore? There was so much he didn't know about her. For a fact, he knew more about her kid brother than he did about Suzanne.

That was definitely going to change! "Well, guess I'd better get cleaned up," he said.

"How long before everyone will be ready to eat?"

"Fifteen minutes should do it."

"Fine, dinner will be on the tables."

Rand left, and Suzanne listened to his footsteps—muffled without his boots—and frowned when he didn't go up the stairs. Hurrying around the counter, she peered down the hall and saw him go through the very last door. Her eyes widened. He slept right next door to the room she'd been assigned? She had thought she was the only one sleeping on this floor!

Disconcerted and pondering what could have been a deliberate deception, she hurried to put the finishing touches on the meal she had cooked.

All day Suzanne had been anticipating a conversation with Mack when the workday was over, but the second he was through eating, he started upstairs.

"Mack, wait." Suzanne stood with one foot on the first step. "We need to talk."

Mack could barely hold his head up. "I can't, Suzanne. I'm beat. Tomorrow, okay?"

Frowning, she watched him slowly ascend the stairs, moving like a very old man. Her lips pursed. He had worked too hard today. Rand should not have permitted it. She had asked him to keep an eye on Mack, and he should have seen how worn-out the boy was getting.

"Excuse us, ma'am." The other men were also going upstairs. Suzanne quickly got out of their way. "Thank you for a good supper," most of them said as they passed by her.

"You're welcome," she murmured several times. Deep in thought, she returned to the kitchen. The counters were laden; apparently the men had brought in their dishes from the dining room. Rand came in carrying several large serving bowls.

"You're a fine cook," he told her. "There's nothing left. We devoured everything in sight."

"Was there enough?" she asked a bit anxiously.

"Since everyone had thirds, I'd say so. Oh, everyone but Mack. He didn't eat much. Too tired, I guess."

"Um, yes, I wanted to talk to you about that. He's overly tired, Rand, and I don't think that's healthy for a boy his age."

Rand set the bowls down. "The only way I could have gotten him to quit working and return to the bunkhouse would have been to bodily drag him in. Should I have done that in front of the men? Suzanne, I know he's only a boy, and we talked a little in the barn and I know he's got some ideas about his future you couldn't possibly agree with. But force is not going to work with Mack."

"What is?" she asked very quietly, very seriously.

"You're worried about him, aren't you? Suzanne, how come he's your responsibility?"

"Our parents were killed in a car accident. Naturally I took him into my home and filed for guardianship. He's my brother, and I love him. I…wish I were able to do better for him. He's very unhappy in Baltimore."

Rand was thrilled they were talking, and he took a shot in the dark to keep the conversational ball rolling. "I kind of got the impression from Mack that you're not so happy, either."

"He told you that?" Surprise widened Suzanne's eyes.

"Not specifically, but I sort of read between the lines— when he first got here and I was questioning him about why he was here and you weren't."

A sense of having just lost her privacy caused a frown to crease Suzanne's forehead. With Mack for a brother, though, should anything surprise her? Besides, was there really any good reason to lie about her troubles in Baltimore?

"If I've been unhappy it's because things have been…well, difficult for some time now," she murmured.

"In what way?" Rand asked.

She wasn't sure she wanted to get that specific, but Rand seemed genuinely concerned, not just morbidly curious, and God knew it would feel good to unload on someone.

"My biggest worry is that I lost my job and haven't been able to find another one," she finally said.

It hit Rand that she had no reason to rush back to Baltimore, and he couldn't help thinking that her misfortune just might be his *good* fortune.

Rand suddenly wasn't feeling exactly calm. Suzanne was

pretty and bright and she was *here!* How could he possibly be miserable over that?

"I wasn't fired from my previous position, the accounting department was downsized," she continued with a note of bitterness in her voice. "A new computer system replaced a few of us."

Despite the wheels spinning in his mind, he managed to speak normally, with just the right amount of concerned interest in her problems. "Meaning the company was reducing its staff."

"Exactly." Suzanne began rinsing dishes for the dishwasher.

"You told George you're a bookkeeper."

"I'm an accountant. I'm not a C.P.A., but I could be with only a few more college credits."

"Is that your goal?"

"When time and money permits, yes. Speaking of George, you must be wondering how he's doing. The phones are still dead, or they were a half hour ago when I last checked them."

Rand forced his thoughts from her to her change of subject. "Yes, I'm concerned, but there's nothing I can do, Suzanne, except to thank God that George took that fall last night instead of today. Only He knows when this storm will blow itself out and the plows will get out this far. To be honest, my biggest concern is that a power line will snap and we'll be without electricity." He saw sudden fear in her eyes and hastened to dispel it. "We'd get by, Suzanne. I didn't tell you that to worry or scare you."

She regarded him silently for a moment, realized she was doing it, decided she couldn't help being nice to such a considerate person, then said, "You're a kind man, aren't you?"

"Why would I ever be unkind to someone like you?" he returned softly. "Why would anyone?"

Their eyes met and held for a very long time. Suzanne felt something warm and lovely creep into her system while looking into Rand Harding's vivid blue eyes, and Rand was thinking that she had to be the most special woman he had ever met, bar none. A caring, warmhearted woman, a woman with ambition and dreams, a woman who had taken in her wayward younger brother and undoubtedly worried herself sick over where he was heading.

"Suzanne," he said quietly. "I'm going to put you on the payroll while you're here."

"I wouldn't hear of it!" she exclaimed. "Mack and I are not guests, we're impositions."

"You could never be an imposition." Rand had to smile. "Mack, now... Just kidding. I like Mack, and I'd like to help you get him pointed in the right direction. Let's both face facts, Suzanne. You can't leave until the weather breaks, and I need a cook *and* a bookkeeper. You can use the money and I can use the help. What do you say?"

"I would continue to do the cooking and any paperwork you want done without pay. Why are you offering me a paycheck?"

"Do you think George and Handy work without one? Do you think I do? Why should you?" He moved closer to her, took her right hand from under the tap water and held it while grinning at her. "It's a pretty slippery way to seal a deal, but it's still a handshake."

Suzanne couldn't help laughing. "All right. I can see you're not going to take no for an answer. Consider me an employee while I'm here."

You're a hell of a lot more than an employee to me, Suzanne Paxton. "Right on," he exclaimed. Slowly he let her hand slip from his, and it pleased him no end that Suzanne hadn't immediately drawn hers back. "Now, let's get this kitchen cleaned up so we can go to the office and get you familiar with George's methods."

"You do not have to help me clean the kitchen. You worked all day and you have to be as tired as the other men."

"The other men wouldn't be tired, either, if they had you to talk to."

Suzanne cocked an eyebrow at him. "Are you flirting with me?"

Rand put his head back and let out a roar of laughter. Damn, she made him feel good.

The myriad problems he had to deal with—the weather, the saboteur, that box of dynamite and having to stay up all night to keep watch—didn't seem nearly as bad right now as they had out in the barn. All because of a watery handshake, a few flirty remarks and the prettiest, most expressive eyes any woman could have.

Life was sometimes an almost unbearable trial, but it did have its moments, didn't it?

Seven

Rand told Suzanne to sit at George's desk. She did so, and he pulled the chair over from the other desk to be near her.

He realized that a discussion on paperwork was necessary if she was going to accomplish anything in this office, but he would much rather talk about her. *Have you always lived in Baltimore? Is there an important man in your life? Do you have any favorable feelings at all about Montana?* Considering the blizzard that had arrived just about the time she had, she probably didn't think much of the area, and could he blame her?

Deciding to get business out of the way before anything else, Rand cleared his throat. "You know more about this than I do, so where should we start?"

"At the beginning," she said with a smile. "The start of any bookkeeping system is the checkbook, Rand."

"Oh. Well, George keeps that in the lower right-hand drawer of that desk."

Suzanne swiveled her chair to the wall shelves behind her, upon which resided a neat row of black-bound books. "And these must be his books of permanent record," she said. She glanced back at Rand. "May I look through them?"

"Anytime you wish."

"I'll just check one of them now so I can tell what accounting system George uses."

"There's more than one kind?"

She smiled and nodded. "Single entry or double entry." She pulled a book labeled Check Register from the shelf and laid it on the desk. Flipping it open, she studied it for a few moments, then said, "Double entry. Good."

"You can tell that fast?"

Suzanne smiled again. "Would you like a lesson on accounting procedures, Rand?"

He shook his head adamantly. "No, thank you."

Suzanne closed the book and looked at him. "I think we should discuss how involved you want me to get with your records. Remember, I won't be here very long. And how will George feel about my even touching his books? Rand, you have to understand something. An accountant feels quite— oh, what's the word?—possessive, maybe, about his or her work."

"Really?" Rand looked dubious.

"Trust me, it's the truth. You must know George's attitudes and personality. Is he going to resent someone else doing his work?"

Rand thought for a moment. "Suzanne, I have to do what's best for the ranch. I honestly don't think George will resent anything you do in here, but if he does…well, I'll deal with that if and when it happens." He paused, thought again for several seconds, then said, "What I need most right now is a payroll."

"When is payday?"

"Tomorrow."

"Tomorrow?" she echoed, her lovely eyes opened wide.

Rand shrugged. "But is there really any hurry? I mean, until the men can leave the ranch, what could they possibly do with their checks?"

"You're absolutely right, we don't even have mail service. But that's not the point, Suzanne. There's never been a late payroll on this ranch while I've been here, and I'd like to keep it that way."

Suzanne nodded. "I understand." Again she turned her chair to survey the black-bound books. Spotting one bearing the label Payroll Records, she took it from the shelf and, moving the Check Register aside, laid it on the desk. After going through it for a few minutes, she raised her eyes to Rand. "George is a methodical accountant. Everything is here. There's a page for each employee, citing salary, social security number and other pertinent information. Also, every check they've received is recorded. Unless you've given someone a raise or changed their status in some way, I can use what's in this book and get your payroll out by noon tomorrow. Is that soon enough?"

Rand sat back. "You're incredible."

From the tone of his voice Suzanne suspected he wasn't just talking about her accounting abilities. Neither was he flirting, as he'd done in the kitchen. His expression was seriously admiring, and she couldn't help responding to it when no one had admired her for anything for a very long time.

It seemed an eternity and she still wasn't able to force her eyes from his, and during that time a great change took place within her. She was immeasurably attracted to this man, and was there any logical reason why she should deny or fight it?

"Am I really?" she quietly asked, belying the quickened beat of her heart.

"You are," Rand said so softly she just barely heard him. She was such a pleasure to look at that he couldn't stop staring. It was as though he were etching her features on his brain so that when she was gone he would be able to remember every detail of her face and form.

Something wonderful is happening here, Suzanne thought as warmth blossomed within her. It had been so long since she'd felt this delicious, potent attraction to and from a man, and she wanted to sustain and protect it. To make it last for a while.

Her hint of a smile was pure female. "Because I understand accounting?"

"No, because you're beautiful and caring, smart and unselfish, and you're also adaptable."

Her smile became broader, slightly teasing. "All of those things? My, I really am incredible, aren't I?"

"You really don't believe it, do you?"

She didn't want to burst his bubble by describing what a truly ordinary woman she was. Certainly she wasn't *beautiful* by any stretch of the imagination. Pretty, maybe, in a quiet sort of way, but not beautiful. And yet it was that very fact that made her absorb Rand's compliment like a thirsty sponge. True or not, it was lovely to hear.

As for the rest of his opinion, if she *weren't* caring, unselfish and adaptable, her life would be even harder than it was. As for Rand's word *smart,* she knew she was very smart in some things and extremely obtuse in others. Perhaps uneducated was a better word than obtuse, as she was thinking of how badly she was failing with Mack and most of that failure was due to an ignorance of teenage boys.

But they weren't discussing Mack right now, were they? And if Rand had any more lovely things to say to her, she wanted to hear them.

"I think you're making me believe it," she said quietly, which wasn't entirely true but neither was it a total lie. Maybe what was happening was that he was making her *want* to believe it.

Rand was thinking that he'd give up a month's pay to kiss her right now. She had sensually full lips, and he could almost taste their texture and warmth. Breathing normally was becoming difficult. A bittersweet ache in his groin was getting more pronounced.

"Suzanne—" he leaned forward "—when I put that ad in that magazine, I never dreamed—I didn't *dare* dream—that it would result in my meeting someone like you."

It was as though someone had suddenly doused Suzanne with ice water. She had actually forgotten that abominable ad! Her pulse rate dropped so fast she saw spots before her eyes. What in God's name had she been doing? Listening to and half believing what could only be flattery for some nefarious reason of Rand's own, forgetting completely that his horrid ad had caused her untold grief and that the worst was yet to come, when she and Mack got back to Baltimore and had to scrimp by to even eat!

Rand felt a sudden influx of shock. The expression on Suzanne's face would dilute the most fiery of emotions. But what did it mean? What was she thinking?

"Suzanne," he said frantically. "What's wrong?"

The anger within herself, *aimed* at herself, expanded to include Rand. "I'm sure you know," she snapped, standing to transfer the black-bound books from the desk to the wall shelf.

Rand, too, got to his feet. "I'm sorry, but I *don't* know."

"Take a wild guess," she said coldly. "Unless there's something else you wish to discuss concerning the work in this office, I'm going to bed." Glaring at him, tapping her toe impatiently, she waited to hear his answer.

Rand couldn't believe this was happening. They'd been getting along so well. Better than well. She'd been so sweetly feminine, so desirable, and now she looked as though one more word from him would start World War III.

He frowned. Surely his mentioning that ad hadn't caused this. It wasn't, after all, something she hadn't known about.

He couldn't let her leave in this state, and his mind raced for something to say to get her talking again.

"Uh, there is something," he said uneasily. "I'd like to put Mack on the payroll. I've been operating shorthanded and—"

"Why?"

"Why what?"

"Why have you been operating shorthanded?" Her eyes were like hard brown icicles.

Rand's stomach sank. Instinct told him that the truth would scare her. Hell, it scared him. They could all be blown up in their sleep; he'd be a fool not to be scared. What he should have done the minute he'd learned about that second box of dynamite was to get everyone off the ranch, then have Reed bring out some other officers and conduct a complete and thorough search of the place.

But the weather had been clear, he'd thought he could find it himself and even Reed hadn't suggested an evacuation. Then the blizzard had struck, changing everything. They were all trapped out here until it was over, and Suzanne worrying about sabotage and dynamite would do no one any earthly good. Rand braced himself for a lie.

"Hands come and go," he said. "It's just one of the things that go along with ranching."

Suzanne inhaled and exhaled slowly, not completely certain he'd been honest with her, although she couldn't put a finger on why she harbored some doubts over what he'd just told her. But what did she know about ranching, and why would he lie about something so mundane?

She put that subject aside and focused her thoughts on her brother. "I don't want Mack on the payroll."

"But he worked as hard as the hired hands today, and

I'm positive he'll be up and ready to do it again tomorrow. Suzanne, he deserves compensation."

Suzanne's eyes flashed angrily. "He *deserves* a swift kick in the seat of his pants! Handing him a paycheck would be as bad as patting him on the back and telling him what he did was all right. It *wasn't* all right, and I don't want anyone even hinting that it was! Do I make myself clear?"

"Very, but I think you're wrong."

"Well, that's just too bad. I personally don't give a damn what you or anyone else might think about my attitude on this matter. Mack will *not* receive a paycheck if we're stuck here for...for two weeks!"

"It won't be that long," Rand said gruffly. He didn't like where his thoughts were taking him. As angry as Suzanne was, he still wanted to kiss her. He wanted to gentle her, hold her and make that sweet smile appear on her beautiful face again.

"Is there anything else?" Suzanne asked stiffly.

Rand thought a moment, then growled, "Yeah, there is." He started around the desk and Suzanne thought he was going to show her something else that had to do with the books on the wall shelf.

Instead, he stopped right in front of her, locked his hands around her waist and pulled her forward. She gasped out loud, but before she could get one word of protest out of her mouth he was kissing her.

The sensation of his mouth on hers caused another, that of her stomach dropping clear to her toes. Objections to this onslaught stacked up in her mind, but they were swiftly overwhelmed by the reactions of her body. While his kiss devoured her lips, he brought her closer, and the chafing of her nipples against his chest shot a whole new wave of response through her system.

She could feel his manhood, huge and hard, pressing into

her abdomen, inarguable evidence of where he hoped this kiss would take them. She tried to think clearly, but it was barely possible to think at all with his tongue in her mouth, one of his hands caressing her buttocks and the other clasping the back of her neck under her hair.

Her hands, her fingers, which had risen to his chest to push him away, began to curl into his shirt. A feverish heat was developing in the pit of her stomach. She gasped for breath and suddenly needed more air than she was getting.

Jerking her head, she tore her mouth free of his and sucked in an enormous breath. Dazed and dizzy, she stayed where she was and looked up into Rand's eyes, which seemed to be darker than usual and burning with a hot light. Seconds passed and neither moved.

Rand spoke first, hoarsely, raggedly. "Suzanne…"

She swallowed hard and took in more air. "I…what are we doing?"

"Making love," he whispered, dipping his head to nuzzle her creamy throat. She smelled delicious, so clean, so femininely fragrant, and his head was spinning from her scent.

Her glassy gaze fell on the black books on the wall shelf. "But…we can't."

Rand raised his head to look at her. "We can't?" He immediately thought the worst. "Is there someone in Baltimore?"

"No…but…" Suzanne was struggling with her own sense of right and wrong. A sexual relationship with Rand could only be an affair, a very *brief* affair, without love, without commitment. Did she want that sort of memory haunting her when she was finally able to go home?

Rand feared he was losing her. Kissing her without her consent had been an extremely bold move. She could have yelled, "Sexual harassment!" and slapped his face, but after her initial shock had passed she had kissed him back with all the ardor any man could hope for. Now he sensed that she was emotionally slipping away, and he knew he would do almost anything to have her clinging to him again.

"Suzanne, this is important to me. *You* are important to me," he said with genuine sincerity.

Suzanne almost lost it. He wasn't leading up to a marriage proposal, was he? Dare she doubt it when he had gone so far as to *advertise* for a wife? she thought with panic destroying every trace of the desire she had nearly drowned in only moments ago.

She had to put an end to this right now, she thought. But she had to do it tactfully. After all, she had kissed him back like a wild woman, and why wouldn't he think it meant more than it did when he was looking for a wife. Why in heaven's name did she keep forgetting that?

Well, it just wasn't her fault, she told herself next, receiving some comfort from doing so. She certainly hadn't started this, he had. She would let him down as easily as she could, but she had to let him know he had gained nothing by kissing her.

"Rand, you have to listen to me for a minute." His arms were still around her, she was still pressed against him, and she gently extricated herself from his embrace, then moved around the desk so it was between them. She saw the look of disappointment on Rand's face, but what could she do about it?

But then, just like that, words escaped her. Instead of the tactful letdown she'd been intending, she found herself thinking of him, of how she'd felt in his arms, of how incredibly handsome he was and how hurt he looked now.

She gave up, mumbled, "Good night," and all but ran from the room.

With a heavy sigh, Rand watched her leave, then listened to the quiet closing of her bedroom door.

His body was tight as a drum, hot and throbbing. It was

just as well that he was planning to lay out his bedroll at the foot of the stairs tonight, because he probably wouldn't get much rest wherever he stretched out.

Suzanne got into her pajamas the second she was in her bedroom, turned off the light and climbed into bed. Huddled under the covers, she heard Rand go into his room and, about ten minutes later, come out of it again.

Lord, what a startling evening this had been, she thought with a nervous shudder. She had come very close to jumping into bed with Rand tonight, and she knew she would have regretted it the moment it was over. Thank God she'd come to her senses in time.

And yet there was the most restless yearning in her body. Well, she *had* become very aroused, she thought in defense of the feeling. And there was no denying Rand's potent appeal. Why couldn't she meet someone like him in Baltimore? Minus that awful advertisement for a wife, of course. How could Rand have done something so utterly ludicrous? He didn't seem at all like the sort of man who would drop his standards to such a low level.

But then did she know him well enough yet to make that judgment? Scratch anyone's surface personality and no telling what you might find.

After a while Suzanne started wondering what Rand was doing. Why hadn't he returned to his room and gone to bed? The bunkhouse was totally silent; the only thing she could hear was the storm outside. Obviously the men were in bed, why wasn't Rand?

Ten minutes of that line of thought was all she could stand. Getting up, she tiptoed to the door, opened it a crack and peered down the hall. Only a dim night-light burned, but it was enough. Her mouth literally dropped open when she saw Rand in a sleeping bag at the foot of the stairs.

Was he crazy, or what? Why would he choose to sleep on the floor in the hall rather than in his bed?

It was a very long time before Suzanne fell asleep that night. She lay there listening to the storm that raged on and on with no break in sight, thinking of herself kissing a crazy man and loving it, worrying about Mack and their future when they finally did manage to get home and, in general, feeling as miserable as a human being could. What horrible thing had she ever done to deserve what she was having to endure in her twenty-fourth year of life?

Rand had been dozing, but he came wide-awake over a sound at the top of the stairs. His eyes opened instantly and he caught the blur of movement. Someone was up and wandering.

Jumping up, he took the stairs three at a time. Everything was quiet, no lights burned. Scowling, he began opening doors and peering into bedrooms. Every man was in his bed and appeared to be sound asleep. Whoever had been roaming had hurried back to his bed when he saw Rand at the foot of the stairs. The man might be fully dressed and in bed with his clothes on, but Rand couldn't wake every man and demand an inspection.

Still, he had stopped someone from pulling any dirty tricks tonight, hadn't he? Feeling good about that, at least, Rand returned to the first floor and crawled back into his sleeping bag.

His eyes narrowed in circumspection. Right now that dynamite could be under a snowbank, but it wasn't likely because the perpetrator would want to keep it dry. Where could it be? Mentally Rand walked through every building on the ranch and visualized every possible hiding place. When he'd actually conducted his search, had he missed anything?

He glanced up the stairs, and his lips thinned grimly. If someone hadn't been up to no good when Rand had spotted movement on the second floor, why hadn't he shown himself?

The constant howl of the wind was beginning to grate on Rand's nerves. Regardless that the blizzard was keeping Suzanne on the ranch, he wished it would stop. Once it did the sun would come out. The earth would be a blanket of glistening white and very beautiful to the eye. He would like her to see that.

He groaned quietly as his thoughts changed directions. Never had he wanted a woman more than he had tonight in the office while holding Suzanne. And she had wanted him just as much. Why had she suddenly turned off on him?

For a while he tortured himself with the fantasy of going into her bedroom, undressing and crawling into bed with her, of taking her in his arms and making love to her. He wanted desperately to kiss her again, and to touch her in all the right places while she touched him.

Muttering a curse, he punched his pillow and told himself to cool off. He was not going into her bedroom uninvited, so why drive himself crazy thinking about it?

It was a long, miserable night for Rand, with only a few catnaps to ease his weariness.

And the wind continued to howl….

Eight

Suzanne awoke even before the men began stirring upstairs. It was very early, still dark and, from the growling wind she could hear outside, still storming. Despondency gripped her. How much longer was she going to be trapped out here?

But there was a trap awaiting her return to Baltimore, too, wasn't there? Her heart beat harder over the possibility of not finding a job right away, which, considering her failure with that effort since being laid off from her previous position, had every chance of being the case. At least here she and Mack had a roof over their heads and plenty to eat. At home her apartment rent was due, utility bills were stacking up and now—after this completely unnecessary trip—there was no longer a family savings account to fall back on. A tear formed in the corner of her eye as she realized how truly dire the situation was.

Her next thought was about how she had phoned the principal of Mack's school the morning she'd left Baltimore to explain that Mack would be absent a few days as he was ill with the flu. It was a lie that could easily catch up with her;

she would bet anything that some conscientious soul from the school had already called the apartment to check on Mack's progress. She shouldn't have lied, she should have told the principal the truth, she thought, her bitter recriminations aimed as much at herself as at Mack. Why protect someone who didn't want protection? Why turn herself into a liar for the sake of a thankless brother?

Because he's only fourteen, you love him and you're worried sick about the direction he's taking with his life, a voice in her head answered.

It was the God's truth. No amount of trouble would ever make her stop loving Mack. She might disown him when he was older if he didn't straighten up his act, but she would always love him.

Hearing movement on the second floor, she jumped out of bed. Maybe she shouldn't accept a paycheck from Rand for doing the cooking and the bookkeeping, but if anyone had ever needed income, it was her.

Hurriedly she washed her face and hands, brushed her teeth and combed her hair. Then she quickly pulled on some clothes. She would shower later, after breakfast. Leaving her bed unmade she hastened to the kitchen, planning a menu as she went. Rand, she noticed, was no longer lying at the foot of the stairs. That still puzzled her, and she shook her head in dismay over such strange behavior.

She had never moved so fast in her life, certainly not in preparing a huge breakfast at this unholy hour. The men began coming downstairs, and she started carrying pots of steaming oatmeal, bowls of scrambled eggs and platters of fried ham and toast to the tables. Sleepy-eyed though they were, most of the men mumbled, "Thank you, ma'am," when she filled their coffee mugs. She was beginning to see these men as individuals, and was able to put names to some of the faces around the tables. Some were old, some quite young. None were boys, like Mack, although it looked as though a few were around twenty.

Dale Carson, for instance, looked young. He had blue eyes and an open, honest-appearing face. Dale smiled at her as she filled his mug, and she smiled back. He caused no romantic feelings within her, but he seemed to be a pleasant person, polite and eager to please.

Rand came in and took his place at one of the long tables. He looked freshly showered and shaved, and he sent Suzanne a smile. Nervous suddenly, unable to think of anything but the intimacy of their kisses in the office last night, she brought the coffeepot over to him. "Good morning."

"Good morning," he returned. "Everything looks and smells wonderful, Suzanne, thank you. You did a fine job."

"Thank you." She filled his mug and moved down the table. Rand affected her much too strongly, she thought uneasily, and her best course was to stay away from him as much as possible. Approaching Mack, she said for his ears alone, "I would like you to find some time to come in and talk to me today."

Mack looked around with an embarrassed expression, and Suzanne realized that he didn't want the men to know his sister had anything to say about his activities. With reddened cheeks, he nodded his head once, then ignored her and dove into a huge helping of scrambled eggs and ham. Sighing because she felt so helpless where Mack was concerned, Suzanne finished filling the men's mugs.

They were eating, and she left them to themselves. In the kitchen, she sat at the counter with a cup of coffee, a slice of toast and a piece of ham. Her worry over Mack was taking a new tack: what if he refused to go home with her? She was his guardian, but if he dug in his heels in stubborn denial, would she take legal measures to force him back to Baltimore? Would it do any good if she did? She couldn't watch

Mack twenty-four hours a day, and she suspected he would run away again the first chance he had. This time it wouldn't be quite so easy for him to do, as he wouldn't have the money to fly anywhere. But the idea of him hitchhiking the many miles back to Montana scared her to death.

She had to talk to him, and she didn't want to wait until *he* decided to suffer through a conversation with her. Actually, she didn't trust him to make that decision at all. In fact, she *knew* he would do everything he could to avoid it.

Rand came in for the coffeepot, and she jumped off the stool. "I'll do that," she said.

"Don't worry about it." He narrowed his eyes on her face. "But you have been in here worrying about something, haven't you? Suzanne, if it's about last night…"

"I wasn't thinking of that," she said without even a hint of a blush as she was still deeply focused on her problems with Mack. It suddenly occurred to her that Rand could help her out, if he would. "Could I impose on you to do something for me?" she asked.

"Name it. Oh, wait just one minute while I take this coffee in to the men."

He was back almost immediately. "What is it you want me to do?"

"Tell Mack to stay behind when the men leave for work. He can join you all later. I need to talk to him. I've mentioned it to him, but I know he'll do everything he can to avoid it. I believe he'll listen to you, and if you tell him—"

"Consider it done." Rand's thoughts were elsewhere. She was even pretty without makeup, and he was thoroughly enjoying the sight of her morning-fresh face. It pained him to remember that she was in as much danger as the rest of them until that box of dynamite was found, and he became more determined than ever to locate it.

"Thank you," Suzanne said with obvious relief. She wished

he wouldn't look at her so intently, but considering what had happened between them last night, his close scrutiny was perhaps justified. After all, she certainly did not look her best this morning, and maybe he was finally realizing how plain a woman she really was.

Her heart sank a little. He looked marvelous and she didn't. It wasn't a pleasant thought, and she had to wonder why it would even enter her mind. Did she care how she looked to him? It hadn't concerned her while getting dressed, but maybe it should have. It would only have taken a very few minutes to put on some makeup, after all.

She was glad when he said, "Well, I'd better go and finish breakfast," and left her alone in the kitchen. Done with her breakfast, she started scrubbing pots and pans at the sink. When the men began bringing in their plates and coffee mugs, she dried her hands, spoke to them if they said something to her and waited for Mack to come in.

He finally showed his face. His first words were surly, his tone of voice resentful. "Everybody's gone to work but me. What d'ya want?"

Suzanne drew a breath. "The first thing I want is your speaking to me like you do to everyone else around here. I deserve no less respect than men you met only a few days ago, Mack."

He slunk to a stool and sat on it. "You're just gonna give me hell, and I don't wanna hear it."

Frowning over his analysis of their relationship, Suzanne filled two fresh mugs with coffee and brought them to the counter. She sat on the stool next to the one Mack occupied.

He poured sugar and milk into his mug and stirred it. Suzanne sipped hers black and set it down.

"Mack, I arrived here angry, but I don't want any anger between us ever again. Can't we just talk?"

He sent her a sideways glance. "If you're not mad, what d'ya wanna talk about?"

"About you, about me, about what each of us wants out of life," she said quietly. "About what each of us can attain with the little we have to start with."

"Uh, what d'ya mean?"

"I have very little money. Do you have any?"

"A few bucks. Do you want it?"

"No. But putting money aside for the moment, what else do you have, Mack?"

He looked puzzled. "My clothes?"

"Your clothes and a few bucks. Mack, is that how you want to spend the rest of your life, with a backpack of clothes and a few bucks in your jeans?"

Mack was beginning to grasp the gist of Suzanne's conversation. "Hey," he said with some of his old anger, "do you think that's all the guys working on this ranch have? Most of them are driving great-looking trucks. You haven't seen 'em 'cause you haven't been able to stick your nose out the door, but I have!"

Suzanne could tell she was not going to diminish Mack's wide-eyed enthusiasm for this life by suggesting he would gain very few possessions from it. Perhaps a little reverse psychology would work better, although it would take some heavy-duty pretense on her part.

"I know why you like it here," she said gently. "I couldn't figure out why you would come to Montana before I got here myself, but I think I understand it now."

"You do?" Mack looked and sounded suspicious.

"Driving from Billings I saw some beautiful country. I wish the storm would pass so I could get outside and look around." That much was true, at least. She shaped a smile. "And you fit the role of cowhand so well."

Mack's suspicious expression vanished in one of his big

grins. "I really do, Suzanne. I'm never gonna leave here. I love this ranch. I wanna learn to ride a horse. I know it's not hard to do, you just have to learn the right way to get on one. I bet Rand could show me in two seconds."

Suzanne gulped. "Did Rand say he would hire you?"

"Uh, no. But I think I can get him to change his mind."

"Perhaps you can. Of course, you would only be able to work part-time until you finish high school. I'm sure Whitehorn has a high school, and there must be buses that pick up the rural students."

Mack leapt off his stool. "I'm not going back to school, and you can't make me!" He ran from the room, stopped in the dining room only long enough to pick up his outside gear and then slammed the door as he left the building.

Suzanne put her head in her hands. She had accomplished nothing, except for learning one thing. She knew now that taking Mack back to Baltimore would only be achieved with a court order. And she didn't have the money to hire a lawyer to even *start* the process.

While the men went in for lunch at noon, Rand stayed away from the bunkhouse and conducted another search of the outbuildings. He cautiously poked mounds of loose hay and straw with a pitchfork. He looked under stacks of folded tarps. He peered into anything and everything that was big enough to hold a case of dynamite, and when it occurred to him that the culprit might have split the case, he went over it all again. Discouraged, he finally had to face facts: the dynamite was *not* stored in the barn, the equipment shed, the small toolshed *or* the storage shed.

That still left an awful lot of possibilities—every rick of hay on the place, for example, the bunkhouse and the main house, although he was the only one on the ranch with a key for it. Not only that, the dynamite could have been buried before the storm hit and was lying under three or more feet of snow, depending on the drifts.

Standing outside the barn thinking it over, Rand suddenly noticed that the wind had died down. Snowflakes were still falling, the sky was still the color of lead, but losing the wind was a definitive sign that the storm was passing.

Normally he would be relieved enough to dance a jig because the end of a blizzard of such ferocity was finally in sight, but not this time. Once the plows cleared the roads, Suzanne would leave, and that prospect hit him like a ton of bricks and created a wrenching sensation in his gut.

Seeing the men starting to come outside again, Rand stepped into the barn, walked clear through it and came out of it by its back door. Circling the other outbuildings to avoid the crew and the questions they might ask about why he hadn't gone in for lunch, he entered the bunkhouse through the door to the laundry.

For a while he just stood there and listened. The only sound in the building came from the kitchen—Suzanne cleaning up. Kicking off his snow-encrusted boots, he also removed his jacket, hat, gloves and scarf. Then he quietly began opening the doors of the cabinets in the laundry and inspected everything they contained. He hadn't really expected to find the dynamite in this room, but he was determined to leave no stone unturned. Finally, satisfied with his search, unproductive as it had been, he padded stocking-footed to the kitchen.

"Suzanne?"

She whirled. "You scared the stuffing out of me!"

"Sorry, that wasn't my intention. Have all the men left?"

Suzanne frowned. "I think so. Why?"

"No reason in particular. Just wondering."

"You didn't come in for lunch. I can heat up the soup and—"

"Maybe later. I, uh, misplaced something and I'm going to look for it." The last thing he would ever tell Suzanne was that there might be dynamite concealed somewhere in the bunkhouse.

"Oh. Well, would you like me to help?"

"Not necessary, but thanks." He knew there was nowhere to hide anything in the dining room, so he ignored it, and also the kitchen for the time being, and strode down the hall to the office. It took about three minutes to scratch the office off his mental list, but he did pick up a telephone to find out if they had phone service yet. No such luck, the line was still dead.

Returning to the hall, he stopped to wonder about Suzanne's room. He knew there was nothing in his own room that shouldn't be there, but what about the one Suzanne was using? And Handy's and George's?

Deciding to leave Suzanne's bedroom until last, he made a quick search of the other two bedrooms, found nothing amiss and then headed up the stairs. From below Suzanne could tell he was moving from room to room on the second floor, and wondered what on earth he was looking for. Was some valuable missing? Goodness, if he found it in one of the men's rooms, did that mean the man was a thief?

Her heart sank considerably. What if Rand found what he was looking for in Mack's room? She could easily picture the chaos *that* would cause, and she suddenly felt as nervous as a cat. It was at that precise moment that she realized the wind was no longer howling. She ran to a window and saw only lazily falling snow.

"It's stopping," she whispered with her hand splayed at the base of her throat. How long would it take for the plows to get out this far? How much longer would she be on the Kincaid Ranch? She had completed the payroll this morning, as she'd promised Rand, but she certainly could not have earned very much money in the few days she'd been here.

Another thought startled her: she wasn't looking forward to going home at all, and not merely because of her dire financial straits in Baltimore, either. It wasn't that she had fallen in love with the ranch—heavens, she'd barely seen it, other than the inside of this bunkhouse—but leaving the ranch meant leaving Rand, and once she left, what possible reason could there ever be for them to see each other again?

She took a slow but startled breath. In spite of her misgivings about Rand's ad, despite her disapproval of his tasteless method of meeting women, Rand had gotten under her skin. How did something like this happen to a woman with her sensible nature?

Totally shaken, Suzanne made quick work of cleaning the kitchen. The payroll checks were lying on George's desk awaiting Rand's signature. Avoiding Rand while she was in this peculiar mood seemed smart, and she hurried down the hall to her bedroom and shut the door.

Upstairs, Rand gave up with a disgruntled sigh. He had gone through every single room on the second floor and come up empty. There was only one room in the building still unsearched and that was Suzanne's room. For his own peace of mind he had to check it out. She was probably still in the kitchen and wouldn't notice, he figured as he tiptoed down the stairs and hall to the door of her bedroom.

But when he opened the door and stepped in, there she was, lying on the bed. "Suzanne!" he exclaimed in surprise.

She sat up with a jerk. "Rand!"

"Uh…" He honestly didn't know what to say, but then something came to him. "I looked everywhere else for…uh, for that thing, and I thought you were still in the kitchen. I swear I would not have walked in like this if I'd known you were in here."

She was beginning to get very uncomfortable about whatever it was he'd torn the bunkhouse apart to find, mostly because of Mack, who she knew wasn't above taking things that didn't belong to him. Money from her purse, for instance. Not large sums, just a dollar or two at a time, but to her stealing was stealing, a concept Mack didn't seem to grasp, or if he did, he thought it didn't pertain to him.

But Rand looking for that mystery object in the room *she'd* been using was a personal affront. Sliding off the bed, she said coldly, "I'm not a thief, Rand."

"God, no!" He was horrified. "Suzanne, I could never think that about you."

"Then why are you in my room?"

"You've only used this room a few days. What I'm looking for has been, uh, missing for about a week."

"Oh. Well, in that case, feel free to look around."

"Are you sure you don't mind?"

"I don't mind," she said, feeling enormous relief. If the article involved had been missing for a week, then Mack couldn't have taken it. For some reason, however, Rand wasn't saying what it was, and that struck her as very odd. Saying nothing to the men about it was understandable—after all, one of them *must* be the thief—but why keep it from her?

Leaning her hips against the dresser, she folded her arms across her chest and watched him peer into the closet. When he looked under the bed, though, a weird urge to giggle rose in her throat. What could possibly be under her bed?

"You know," she said around a smile she couldn't suppress, "if you would tell me what you're looking for, I might be able to help."

It was the second time she'd offered her help, and he hated having to refuse it again. But what else could he do?

"Thanks, but I have to do this myself."

He was so serious that Suzanne laughed. "Goodness, one would think your missing item is necessary to national security."

Rand had spotted what appeared to be a boot box under the bed. It wasn't big enough to contain a whole case of dynamite, but he had already wondered about the case having been opened and the dynamite divided and hidden in a dozen different places.

He stared at that box with a knot in his gut. Suzanne was standing by, watching him, and he didn't want to alarm her by asking her to leave her own room. Unless it became necessary, of course. Stretching out on his belly, he reached under the bed and cautiously slid the box's lid aside. He breathed a silent sigh of relief; the box contained an old pair of boots. Obviously someone who'd been using this room at one time or another had purchased new boots and left the old ones behind.

"Did you find what you've been looking for under my bed?" Suzanne asked with laughter lurking in her voice.

Rand left the box where it was and got to his feet. He was satisfied that the dynamite was nowhere in the bunkhouse, which at least relieved him of one very grave concern. He was beginning to think that the man who'd ordered that second box of dynamite had furtively taken it out to some far-off pasture and buried it, which meant that Rand would never find it. Certainly he couldn't cover every foot of Kincaid ground to look for it, especially with the snow concealing any disturbed dirt.

"Well, I guess that does it," he said to Suzanne.

"You didn't check the bathroom," she stated with a tongue-in-cheek smile.

Rand smiled back. She hadn't taken his search seriously, and that was best.

"Nor the bureau drawers," Suzanne added teasingly.

Her teasing tone thrilled Rand. His ransacking the entire building in search of some mysterious object was apparently amusing to her, and now that he knew the bunkhouse was safe, he was more than willing to participate in any game she might want to play.

In a deliberately somber voice he said, "You're right." Striding into her bathroom, he pulled back the shower curtain to check the stall, then opened the few drawers in the sink cabinet. Her small cache of cosmetics, toothbrush and toothpaste were in one drawer, her hair dryer in another.

He returned to the bedroom, sent her a grin and opened the top drawer of the dresser. Folded neatly within the drawer was a stack of silky panties and bras. He slowly turned his face to her, his left eyebrow raised in friendly good humor.

"Dare I look *beneath* these dainty things?" he asked.

Suzanne laughed. "I think you'd dare anything you thought you could get away with, Mr. Harding."

"Do you really?" Pushing the drawer closed, Rand walked over to her.

Suzanne's pulse leapt. Only a short time ago in the dining room she had decided that maintaining distance between her and Rand was her best course. Now she'd been bandying words with him and teasing him over his searching her room. He'd been teasing, too, but right this moment he didn't look all that playful.

"Um, you haven't looked in the other drawers," she stammered, nervous suddenly.

"No, but I bet you have. Is there anything in them?"

"Uh, they're all empty except for the top two."

"Figured as much."

An idea so startling that she nearly gasped right out loud suddenly raced through Suzanne's mind: Rand could be the solution to every single one of her problems! He liked her, he wanted a wife badly enough to advertise for one and she had nothing in Baltimore to go home to. Plus, there was Mack, who no longer listened to her concerns for his welfare and future, nor did he heed any advice she might offer him on any given topic. What Mack needed was a father image, a strong man that wouldn't take any teenage guff and bluster, especially about his not finishing high school.

As for her own needs, so what if she and Rand weren't in love with each other? There was *something* between them, and besides, when she *had* married for love, the liaison had been an abysmal failure.

She could tell that Rand was thinking about kissing her. It was in his eyes, in the very air they were both breathing.

Well, there was nothing wrong with a few kisses, she resolutely told herself, and she tilted her chin and parted her lips in blatant invitation.

Rand didn't need her encouragement spelled out any clearer. He took one step, slid his hands down her back and brought her forward. His lips glided over her face in mute appreciation of her participation, then stopped on her mouth. At first his lips moved very gently on hers, and that gentleness was extremely effective in igniting Suzanne's passion, although Rand hadn't planned or thought ahead to that result. It was just such a pleasure to kiss her that he was taking his time and savoring every moment.

It was Suzanne who really got them rolling. Wrapping her arms around his waist, she snuggled her body into his, drew his tongue into her mouth and started sucking on it.

Rand was hard in two seconds flat. His kisses began eating her up, and he didn't even try to keep his hands away from the intimate spots of her body. Last night she had stopped him after a couple of kisses; he knew in his soul that she wasn't going to stop him today. Her feverish excitement blew his mind, and he started undressing her by pushing the unbuttoned sweater from her shoulders.

"Yes, oh, yes," she whispered, and went for the buttons on his shirt, then for his belt buckle.

Rand didn't care what had happened to change her mind

between last night and today. A man didn't question a
woman's feelings or motives at a time like this. All he could
think of was getting them both naked and in that bed.

He did pause for a moment to look at her without clothes,
however. She was slender from her smooth, creamy throat to
the tips of her toes. Her breasts were not large, but they were
beautifully shaped and had rosy-pink nipples. Her waist was
tiny, her hips were narrow and her legs were thrillingly long.
He wanted to feel them wrapped around him. He wanted to be
inside her, with those long, gorgeous legs locked around him.

Suzanne was doing some looking of her own. There was
only a small patch of dark hair on Rand's muscular chest—
she liked that—and his body was superb, every inch of it. She
nestled herself against him, and closed her eyes to absorb the
incredible sensation of his bare skin embracing hers.

"You're hot," she whispered, pressing a kiss to his chest.

Rand chuckled deep in his throat. "Hot for you, Suz."

"No, I meant your skin is hot." She smiled because he had
shortened her name.

"So is yours." Rand let his hand drift down her back, then
slid it around her hip to touch her intimately. "You're hot here,
too," he said hoarsely. "And wet. Oh, Suz, kiss me. Touch me.
I want you so much. You're so beautiful."

She raised her head from his chest and stood on tiptoe to
kiss his mouth. She might not have fallen in love with Rand—
that took more than a few days, didn't it?—but she could
honestly say she had never wanted a man more.

They fell to the bed and somehow managed to maneuver
themselves under the covers while still kissing and caressing
each other. Rand took her hand and placed it on his manhood.
A shiver of utter delight rippled her spine as she explored its
velvety texture. *His* hand was between her legs, and so much
erotic foreplay was bringing them both to the brink.

"I have a condom," Rand growled. Reaching to the floor

for his jeans, he pulled out his wallet and took out a foil packet.

Suzanne was glad *he* had the good sense to be cautious, because it hadn't even entered her mind. She wanted at least one child someday, but not like this, not when her life was in turmoil and she had too many problems to count. Again it flashed through her mind that Rand might be the answer to everything, but it was a brief thought as he had quickly put on the condom and was back to kissing her with a hunger that took her breath.

They writhed together under those covers, creating a cocoon of heat and ecstatic feelings. And then he eased himself on top of her. She opened her legs for him. He thrust into her. She closed her eyes as he began moving, and silently prayed that he was the kind of man to make sure the woman under him reached fulfillment before he took his own pleasure. Since her divorce—even before it—she had given so little thought to sex that the intensity of her desire now was startling. If Rand left her hanging she would not be able to forgive him.

A long time later, sweating and weeping, she kissed him again and again. She had never before experienced such an overwhelming climax, and she knew in her heart that in this, at least, they were soul mates.

Nine

Every cell in Suzanne's body felt loose and languorous. Mentally she added *incredible lover* to her list of Rand's good points. She liked the way he was curled around her now, spoon-fashion, and that he hadn't immediately jumped up and returned to work after making love. Dreamily, she smiled. Could a city-born-and-bred woman find happiness on a ranch in Montana with a man she barely knew?

"Hmm," she murmured, realizing that her disdain for the idea of advertising for a spouse was losing impact. Different strokes for different folks, after all. Nevertheless, she would like to know what had prompted Rand to join those particular ranks when he seemed to have so much to offer a life-partner. Maybe if she talked some about herself, she mused, Rand would offer some information about his own past.

She was facing the wall and could feel Rand's warm breath on the back of her hair. He had one arm buried beneath her pillow, the other around her waist. She was lazily comfortable, more so than she'd ever been with any man, even with her husband, as Les had been a nervous sort and forever fid-geting. Rand seemed perfectly content to lie still, as Suzanne was doing, which in her estimation was another point in his favor.

"Rand?" she said softly, a little tentatively.

"Yes?"

"Did Mack tell you about my marriage and divorce?"

Rand was silent a moment, digesting the information. It wasn't a shock, by any means, but it wasn't something he had speculated about, either. He finally spoke, quietly. "No, he never mentioned it. What happened? I mean, if you don't mind my asking, how come it didn't last?"

Suzanne sighed. "A thousand reasons. I think what really happened is that we just fell out of love."

Rand had an immediate answer for that observation. "Love isn't all it's cracked up to be, anyway." There was a touch of bitterness in his voice that gave Suzanne a start. "I think if two people like and respect each other it's a lot more impor-tant than love," he added.

So that's it, Suzanne thought. Rand had experienced love and some sort of subsequent failure, and now he was gun-shy. Well, could she blame him? Didn't she have similar misgiv-ings? The death of a relationship, whatever its causes or whoever had been to blame, was terribly traumatic. She didn't love Les anymore, but she wasn't completely over the pain of the divorce, either.

Her insight, however, did not cover all the bases. "Were you married?"

"No." Rand never talked about his having been jilted prac-tically at the altar. It was probably the most emotionally wrenching event of his life, but it was in the past and he intended keeping it there. Certainly something within himself rebelled at the thought of relating it to Suzanne.

His terse reply told Suzanne that she had heard all he was

going to say on that subject. She wasn't offended, as she didn't enjoy talking about her abysmal love life, either. Besides, considering that she was in bed right now with a man who had just taken her to the stars, maybe *abysmal* was no longer applicable.

She was thinking hard. Rand wasn't out romancing women in his search for a wife because of a bad experience with love. Ergo, the ad, which she had totally misinterpreted. She wasn't looking for love, either, although, in all honesty, she wasn't as dead set against it as Rand seemed to be. Bottom line:

they had a lot in common, and was there really anything wrong with a marriage based on mutual liking and respect? Actually, they had more than those things going for them; a powerful attraction and perfect sex was nothing to sneeze at.

"Let me ask you something," she said slowly. "If Mack had sent you a photo of me instead of the one he did send, would you still have answered his letter?"

Rand raised his head to peer around her and look into her eyes. "In a heartbeat." He grinned and then chuckled. "Would you like to see the picture he *did* send?"

"You still have it?"

"It's in my room."

Suzanne grimaced. "Let me guess. The woman in the picture is only partially dressed."

"Good guess. She's blond, voluptuous and wearing a skimpy bathing suit."

Suzanne groaned. "What did I ever do to deserve a kid brother like Mack? Sometimes I wonder if he has any sense at all. Didn't it occur to him that if you and I ever did meet, you would immediately know I wasn't the woman in that photo?"

"It would have occurred to an adult, Suz, but Mack thinks like a fourteen-year-old." Rand hesitated, then added, "You know, I can't be angry about what he did when it brought you to Montana. You're exactly the kind of woman I was hoping my ad would attract."

Suzanne turned her head to give Rand a quixotic look. He had written virtually those same words in his letter when he'd believed she was a nudie-cutie. What should she believe now?

"It's true," Rand said solemnly. "On my honor, Suzanne."

She turned her face away again. And if Mack hadn't brought the two of us together and another woman had answered your ad, you would probably be saying the same thing to her. Suzanne wasn't overly thrilled with that theory, but it was much too clear in her mind to ignore. Truth was, she liked Rand. A lot. But even though she now had some understanding of what had prompted him to advertise for a wife, and even though she didn't find the concept nearly as distasteful as she had, some part of herself couldn't let this conversation end up where she was beginning to suspect it was leading.

It's my fault as much as his, she thought apprehensively, fearing that Rand was on the verge of offering marriage. Even though she herself had been thinking only a moment ago that a marriage based on friendship might work, a part of her rebelled at the idea of settling for that sort of one-size-fits-all relationship. I never should have asked him about the ad, or the photo, or anything at all about what Mack might have told him, she thought, terribly uneasy with the whole thing. Obviously she had given Rand some very serious notions by sleeping with him; it was up to her now to dispel those ideas without hurting his feelings. He had, after all, taken his cue from her; she could have said no and hadn't.

She tried to wriggle free of his embrace and move to the edge of the bed.

"Hey, where're you going?" Rand asked in surprise.

"I have things to do. So do you," she said calmly, as she was determined to keep this friendly. Frowning, he watched her get off the bed and start picking up her clothes. "I've noticed how the wind has died," she said while heading for the bathroom. "Does that mean the storm is coming to an end?"

"Probably," Rand mumbled. They had gotten very close to a serious conversation, and he wasn't at all happy over Suzanne's unexpected and rather sudden decision to avoid it. Reluctantly he got up and began dressing.

In the small bathroom, Suzanne refreshed herself, got dressed and marveled that she felt absolutely no remorse or embarrassment. It was probably because making love with Rand was so explainable, she decided. She had lived a celibate life for a long time and she liked and admired Rand. She was a logical thinker—most of the time—and what had happened between them today seemed perfectly logical.

That was the perspective she must maintain, she told herself while brushing her hair in front of the mirror. The storm was dying, and she and Mack would be leaving as soon as the roads were plowed. This romantic little interlude with Rand would be a pleasant memory when she got home. At least that was how she would try to view it.

But then concern about Mack willingly going back to Baltimore buffeted her again, and she stopped brushing her hair to stare into her own eyes. It hit her abruptly that Rand might have some suggestions to help her convince Mack that he simply could not stay in Montana by himself. She had to talk to him before he returned to work.

Dropping the hairbrush, she hurriedly opened the door to the bedroom and saw Rand, fully dressed, straightening the bedclothes. He turned when he heard her come in.

"I—I have a problem," she said.

"Don't we all?" he drawled cynically.

Suzanne blinked. "Are you angry about something?"

"Me, angry? Why would you think that? I don't have any reason to be angry, do I?"

Suzanne's spine stiffened. She knew exactly what was behind Rand's attitude, and while some resentment on his part might be justified, he was an adult and had to take life's hard knocks, same as her. She wanted very much to keep this amicable, but maybe that was asking too much, given the circumstances, she thought unhappily.

"No, you do not," she said, maintaining a neutrality in her voice in a last-ditch effort at congeniality. "Rand, both of us have to look at what happened here today sensibly. Sleeping together did not give either of us any kind of hold over the other."

"It would if we wanted it that way."

She hesitated a moment to think and discovered she couldn't disagree with his point. "You're right. It would if we both wanted it that way."

"Meaning you don't."

In spite of her good intentions, her voice rose. "Meaning I'm getting more confused by the minute with you, Rand!"

"And you're blaming me? What in hell have I done to confuse you?"

The anger in the air rocked them both, and they fell silent and looked uncomfortable and a little sheepish.

Rand moved first, taking a few directionless steps around the room. "I'm sorry," he said, sounding almost helpless. "It's just that…" Heaving a sigh, he let his voice trail off and looked at her. "What were you saying about a problem?"

It took a moment for her to recall what she'd said before that flash-fire explosion between them. At least he had apologized, and could she do any less?

"I'm sorry, too," she said with genuine chagrin. "You don't…you couldn't possibly…understand where I'm coming from."

"Granted," Rand said dryly. "But I'm willing to listen." He cocked a hopeful eyebrow. "Am I your problem, Suzanne?"

"I…you weren't." She walked to the window to draw back the drape and glance outside. "Maybe you are now," she said with a sigh, and dropped the drape to turn and face him. "But when I said I had a problem I was referring to Mack."

"Mack," Rand echoed, disappointment knotting his gut. It hurt that Suzanne could make such uninhibited love with him and then write it off so casually. And yet she'd admitted he might be a problem now, too. Damn, was there ever a man alive who truly understood women?

"What about Mack?" he asked gruffly. He already knew the boy was a worry for Suzanne, but she didn't appear to be thinking in generalities at the moment.

"Do you have time for this?"

"A few more minutes won't matter."

Suzanne was biting her lower lip and frowning. "Thank you. I need to talk to someone about this. I—I'm afraid Mack won't go home with me."

Rand winced over her reference to going home—today really hadn't meant anything to her—but he stuck to the subject. "You're his guardian. He has to do what you say."

"He rarely does," Suzanne said, sounding weary of the family battle. "Rand, if he digs in his heels and refuses—he's already told me he isn't going back to school—what can I do about it? He's not a child I can pick up and carry to the car."

"Are you asking me to put him in the car for you?"

She shook her head almost impatiently. "That's not the answer. You said yourself that force wouldn't work with Mack. I guess I was hoping you had an alternative suggestion."

Rand sat his hips on the edge of the dresser. "I could kick him off the ranch. He'd have no choice but to go with you."

"Rand, if he doesn't go willingly, he won't stay. He has this…this romanticized idea of a cowboy's life stuck in his head—and maybe his heart—and I can't think of anything in Baltimore to take its place."

"There isn't anything to take its place," Rand said flatly. "Cowboying isn't just a job, Suzanne, it's a way of life. If you get bitten by that particular bug, you rarely get over it. I'll tell you something else, too. Mack's seen ranching at its worst since he got here, and if this storm and working his tail off in frigid weather and deep snow didn't turn him off, nothing will."

Suzanne's expression grew grim as Rand talked. "That's not exactly what I had hoped to hear from you."

"I'm sure it's not, but did you want a pretty story or the truth?"

After a second she said with a discouraged sigh, "The truth."

He was thinking of how much he didn't want her leaving the second the weather turned and the roads were passable. "Suzanne, I think you need to give Mack a little more time out here. He's doing the work of a man. Maybe he'll start thinking and behaving like one."

"I don't have any time to give him! I told you about my job situation."

"My point, exactly. Look, if the weather turned sunny and the plows cleared the roads tomorrow morning, I'd still be without a cook and bookkeeper. We know George is going to be laid up for a while, and I have no idea when Handy will be back. Depends on his sister's health, I'm sure. Anyhow, what I'm getting at is, why don't you think about staying on and working here until things return to normal? Could be a couple of weeks, and by then who knows? Maybe Mack will have his fill of working from dawn to dusk."

"And I should just forget about his education?"

"Absolutely not. The day the school bus passes by the Kincaid driveway, Mack will be out there waiting for it. I guarantee it."

"Then how would he be working from dawn to dusk?"

Rand grinned. "By putting in several hours after school

every day and working weekends. That's the way a lot of ranch kids live, Suzanne. I know, because it's how I grew up."

"And you think that routine might disenchant him," Suzanne murmured, as much to herself as to Rand.

"It's a possibility." Rand didn't believe anything of the kind. Mack was champing at the bit to learn to ride a horse, which, so far, no one had had the time to teach him. Once the weather broke, duties and chores would lessen, and most any of the hands would get a kick out of showing Mack the ropes, undoubtedly teasing him unmercifully in the process. But that, too, was part of this life-style—male camaraderie, good-natured ribbing, a sense of fraternity. Mack, Rand suspected, would eat it up.

But Rand knew he would say almost anything to keep Suzanne from bolting at the first sign of a snowplow. As much as he despised lies and liars, he was willing to bend his principles to keep Suzanne around for a while longer. She'd proved their mutual attraction today in the most elemental way possible, and he wasn't going to simply stand by and do nothing while she made plans to leave.

He saw her take a very long, very deep breath. "You feel certain that you can get him to go back to school?" she asked.

"If he wants to work on this ranch, believe me, he'll go to school," Rand replied. After a moment he asked, "So, what do you say? Have we got a deal?"

Returning to Baltimore practically penniless versus returning with some money really was no contest. Maybe the wisdom of putting Mack into a new school for such a short time was debatable, but at least he would be attending *some* school, which was vastly superior to what he was doing now.

As for Rand and herself, surely she could keep her emotions in better control than she had today.

"All right," she said. "I'll work here until your people get back and can resume their jobs."

A frisson of excitement danced up Rand's spine, but he merely nodded and pushed himself away from the dresser. "Great, and don't forget, you'll be doing two jobs and paid accordingly."

Suzanne's eyes lit up. "Really?"

"Darned right." She looked so pretty he could hardly stop himself from going to her and making another pass. He knew too much about her now to think of her as just another woman. It was as though he could see through her clothes, and he knew that whenever he looked at her from this moment on he would remember her naked, flushed with passion and in his arms.

He was suddenly overheated and edgy. "Well, guess I'd better get back to the men. They're probably wondering what I've been doing for so long."

Suzanne's cheeks got pink. "You…you won't tell them, will you? About us, I mean."

"No way. What happened between us is strictly off-limits to anyone else."

She swallowed her nervousness regarding that topic. "Thank you."

Rand walked to the door, paused to send her a heartfelt smile and then left. With knees that had suddenly gotten weaker, Suzanne sank to the edge of the bed. If just a man's smile could make her knees go weak, wasn't she playing a rather dangerous game of chance with her heart?

But did she have a choice? Why, she might earn a thousand dollars or more before Handy and George got back.

And wouldn't it be wonderful if Rand was right about Mack becoming disenchanted with ranch life after a few grueling weeks of hard work?

It was a risk worth taking, Suzanne decided. Her first priority right now was money, her second was Mack. At this crucial time of her life, any feelings she might have about anything, especially a man, came in at a very feeble third. All she could do was vow to survive Rand Harding's almost fatal charm and leave it at that.

Again, what choice did she have?

Rand noticed that J.D. now had two admirers, Dale Carson *and* Mack. Working together that afternoon, he also noticed that Mack didn't seem to mind that Dale was also dogging J.D.'s footsteps, but Dale was getting surly about Mack's presence.

"What 'cha doing here, anyhow, kid?" Dale threw at the boy in a nasty, snide voice. "You should still be at home sucking the hind teat."

Mack got red in the face, but he stood his ground. "You got a problem, Carson?"

"Oh, tough guy, huh? Well, why don't you show me what you're really made of, Paxton."

Rand interrupted. "Hold on there, you two. Dale, get back to work. Mack, come over here."

Mack waded through the snow to Rand. "He started it, Rand."

"And what were you planning to do, finish it? Listen, Mack, Dale might not be very tall, but he's strong as an ox."

"I ain't afraid of him," Mack said, wiping his runny nose on the sleeve of his jacket.

Rand just looked at him. Mack was a boy trying to be a man, no doubt wishing with all his heart that he was older than his age. Rand could remember himself at fourteen, and also the confusion of feeling like a kid one minute and a grown-up the next.

But the similarity stopped there. When Rand was fourteen his parents had still been alive. He'd had roots and stability, and while his folks hadn't been particularly affectionate people, he'd known they were there for him. Mack had Suzanne, and damned lucky he was to have her, too, but he didn't realize that yet. Someday he would, but reason and good sense sometimes came too late to save unnecessary pain.

Yes, Rand thought with a sigh, Suzanne would go on beating her brains out trying to get her kid brother on the right track, and Mack would keep on being a pain in the neck—possibly worse—until time made it all obsolete. Neither of them should have to go through it.

"Your being unafraid is immaterial, Mack," Rand said. "If you tied into Dale, he'd beat you black and blue. That's a fact, and I don't believe you're stupid enough to ignore facts." Rand studied the boy's face. "Are you?"

"No, but I ain't backing down like no yellow coward, either."

Mack's fractured English made Rand wince. If anyone needed schooling, it was this boy. Not that perfect grammar was the norm among cowpokes, but they were grown men and their school years were behind them. Mack's education was still ahead of him, and Rand vowed on the spot that if he had anything to say about it, Mack Paxton was going to school. At least while he was in Montana, he was.

"Mack, if you're going to work with men like these, you're going to have to learn when to fight and when to laugh. Do you get my meaning?"

"You think I should have laughed when Dale said I should be home sucking on the hind teat?"

"I think you should have recognized that he was deliberately goading you, and yes, I think you should have laughed. It would have diffused the whole thing and it would have been over with. Mack, you're young, the only kid on the block, so to speak, and you're going to get a lot of ribbing from the crew. It goes with the territory. Tease them back, make *them* laugh. That's what they're looking for."

"Dale wasn't. I been in enough fights to know when a guy wants to punch your lights out."

Rand agreed, although it wasn't a concession he could give Mack. Dale was a tough little nut, and Rand didn't want to see Mack with a broken nose, or worse. "I can tell I'm not really getting through to you," Rand said. "Let me put it another way. If you want to work on this ranch, you'll hold your temper. If I hear of you getting into a fistfight with *any* of the men, you're through. Now, is that clear enough?"

Mack looked startled, then excited. "You're gonna hire me! I knew it! I told Suzanne you would. I told her!"

"Only for as long as the two of you stay in Montana," Rand warned. For the merest fraction of time he thought of enlisting Mack's aid to help him keep Suzanne in Montana. But it was such deceitful business, pitting brother against sister, and he couldn't do it. Drawing a breath, he went on with what he could say. "And there's more. You'll go to school in Whitehorn. You'll start the first day the buses run again."

Mack's mouth hung open. "But...but..."

"No buts, Mack. School and a job on the ranch or neither. It's your decision."

Mack was visibly shaken. He looked off across the snow-covered fields while Rand looked at him. A soft spot for this lost and wayward youth developed in Rand's chest, making him speak more gently.

"Me or one of the other men will teach you to ride and anything else you want to learn about ranching, Mack."

"I hate school," Mack mumbled, clearly on the verge of tears. "Why can't I just work?"

Rand deliberately inserted a hard note in his voice again. He was not going to argue with Mack about this. "Take it or leave it, Mack," he said as he walked away to rejoin his crew of men.

A short time later J.D. said to Rand, speaking quietly, "The boy's going through a bad time, isn't he?"

Mack was back to work and still looked as though tears

were imminent. "He'll make it," Rand said. It was all he could say without bringing Suzanne's name into the conversation, which he would not do with J.D. or anyone else.

Still, while pitching hay from the sled, he kept a close eye on Mack. He felt something important, a bonding with that sad-faced young man, and he passionately hoped he would have the chance to help him.

It could only happen if the Paxtons stayed in Montana, of course. Rand leaned on his pitchfork for a minute, his expression deeply introspective. If he could somehow convince Suzanne to stay—to marry him—wouldn't all three of them be better off than they were now? Mack certainly would be, *he* would be…and Suzanne? Well, she would never have to worry about finding a job again, and how could that be a detriment?

Yes, she would definitely be better off as far as having to support herself and Mack went. He should be able to convince her of that much, at least. He decided then and there that he was going to give it his best shot. After all, what did he have to lose?

Supper was roast pork, sage dressing and a half-dozen side dishes. Suzanne was getting the hang of cooking large meals and was especially proud of tonight's menu. She still ate alone in the kitchen, and could hear the men talking and laughing. It was no longer snowing, there was a definite rise in temperature and everyone was elated about it.

She was surprised when Mack came in carrying his plate and glass of milk. "Uh, is it okay if I sit with you tonight?" he asked.

"Of course it's okay. Pull up a stool." My Lord, she thought, was Rand's theory working already? Was Mack any less thrilled with ranching than he'd been? Why else would he leave the men and eat with her?

He ate for a few minutes, shoveling it in and saying nothing, and Suzanne let the silence stretch, knowing that if he had something to tell her, he would get to it in his own good time.

Finally he mumbled, "Good supper, sis. Really good."

She smiled. "Thanks. I'm glad you like it."

He took a swallow of milk. "Uh, Rand hired me today."

Suzanne's stomach sank, and she laid her fork on her plate. This wasn't quite what she'd been hoping to hear. "Oh?"

"It's part-time, though. He said I have to go to school if I want to work for him."

Suzanne quietly cleared her throat. "And how do you feel about that?"

Mack was looking down at his plate. "I don't know why he wants me to go to school. I was sort of hoping you'd talk to him about it."

"Let me get this straight. You want me to tell Rand you don't need to finish your education? Mack, you know how I feel about your quitting school. How could you ask me to do something that is in direct opposition to my own standards?"

Mack cast her a sullen look. "You won't do it, then?"

"No, I will not."

Mack slumped back on the stool. "I hate being a kid."

Rand walked in and heard him. "Sounds to me like you hate quite a few things, Mack. Besides school and your age, what else do you hate?"

Just the sight of Rand had Suzanne's pulse racing. Was this going to be her reaction every time they ran into each other? she thought in horror. Why, oh, why had she made love with him today? she asked herself with a silent groan. She was going to pay for that error in judgment for as long as she was in Montana, make no mistake.

Mack's face was red. "I got a right to hate school," he muttered.

"And you have a right to hate your age, but does it do you

or anyone else any good?" Rand asked him. "It's certainly not going to make you older overnight."

"Didn't say it would." Mack slid off the stool. "I'm going upstairs."

Rand watched him go, then shook his head. "That is one unhappy boy, Suz."

His shortening her name, as he'd done in her bed today, ignited a fire in the pit of Suzanne's stomach. "I know," she said in the quietest possible tone.

"I thought he liked me. He did when he first came," Rand said thoughtfully.

"He probably still does. What he doesn't like is being told what to do."

"But we're all told what to do, in one way or another."

"So speaketh a mature man," Suzanne murmured. "He said you hired him today, with the condition that he attend school."

"I did." Rand moved closer and leaned his elbows on the counter, thereby putting his face only inches from hers. "Suz, will you marry me?"

Ten

"Rand...please don't," Suzanne whispered, wary of someone overhearing this embarrassing discussion.

"You don't believe I'm serious, do you?" Rand laid his hand over hers where it rested on the counter next to her plate.

"I don't see how you could be." She tried to slide her hand from under his, but he curled his fingers around it and held on. "Rand!"

"Simmer down and talk to me for a minute. Do you have any reason to go back to Baltimore? Something I don't know about?"

"It's my home. Do I need a better reason?"

"But you live in an apartment. What kind of home is that?"

"There's nothing wrong with my apartment. And, if you'd care to think about it, it's full of furniture that belongs to me. I also have a car."

"Your car and furniture could be shipped to Montana." He probed the depths of her eyes. "Is there anything else?"

She dropped her gaze. "You know there isn't. But..."

"Let me finish. You have nothing to go back to, and neither does Mack. The three of us could have a good life together. I have plans. I inherited a little money from my parents, and I've been saving most of my pay for a long time. I'm going to have my own ranch someday, probably in another few years. There's cheap land for sale out there, but I want a good place, with grass and water and a decent house. Nothing I could afford will be perfect, I know that. But if I start out with the basics, I can make it perfect. I'd like you to make it perfect with me. You're smart and capable, Suz, and if you'd be willing to handle the paperwork and take care of the house and meals, me and Mack could do the rest. I believe the three of us would make a damned good team."

"A damned good team," she repeated slowly. "Yes, I can see why you might feel that way. But from where I'm sitting, it sounds like you're offering a business arrangement rather than marriage."

Rand thought a moment. "Guess I'm offering both." He squeezed her hand. "What do you say, Suz? I think it would work. What do you think?"

Financially speaking, it was the best offer she'd ever received. So why didn't she immediately grab it? Why did she feel slightly sick to her stomach instead of elated? Rand was a good man, handsome, clean, hardworking, and she couldn't deny the physical attraction between them.

But there *was* denial in her system, strong and potent. Total rejection of his plans. Revulsion that he would think she would be receptive to such a callous marriage proposal.

"I…" She was about to tell him no deal, as tactfully as she could, of course, when the men began filing in with their dirty dishes.

Rand let go of her hand and straightened his back. "We'll talk again later," he said in a conspiratorial undertone.

She managed a weak, thin smile as she got off her stool and rounded the counter to begin cleaning up. It was all she could give Rand in her present state of confusion.

Suzanne had no intention of taking up that conversation where it had left off, and the minute the kitchen was in order, she hurried down the hall to her bedroom. She realized that she'd been no more emotionally shaken during her divorce than she was now, and she considered divorce to be one of the best examples of human-caused misery in today's rash and reckless world.

But a marriage proposal without so much as a hint of feelings topped the emotionless legal proceedings for a divorce, she felt now. With her stomach churning she showered and got ready for bed, all the while wondering and worrying how she was going to elude another discussion of marriage with Rand. Avoiding him completely was out of the question, especially if he deliberately sought her out, which she knew in her soul he was going to do. Worse, she suspected he would not take a simple no for an answer, and would keep on trying to make her see his long-term plan for their future as sensible.

The trouble was that it *was* sensible. If she was looking for a man to feed, house and clothe her and Mack, then Rand was a ready-made patsy. But what about love? What about caring for a man so much you put his well-being before your own? Didn't Rand ever want to feel that way about a woman?

Her own thoughts sickened her. What was so great about love? Why was she so stubbornly opposed to a loveless marriage when the supposed love of her life had turned out to be a grade-A jerk?

She wiped a circle of steam off the mirror above the sink and took stock of herself. Looking into her own dark eyes she questioned her ambiguity. She, herself, had thought that Rand was the answer to her problems only yesterday, then, after they had made love, her attitude had taken a major change. She was still going back and forth on it. Why in God's name couldn't she settle on one opinion and stick with it?

With a disgusted shake of her head and a soulful sigh, she dug out her hair dryer and plugged it in. Ten minutes later, with her hair dry and wearing her pajamas and robe, she walked from the bathroom into the bedroom.

Her mouth dropped open. Rand was sitting in the room's one chair, his right ankle resting on his left knee. He looked as settled in and as comfortable as anyone she'd ever seen, as though he had every right to enter her room without permission!

"Hi," he said, untangling his legs and getting to his feet. "I was in the office when you rushed by. Looks like you're ready to go to bed. I was hoping we could do a little more talking."

She was so upset that she couldn't speak any way but stiffly. "This is the second time you've walked into this room without knocking. Should I expect that to be the norm?"

"I knocked, you just didn't hear me."

"I happened to have been in the shower," she said sharply.

"I figured that out for myself. You're mad at me." He took a step toward her. "Don't be mad, Suz. If I'd been up to no good, I would have joined you in the shower." He grinned slightly and looked adorably boyish, which Suzanne tried hard to ignore. His voice softened. "Maybe you wouldn't have minded."

"I most certainly would have," she retorted, although she wasn't sure it was true. It wasn't at all comforting to realize that with Rand she didn't know what was truth or utter nonsense! Certainly it was true that he affected her physically, and it was true that she liked him as a person. But it was also true that she didn't seem to know right from wrong anymore, although in her response to Rand she wondered if there was any difference.

Rand chuckled over her quick comeback. "I wonder if you're just saying that to get a rise out of me. After what happened between us…"

She flushed. "I told you sleeping together gave neither of us a hold over the other."

"I remember, but the thing is, Suz, we didn't do any sleeping."

She had to change the subject. This was getting out of hand. "Speaking of sleeping," she said, "why did you sleep at the foot of the stairs last night instead of in your room?"

Her question took Rand so by surprise he couldn't immediately come up with a deceptive but reasonable answer. "Uh…you wouldn't understand."

"Try me," she taunted.

Rand shook his head. "Sorry."

"Don't make the mistake of thinking I'm dull-witted, Rand. Don't you think I've wondered about men guarding the place at night, about your searching every nook and cranny of this building for some mysterious object and then your sleeping on the floor? All those things are connected, aren't they? There's something going on you won't talk about. Don't bother to lie about it, I know there is. It probably has something to do with the murders of the Kincaid family."

At Rand's surprised expression, she added, "Yes, I heard about that grisly affair, about ten minutes after I landed in Billings."

"It's no secret," Rand said calmly.

"Well?"

"Well, what?"

"Is what's going on now connected to the Kincaid murders?"

"No." He'd spoken firmly, positively, but Suzanne's question had opened a brand-new school of thought. Was the sabotage somehow related to the Kincaid murders? How could it be? *Why* would it be? Most of the players in that awful chapter of Whitehorn history were dead.

Except for baby Jennifer.

Well, a small child certainly wasn't responsible for the reprehensible acts on this ranch. The whole idea was preposterous.

And he was on to Suzanne's evasive tactics, too. "You're bringing up anything you can think of to avoid talking about marrying me, aren't you? Why, Suz? Don't you like the idea?"

Suzanne's bluster vanished like a puff of smoke. Her mind raced for some way around a direct answer.

She even attempted a small laugh. "Rand, I don't even know if I like Montana. What have I seen of it? I drove from Billings, most of the way in the dark. I got out of the car and skidded myself through the snow to the door of this building, and I haven't left it since. I haven't even seen the ranch, although I can vouch for it having a remarkable kitchen and a so-so office."

"But you *will* see the ranch," Rand said eagerly. "When the sun comes out and the snow starts melting, you won't believe how beautiful it is. Wildflowers and new grass will start popping up through the snow. The sky will be so blue you'll need dark glasses to look at it."

He suddenly stopped talking to listen. "Do you hear that?"

"I hear something. What is it?"

Rand was thinking the worst. "Stay here," he told her. "I'll go find out what it is."

Suzanne thought he would dash from the room, but instead he gingerly opened the door a crack to peer down the hall. Then he sidled through the crack and hugged the wall as he made his way to the front door.

"Good grief," Suzanne mumbled over such histrionics. Whatever was happening on this ranch, it had Rand Harding, whom she was positive was afraid of nothing, acting like a private eye in a grade-B movie.

She watched from her door. Apparently when Rand reached the outside door he could better tell what the sounds were because he pulled it open without any more drama.

In rushed a scraggly dog, whimpering and wriggling his scruffy body all over the place. Rand knelt down, and the mutt licked his face.

"And who might you be?" Rand asked, scratching the dog's ears. There were clumps of frozen snow matted in the animal's dingy white coat, and he looked half-starved. Suddenly the dog took off up the stairs so fast that Rand ended up on his seat on the floor. "What in hell? Where're you going?" he yelled at the speeding dog.

Getting up, Rand took the stairs three at a time to chase down the stray before he woke up every man on the second floor.

But the dog woke only one man—J. D. Cade. Evidently J.D. hadn't latched his door securely before retiring, because the dog nudged it open, ran into the room and jumped right onto J.D.'s bed, landing squarely on the man's chest. J.D. came awake snorting and cussing.

Rand arrived. "J.D., I'm sorry as hell. This here mutt…" He stopped, noticing how J.D. was petting and hugging the mangy animal.

"Freeway, how in hell did you find me?" J.D. looked at Rand. "He's mine, Rand. For a while he was, anyhow. Then, just before I got here, I lost him at a truck stop. Don't know how it happened. I looked everywhere for him, and the only thing I could think of was that he'd gotten in a truck with some friendly guy."

Rand grinned. "Did I hear you call him Freeway?"

"That's what I named him, 'cause I found him wandering a highway. What I can't figure out is how he found me now. That truck stop is a hundred miles from here."

"I've heard of things like this, J.D., where a dog or cat will track its master for hundreds of miles. That's what Freeway must have done. The storm probably slowed him down or he would have been here long before this. Well, there's plenty of dog food in the barn with Daisy and her pups," Rand said. "Help yourself."

"Thanks, I will. Is it okay if he sleeps in here, though?"

"If his smell doesn't bother you, it won't bother me," Rand said with a laugh. "Night, J.D."

"Good night, Rand, and thanks."

When Rand left, J.D. was up and getting dressed. Rand went back downstairs and knocked softly on Suzanne's door. It was hard for him not to go back in her room, but he quickly explained about the dog, then wished her a good-night. She stared at him with a puzzled expression for a moment, then said good-night and shut her door. Feeling all mixed up, sweetheart? Rand thought. Well, join the club.

Maybe Freeway's arrival hadn't been timed the best, but he hadn't really been getting anywhere with his marriage discussion, anyway, Rand told himself as he detoured to the kitchen for a glass of milk before going to bed.

After pouring it, he sat on a stool at the counter and let his thoughts ramble. There were two men on guard duty tonight, so he'd be able to sleep in his own bed. He'd sent them to the bunkhouse early this afternoon to get some rest because of their having to stay awake all night. Too damned many people were losing sleep because of one rotten apple, he thought with an onslaught of bitter feelings.

At least he'd been believing he was dealing with only one man. He took a swallow of milk, thinking there could be more than one. His mind began working on that angle. Were there any two men in the crew who were really close?

He couldn't think of any. Oh, some were friendlier than others, that was only natural. But none struck him as a team.

Then there was that startling question of Suzanne's to ponder: is what's going on now connected to the Kincaid murders? His eyes narrowed. Was it possible?

It didn't make any sense to him, and after a few minutes of puzzling over it he moved from that topic to Suzanne. At once his body felt warmer, more alive. Thinking of their intimate interlude in her bedroom today caused a predictable reaction, and he squirmed on the stool to strategically loosen his jeans.

She liked him, he knew she did, so why wouldn't she talk about marriage? Hell, he'd offered her everything he had, what more could he do? And she had to know how much better off Mack would be with a stable home. She *was* going to have trouble in getting the boy to leave Montana, no doubt about it, and she knew it, too, or she wouldn't have asked for his advice today. So why didn't she just add up the pluses, accept his marriage proposal and let it go at that?

Rand finished off his milk, sat there pondering all that was happening for a few minutes longer, then sighed and got off the stool. He was beat. It was time for bed.

He headed for his room.

Suzanne was up before daybreak the next morning, but as the men left for work after breakfast she noticed the breaking of dawn on the eastern horizon and realized the sky was clear. Her spirits took a decided jump upward. Today she was going to see the sun! The storm was over, and already dripping icicles were forming on the eaves as the snow on the roof began melting.

She stood at one of the windows in the dining room and watched the sun rise, and as it got lighter and brighter outside, she got her first completely unobstructed look at the ranch compound. Sun-speckled snow covered everything, giving the scene a fairy-tale quality. Only a small portion of the lower half of the trunk of her blue rental car was bare, and if she didn't know she was looking at a car, she wouldn't have any idea what lay under that smoothly rounded mound of snow.

Next to it was another large mound, but she could tell it was a vehicle. Craning her neck she looked for other vehicles, those "great" trucks Mack had told her the men drove.

"Must be another parking place somewhere," she murmured.

Perhaps what she found most intriguing on this beautiful morning was the Kincaid mansion. Questions about it arose in her mind as she studied it. Had the Kincaids been murdered in that lovely, lonely-looking house? How many Kincaids had there been? Who was the woman who had supposedly done the murders, and how had she died?

The ringing of telephones startled her, and she dashed to answer the kitchen extension. Thrilled that the phones were working again, she breathlessly said, "Kincaid Ranch. Good morning."

"Good morning, ma'am. This is Sterling McCallum. May I ask who you are?"

"Certainly, Mr. McCallum. I'm Suzanne Paxton. I am so glad the phones are working again. It must have just happened, because I tried them only a short time ago."

"Yes, things are finally getting back to normal, Ms. Paxton. You should see snowplows out that way some time today. Are you from around here?"

Obviously Mr. McCallum, whoever he was, hadn't expected a woman to answer his call, Suzanne thought with a small smile.

"I live in Baltimore, Mr. McCallum."

"Got caught in the storm, I expect."

Suzanne didn't think an explanation of why she'd gotten trapped on the Kincaid Ranch was necessary, so her answer was brief. "That I did."

"I would imagine you're relieved to see the end of that blizzard."

"Very relieved."

"By any chance is Rand Harding around?"

"No, sir, he's not. I'll tell him you called the minute he comes in, if you wish."

"Please do that. He has my number. Oh, if for some reason he doesn't come in until late, tell him to call me at home. He also has that number."

"I'm writing your message down as we speak, Mr. McCallum."

"Thank you."

"You're welcome. Goodbye."

Suzanne had no more than put the phone down when it rang again. She answered as she had before. "Kincaid Ranch."

A high-pitched female voice stammered, "Uh, hello. I didn't know there was a woman on the ranch."

"I got caught in the storm," Suzanne said, deciding to stick with that simple explanation of her presence.

"Oh, too bad. Well, I'm Janie Carson. One of the men working out there is my brother. Do you know Dale?"

"I know him, yes."

"Is he all right? I've been terribly worried. The storm was so awful, and the phone lines were down, and I've been going a little crazy wondering if Dale is all right."

How well Suzanne understood a sister worrying about a brother! "He's fine, Janie," she said gently. "Everyone is. I'm Suzanne, by the way, Suzanne Paxton."

"I heard George Davenport got hurt and is in the hospital."

"That's true. He took a fall at the onset of the blizzard, but his was the only injury. Everyone else survived intact. Would you like me to ask Dale to call you when he comes in?"

"Yes, please. Tell him I'll be at work at the café until seven tonight. He has the number."

"Consider it done. Was the storm as bad in town as it was out here, Janie?"

"The storm was awful, one of the worst I've seen, Suzanne, but we didn't lose the phones and our streets were plowed. Some of them only had one lane open but most people were able to get to their jobs. A few businesses shut their doors, and the schools have been closed, of course. The kids liked that," Janie added with a laugh.

"I'm sure they did."

"Their freedom is over, though. I heard there would be school as usual tomorrow."

"Someone told me a few minutes ago that we could expect to see plows out this way today. Does that mean the school buses will run?"

"Oh, yes. If the roads are open, the buses will run. Why do you ask?"

Suzanne hedged, not wanting to tell her problems to a complete stranger, as nice as Janie Carson seemed to be. "I guess I was thinking more of the mail. If the buses can get through, so will the mail trucks, wouldn't you say?"

"That's right, the ranch hasn't been getting any mail, has it? No phones, no mail, goodness. I've never been cut off from the rest of the world that way. Must be an awful feeling."

Suzanne was about to agree when she realized it hadn't been awful at all. In fact, now that she really thought about it, the isolation had been peaceful. Soothing to her frazzled nerves.

"It wasn't so bad," she told Janie. "I rather enjoyed it, to be honest." Suzanne saw Rand walk in and watched his face light up as he realized the phone was working. "I have to run, Janie. I'll give Dale your message when I see him."

"Thanks, Suzanne. Maybe we'll meet. When the roads are open, I just might drive out there to see Dale. Bye for now."

"Bye, Janie." Suzanne put down the phone and looked at Rand. "That was Dale's sister. She wants him to call her."

"When did the phones start working?"

"About fifteen minutes ago. The first call that came through was from Sterling McCallum. He asked that you call him. Said you have his number."

"I do. Thanks." Rand walked out, saying as he left, "I'll use the office phone." He had come in to talk to Suzanne. With the drastic turn in the weather, he knew the roads would be open very soon, possibly even today, and he couldn't let Suzanne take the notion to leave without making at least one more attempt to change her mind about marrying him.

But first things first, he thought, unbuttoning his heavy jacket as he traversed the hall to the office. Laying his gloves, hat and scarf on his desk, he sat down and dialed the White-horn Police Department.

"Hello, Shelley," he said to the receptionist. "This is Rand Harding. I'm returning a call from Sterling."

"I'll put you through, Rand. Did everyone out there survive the storm?"

"Sure did. We're digging ourselves out now. It's going to be a mess for a while, but we'll make it."

"I'm sure you will. Hold on and I'll ring Sterling's desk."

Sterling came on the line. "Rand, how's everything out there?"

While Rand talked to Sterling, Suzanne found herself battling a powerful urge to go outdoors and soak up some of that sunshine. Her biggest deterrent was something warm for her feet. She had a coat and gloves, but the shoes she had with her would provide very little protection in such deep snow.

Suddenly recalling the old boots that Rand had stumbled upon under her bed, she ran down the hall to her room to check them out. Kicking off her loafers, she tried them on. They were at least three sizes too big, but if she put on extra stockings they would work, she decided with an impish grin. Pulling on the stockings, then every sweater she'd brought with her, she donned the boots, her coat and gloves and left the building.

Rand thought he heard the closing of a door, but he was engrossed in his conversation with Sterling and paid it no mind.

"No, everything's been quiet, Sterling. Guess the storm kept our saboteur indoors. The storm and the fact that someone's been on guard duty every night."

"You're thinking it's been a little too quiet, aren't you?" Sterling said.

"I'm hoping for the best and expecting the worst, Sterling. I wouldn't be so antsy if that box of dynamite wasn't on the place. I've searched every building twice and three times, including the bunkhouse. I honestly don't know where else to look, not until this snow melts, anyway."

"I've talked to Wendell about it several times, and he's worried as hell."

"Really? He didn't sound worried as hell when *I* talked to him about it."

"He didn't?"

"Sterling, when you were in Washington, I called Wendell and told him about it, thinking he'd be as alarmed as I was. He started talking about us having a thief on the place because the perp charged the dynamite to the ranch. He didn't seem one bit concerned that someone might be planning to blow us all to kingdom come."

"That's odd. He's certainly given me a much different impression. In fact, I'd say he's gone out of his way to let me know how deeply concerned he is. Rand, are you worried enough about it to evacuate the ranch? I talked to the County Highway Department early this morning, and they're planning to plow out that way today. By tonight we could have everyone off the place. How do you feel about that?"

"Sterling, you're the boss and a cop, to boot. How do *you* feel about it?"

"Well, we'll never catch the bastard if we move him to town, that's for sure."

"And what about the animals? There's still far too much snow for them to reach the grass under it, Sterling. We have to keep on feeding until we lose some of this snow."

"This is a hell of a mess."

"Yes, it is," Rand agreed. "I'll tell you, Sterling, when I find out who's behind the trouble out here, I'm going to kick his butt all the way to the county jail." Rand took a breath. "You know, we keep talking like we're dealing with only one man, but there could be two or even three."

"True," Sterling said, sounding disgruntled. "On another tack, Rand, a woman named Suzanne Paxton answered your phone this morning. She said she was there because she'd been caught by the storm. You might have to keep the crew on the ranch to tend the animals, but that woman should be out of there the minute the roads are clear."

Rand's stomach sank. If he sent Suzanne away, she might never come back. But Sterling was right. Suzanne's safety was vastly more important than his love life.

"I'll see that she leaves," he said stoically, belying the sickish feeling he felt in his gut at the thought of telling Suzanne to leave. Mack, too. The boy shouldn't be exposed to a maniac's instability, either.

But then, neither should any of the good, honest men working on the ranch. On that, however, Rand's hands were tied. He couldn't leave the cattle and horses and let them go hungry until the snow melted, nor could he or any other one person see to the hay drops by himself. Besides, what would actually be accomplished by a temporary evacuation? Eventually the crew would return to work, including the man who'd ordered that second case of dynamite.

Outside, Suzanne was trudging through the snow in her oversize boots, tittering like a schoolgirl and lifting her face to the sun. Rand hadn't exaggerated, she thought. Never had she seen such a dazzling blue sky.

Automatically, so it seemed, she headed for the mansion. It fascinated her, sitting there so still and silent in a field of sparkling white. Most of the windows were covered, she noted, but then she spotted one that was undraped. Standing on tiptoe, she put her face to the glass and peered into a small dining room.

"Oh, it's gorgeous," she whispered, wishing ardently that she could go in and look at all the rooms.

Circling the house in hopes of finding another bare window, she came upon a side door. It couldn't possibly be unlocked, she thought. But if it was and she went in and looked around, why would anyone care? She tried the door, and to her amazement the knob turned. Quickly, before she could tell herself she had no right to enter this house, she went in and shut the door behind her.

It took a moment for her to realize that the house wasn't cold. Apparently the heat had been left on low, and she was able to loosen her coat in comfort. Her next surprise was that while walking from room to room, she discovered the house wasn't nearly as gorgeous as she'd thought. Oh, it wasn't the house itself, it was the decor. Whoever had decorated this marvelous home had used too many frills. It was tastelessly overdone with flowered wallpapers and fussy furniture. What a pity.

She allowed herself about fifteen minutes in the house, then exited by the same side door and trudged back toward the bunkhouse.

Spotting Rand coming out through the dining room door, she waved and called, "I love this sunshine!"

Rand waved back. She looked like a young girl cavorting in the snow, pretty as a picture and one to warm any bachelor's heart. Grinning, he walked out to meet her.

Her cheeks were pink from the crisp, fresh air, and he gave in to impulse and put his arms around her to pick her up and swing her around and around. Her laughter rang out, as did Rand's, and then he floundered in the deep snow and they landed in a drift.

They lay on their backs and laughed over their own antics,

and Rand couldn't remember when he'd been this happy. She *had* to stay in his life; how was he going to make her understand that his request that she leave for a while had nothing at all to do with the two of them?

But it had to be done, and now was as good a time as any to attempt that explanation.

He turned to look at her, and his gaze roamed her body from head to foot. He started to laugh again when he saw the boots she was wearing.

"Are those the latest style in women's footwear?" he asked with a merry, teasing twinkle in his eyes.

Suzanne laughed again. "They might not be stylish and they're much too big, but they've kept my feet warm and dry. I just had to get outside, Rand. I'm not used to being cooped up."

Rand smiled at her. "Do you know you're a very sweet woman?"

"Sweet?" Suzanne's expression softened as she looked into his eyes. "What a nice compliment. Thank you."

He looked away from her for a moment and noticed, for the first time, the direction of her tracks in the snow.

"What've you been doing?" he asked.

"Looking at the house. You don't mind, do you?"

He raised one shoulder in a shrug. "There's not much to see when you can't get inside."

She hesitated, but his comment indicated that all the doors of the house were locked and one wasn't. He should know.

"Rand, I got in. There's an unlocked side door, and couldn't resist seeing…" She gaped when Rand jumped up and took off running for the big house. "Well, good heavens," she muttered. "I didn't touch anything," she shouted at his back.

Shaking her head at his peculiar, completely unpredictable behavior, she got up, brushed snow from her coat, walked to the bunkhouse and went inside.

Eleven

During the lunch hour, Suzanne, from the kitchen, could hear the men laughing about J.D.'s dog.

"You should have seen old Freeway hightailing it out of the barn. Daisy must have put the fear of God into him," one man said. "Freeway was moving so fast he was smoking."

"Daisy's mighty protective of those pups of hers," someone else said.

"Freeway will make friends with her, you'll see." Suzanne recognized that calm, collected voice as J.D.'s.

"Not as long as she's got those pups, he won't," Dale Carson said with a snide little laugh.

Suzanne frowned. She had listened to table talk among the men before, and it seemed to her that Dale deliberately tried to rile J.D. Not that J.D. couldn't take care of himself. He either ignored Dale completely or put him in his place with a few well-chosen words. The younger man always backed off, so why did he keep baiting J.D.? Suzanne wondered.

She also wondered why Rand hadn't come in for lunch

again. She'd seen nothing of him since he'd taken off running toward the big house. She couldn't possibly imagine a reason for him spending hours in it, but neither could she imagine where else he might have gone. Surely he wasn't inspecting every little thing in it, thinking that she might have disturbed something. Goodness, she'd made sure that even her coat hadn't brushed up against any of the furniture or woodwork. She hadn't, as she'd told him, touched one single thing in the entire house, but it still made her nervous that he might have thought differently. She wished now that she hadn't gone near the place.

Rand was glad she had. Cursing his own lack of foresight—he'd been so positive the house was locked up tightly—he had spent hours going from room to room in search of that dynamite. Obviously someone had neatly picked the lock on that side door, as there was no sign of forced entry. Why the creep had left it unlocked remained a question in Rand's mind—maybe so he could get to the dynamite fast when he felt the time was right, maybe because he was willing to take the chance that no one would notice one unlocked door or maybe because he was just plain stupid.

At any rate, Rand was certain the dynamite was somewhere in this house. He would have interrupted his search for lunch except for one thing—Suzanne's and his tracks in the snow. He wanted to find the dynamite before the culprit noticed the tracks and realized that Rand was on to his bag of dirty tricks.

The house had a basement, most of which was taken up by a huge recreation room. There was a long bar of polished mahogany and a striking antique billiard table. The paneled walls contained numerous hunting trophies, mounted heads of elk, deer, moose and bear, and there was a large, locked gun cabinet with an impressive display of hunting rifles. Rand remembered the conversation he'd had with Sterling after he'd worked on the ranch for about a month.

"Sterling, that house is a burglary waiting to happen. At least take the guns out of it."

"That house is part of my daughter's history, Rand," Sterling had told him. "Someday she's going to want to know about her birth family. Jessica and I have discussed Jennifer's inheritance at great length, and we agree that the house and everything in it should remain just as it is. It tells a story, which Jenny will someday want to know. The only items removed since Mary Jo's arrest were the Native American artifacts she used in one of her crimes. After they were utilized as evidence against her in court, we donated them to the museum on the reservation. Everything else is as it was when Jeremiah was alive. It's the way we want it."

Rand had never mentioned it again, but the house had continued to worry him. It was stuffed with valuables, good paintings, sterling silver flatware, china patterns galore and every electronic gadget money could buy. He didn't care much for the way Mary Jo Kincaid had decorated it, but there was no question about the house and its contents being worth a great deal of money.

He looked around the rec room without a whole lot of hope. Other than the gun and liquor cabinets, there really wasn't anything that wasn't in plain sight.

After checking the cabinets, his gaze fell upon a door in the paneling, which he knew led to a storage room. He had glanced into the room only one time, and he recalled now that it had been crammed with discarded furniture and cardboard boxes.

Grimly, he opened the door and stepped into the room. An alarm bell instantly went off in his head; someone had been in here, boxes had been moved!

He began moving some himself. It took about ten minutes of shifting things around before he found it—a brand-new unopened case of dynamite.

"Bingo," he exclaimed as satisfaction coursed through his veins.

And he knew exactly what he was going to do with his dangerous find, too. The men were still in the bunkhouse having lunch. If he hurried, he could take care of this problem before they came outside for the afternoon shift.

He swiftly set to work.

Rand came rushing into the bunkhouse while Suzanne was still cleaning up after lunch. The men had returned to work; the building was quiet. She froze, fearing he was coming to the kitchen. She felt more defensive than guilty about having invaded the big house, and if he said something to her about it, she was apt to get angry.

But he went directly to the office and she breathed a sigh of relief and went on with her work.

In his office, Rand threw off his jacket and plopped down at his desk. Immediately he dialed a number. Rand got Sterling right away.

"Yes, Rand?"

"I found it. It was in the storage room in the basement of the house. Someone picked a side-door lock. I hauled it out to that big stand of pines behind the house and buried it. Then I took a horse and rode it back and forth in the snow so many times no one could possibly locate it by following my tracks."

"Damn, that's good news!" Sterling exclaimed. "The lock was picked, you say?"

"Had to have been. Either that or someone besides myself has a key. There isn't a mark on the door or the jamb that shouldn't be there. Sterling, I need some advice. Should I leave that door unlocked or what? Somebody's going to go looking for that dynamite, and if the door's locked he might break in next time. What's your feeling on that?"

"What I'm wondering right now is who's clever enough

out there to pick the good security locks that are on every door of that house. Know anyone with that kind of expertise?"

"No, I don't, but then we don't exactly screen applicants for a cowhand's job, do we? Hell, in the past three months all a man had to do was breathe and walk upright to get hired."

"You did what you had to, so don't go laying any of the blame on yourself," Sterling said gruffly. "Rand, here's what I want you to do. Find a big piece of paper, and I mean big. On it, write with one of those heavy black markers, I Found It, You Son Of A Bitch, So Don't Bother Going In. Sign your name and nail it to that side door. And lock it. That should shake some of the cockiness out of the bastard."

Rand chuckled. "That it should. Okay, I'll do it right away. Thanks, Sterling."

"Call anytime, Rand. And listen, I think Reed should make another trip out there when the roads are open. I'll call him myself."

"Good idea. Talk to you later, Sterling."

"Oh, Rand? Winona Cobb dropped in to see me this morning. You know who she is, don't you?"

"That woman who runs the junkyard outside of town? What's it called again?"

"The Stop-n-Swap," Sterling replied.

"Oh, yeah. Right." Rand laughed. "I heard she says she's psychic or some such bull."

"I'm not so sure she isn't. She's hit the nail on the head quite a few times in the past, and it couldn't all be guesswork. Anyhow, she made a special trip to town to tell me that there are dark clouds on the horizon for Whitehorn. Warned me about a disturbance in the town's aura and mentioned it could encompass some outlying areas. Talked about strangers wearing masks, or some such gibberish, but I immediately thought of the ranch and the strangers you've been hiring. There's nothing you can do about it, but I just thought you should know."

"Hell, Sterling, it's really just more gossip about the trouble out here, wouldn't you say? That old lady's nuttier than a fruit-cake."

"If it was anyone else doing the talking I'd agree, and Winona is surely a strange duck. But, like I said, she's come up with some pretty accurate predictions in the past. Remind me to tell you about some of the things she said about Mary Jo Kincaid when we have the time. Right now I'm swamped."

"Yes, we'll talk about it sometime, Sterling. I'll sign off now and let you get back to work. Bye." Rand grinned a little as he hung up. It was hard for him to believe that a man of Sterling McCallum's caliber would even listen to psychic mumbo-jumbo, let alone give it any credence. Oh, well, he thought, to each his own.

After opening a dozen drawers in the desks and cabinets in the room, Rand found a large piece of white pasteboard. He wrote on it what Sterling had told him to write, chuckled again over the message, got into his jacket again, took the sign and went outside to secure it on that side door of the house.

Walking back to the bunkhouse, Rand felt hunger pangs in his stomach. He also felt so lighthearted, he almost whooped with glee. Not only would he sleep easier tonight, but he didn't have to tell Suzanne and Mack to leave the ranch. At the bunkhouse, he shed his outside gear and headed for the kitchen and something to eat.

Suzanne heard him coming and stiffened. She finished drying her hands on a cotton towel and was hanging it up when Rand walked in. His big smile surprised her, but not nearly so much as what he did next. Rounding the counter in three long strides, he put his hands on her waist, picked her up so that her face was on a level with his and planted a warm, squishy kiss on her lips.

She drew her head back and glared at him. "What on earth are you doing? Put me down, for heaven's sake! What if someone should come in? Maybe you don't give a whit about my reputation, but I do."

He laughed as though he didn't have a care in the world, which was exactly how he felt. Finding and burying that dynamite had relieved a ten-ton burden.

"Good things are happening today," he declared. "The sun's out, the snow is melting, the phone's are working and you've been just waiting for me to come in so you could tell me you're going to marry me, right?"

Suzanne realized that he was feeling full of the devil, for some reason, and decided to tease him back.

With a perfectly straight face she said, "How did you know?"

Probably because of Sterling talking about Winona Cobb, Rand said, "I'm psychic, that's how."

"Yeah, right," Suzanne drawled. "And I'm the tooth fairy."

"I knew that."

She couldn't help laughing. "You big fake. You're about as psychic as that dishwasher over there. Now, please put me down and I'll fix you some lunch."

Chuckling, Rand lowered her so that her feet were on the floor.

"What put you in such a good mood?" Suzanne asked as she turned on the burner under the pot of soup she'd left out to warm up for him.

"Told you good things were happening today." Rand perched on a counter stool to watch her gracefully move around the kitchen. She seemed completely at home, as though she'd been cooking for a crew of men for months instead of a few days. The word *adaptable* entered his mind again. Adaptability was a necessary trait for anyone trying his luck with cattle ranching, he believed. The fluctuations of weather and beef prices, the hard work seven days a week, month after month, the way cowhands came and went, and the isolation most ranchers lived with weeded out the weak-willed and unconformable very quickly. Either that or people lived in misery.

Suzanne didn't seem at all miserable. In fact, she didn't even seem worried now, as she'd so obviously been when she got here.

"You like it here, don't you?" Rand said.

Suzanne turned her head to send him a glance. "I don't dislike it."

"Come on, tell the truth. Isn't there something about this place that makes you happy? You seem happy, you look happy. Shouldn't I assume you *are* happy?"

"I do feel…less stressed out than when I came," she admitted thoughtfully. "Maybe it's because I've been busy. I always feel best when I have something productive to do."

"Maybe you're feeling good because of me."

She brought a sandwich on a plate to the counter and set it in front of him. "And maybe I'm feeling good because of the sunshine. I'll get your soup."

"You won't face it, will you? Why not, Suzanne? Why can't you look me in the eye and admit that marrying me would solve all your problems?"

She was ladling soup into a bowl, and she stopped to send him a raised-eyebrow look. "Is that what you want to hear? All right, I can easily admit that marrying you would solve my *financial* problems, and probably help out with Mack. Does that answer satisfy you?"

"Not entirely, but it's a start."

She brought the bowl of soup to the counter. "It's a bad start, Rand, which you'd know if you had been married before."

"Don't judge what you and I could have on your first marriage, Suz. We have fun together, don't we? Like we had in the snow this morning?"

"That's your problem, Rand. You think marriage is all fun and games. Believe me, it isn't."

He grabbed her hand across the counter and looked into her eyes. "But it could be. With you and me it could be."

As she stared into his gorgeous blue eyes, the strangest sensation struck Suzanne. It was a startling flash of insight; if he said one word about having fallen in love with her, everything would change so fast her head would spin. She, it appeared, had fallen in love with him!

She looked down and tried to swallow the lump that suddenly clogged her throat. How in God's name had this happened? She hadn't been looking to fall in love with any man, for certain not with one who thought of marriage as a game. Rand was going to have to learn the facts of life the hard way, by experiencing the realities of marriage himself.

But not through her. He was going to have to find a woman who thought no more of love than he did. So there was an ache in her chest. She'd get over it. People didn't die of unrequited love. It wasn't a disease, after all; it just felt like one.

"I—I don't want to talk about this any longer," she said, pulling her hand from his.

Rand's eyes narrowed on her as she busied herself by picking up pot holders and laying them down again, nervously, it seemed to him. "You sure can run hot and cold."

"Maybe I'm not as sweet as you thought," she said without looking at him. "Eat your lunch. Your soup is getting cold." Dampening a dishcloth at the faucet, she began wiping down the countertops. Her mind was full of bitter thoughts. She was in love with Rand Harding and she didn't deserve that kind of heartache. Hadn't life already played enough foul tricks on her? How much more could she take?

If her only consideration was herself, she would leave this ranch the minute the roads were plowed. But she had Mack to reckon with, and dare she forget how little money she had? Every day that she worked here would increase the cash she could take with her to Baltimore. It was a crucial factor and not to be overlooked or diminished by emotional distress.

Rand ate and pondered Suzanne's changeable moods. At moments he felt so close to her, as though they were functioning on the same wavelength. It had happened in the snow this morning, and it had happened again just a moment ago. Now she looked as distant as the stars. Was it something he'd said?

Maybe if he got her talking again—any subject would do—she wouldn't look so cold and forbidding.

"What did you think of the house?" he asked.

"The house?" What was he going to do now, chastise her for daring to enter that sacred domicile? If he did, he was going to get an earful, she decided. She was not a child and was not going to meekly accept a dressing down for giving in to simple curiosity.

"The Kincaid house. What did you think of it?" Rand repeated.

Suzanne tossed the dishcloth into the sink and put her hands on her hips in a militant stance. "I did not touch one single thing in that house."

Rand lowered his soupspoon. "All I asked was what you thought of it. I couldn't care less if you had touched every stick of furniture and every piece of china in the place. Why would I?"

"I—I thought…" She took a breath. "Sorry, I thought you were upset because I went inside."

"Well, I'm not. The house is normally locked to keep people from wandering through it, but if I'd known you wanted to see it, I would have taken you over there myself. I'll still do it if you want to take a better look. Wouldn't bother me a bit."

"Rand, that one door was not locked. I swear it."

"I know it wasn't. Do you know how to pick locks?"

"Of course not. Is that what someone did?"

"Yes, that's exactly what someone did."

"This is another segment of your ongoing mystery out here, isn't it? And it *must* be connected to the Kincaid murders. Why else would someone break into their house? Was anything stolen?"

Since he didn't want to tell her about the current rash of trouble on the ranch, he resorted to history. "You're curious about those murders, aren't you?"

"It's only natural, don't you think? Did you know the Kincaids?"

At least she was talking to him again, Rand thought, and he didn't mind relating what he knew about the Kincaids.

"No, never met a one of them, except for baby Jennifer. She's three years old now and the sole owner of this ranch, among other things. Jennifer was adopted by Sterling and Jessica McCallum—he's a detective with the Whitehorn Police Department—and Sterling and an attorney, Wendell Hargrove, are trustees of Jennifer's estate."

"A toddler owns this ranch? How...strange," Suzanne murmured.

"Unusual, at least."

"Was she orphaned because her parents were, uh, murdered?" It was a hard word to say now that she was talking about specific people, Suzanne realized.

"Not exactly. It's really a convoluted story, and I don't know all the details. What I do know is that a woman named Lexine Baxter grew up around here, left the area for a number of years and then returned with a face full of plastic surgery and a fictitious name, Mary Jo Plumber. She lured Dugin Kincaid, who was the son of Jeremiah, into marrying her. There was another son, but I heard he died in Vietnam. Mary Jo was a real mental case and ended up murdering her husband, her father-in-law and three or four other people."

Suzanne gasped. "On this ranch?"

"I think only Jeremiah died on the ranch. I'm not real sure about that, though."

"And how is Jennifer related?"

"She's Jeremiah's illegitimate daughter. Seems the old guy was quite a ladies' man."

"What happened to his wife? I mean, if he had two legitimate sons…"

"She died from cancer. I got the impression from people who've talked to me about it that her sons weren't very old when she died. Dugin wasn't, anyway. I'm not sure about the other one."

"That's terrible and sad, but at least she wasn't murdered," Suzanne said with a shiver. "How did Mary Jo die?"

"I don't think she did. Last I heard, she was in jail." By this time Suzanne was hanging on the counter, no more than a foot away and intent on Rand's every word. He liked her nearness and the fact that he could inhale the subtle scent of her cologne. He wracked his brain trying to remember more about the Kincaids, just to keep Suzanne's interest.

"Murder wasn't the only crime she committed," he said. "She kidnapped several people, baby Jennifer included."

"She kidnapped Jennifer? My God, what was driving her? What was her motive?"

"Money. I also think there had been some kind of dispute between her father and Jeremiah over valuable land—a sapphire mine, or something. I don't know all the details, but the Kincaids were very wealthy. She thought she'd gotten rid of all of them and then found out that Jennifer was Jeremiah's child. In order to secure her own inheritance, she had to get rid of Jennifer, too."

"How on earth was she stopped?"

"It took damned good police work to do it, I can tell you. She might have been demented, but she wasn't stupid, and she stopped at nothing to cover her tracks. You know, that's what gives criminals an edge, their total lack of compassion for anyone or anything but themselves." Rand wondered if he weren't also talking about the person or persons causing so much trouble on the ranch at the present. If he or they were the same sort as Mary Jo Kincaid, heaven help them all.

"It's a horrible story, Rand."

"Yes, it is."

"And that big house just sits there empty and lifeless. Do you think anyone will ever live in it again?"

Rand shrugged. "I really don't know. Sterling said he and his wife want to keep it intact for Jennifer, because it will give her some idea of her birth family."

"Her father, anyhow. Who was her mother?"

"A woman named Marie, uh, Marie something. I can't remember her last name. She's dead, too."

"Not by Mary Jo's hand!"

"Afraid so. That was sort of an accident, though, because Mary Jo was really after a private detective who was getting a little too close on her trail for comfort. She blew up his car and killed Marie instead."

Suzanne shook her head in horrified astonishment. "Mary Jo was a monster! Are you positive she's safely incarcerated? The thought of running into her gives me the creeps."

Rand smiled, reached out and tucked a strand of her dark hair behind her ear. "I swear to protect you from any and all monsters that might threaten your well-being."

His touch sent a delicious tingle throughout Suzanne's system. She had become so engrossed in the lurid twists and turns of Mary Jo's story that she'd completely dropped her guard. Rand was not above taking advantage of her proximity, but she'd already known that and should have stayed on the other side of the room. At the very least she shouldn't be leaning on the counter with her face practically in his!

The look in his eyes said that he would touch her for as

long as she would let him, and her own body was telling her to stay right where she was and savor the sensation.

Was she destined to forever love men who didn't love her? she thought with a heavy heart. Oh, Les had said all the pretty words, but when push came to shove, and responsibility had caught up to her in the form of her kid brother, Les had shown his true colors by turning into the weasel he must have always been.

What would Rand turn into if she gave in to his physically exciting pressure and married him? How would he treat both Mack and herself after six months, a year? Mack could try the patience of a saint, and even while admitting love for Rand Harding, if only to herself, she didn't think he was sainthood material.

She pushed away from the counter—and Rand's hand— and saw the light go out of his eyes.

"Did I offend you?" he asked quietly.

"No, I just…" She heard a far-off motor noise, and jumped to use it for an excuse. "I just heard something. Listen, don't you hear it?"

Rand cocked his head, then grinned. "It's a snowplow, and it's passing our driveway right about now!" Getting up, he ran for his jacket and out the door.

Suzanne stepped outside, but stayed on the stoop. The sound was louder outdoors, and she kept waiting for the elation she had expected to feel when the roads were finally plowed.

It never came. Rand had disappeared around the building, and she stood there in the fresh, clean air, with the sun beaming down and warming her arms, and thought about it being over with. She could stay on, of course—Rand had made that very clear—and she probably would, just to accumulate a little more money, but it wouldn't be the same.

It would never be the same again. Sighing, she went in and closed the door.

Twelve

Suzanne lay in bed that night and listened to nothing. There wasn't a sound inside or out. After sleeping with a howling wind since she got to the ranch, the complete silence was keeping her awake. Even the icicles along the eaves, which had dripped all day, were silent, as they had frozen again when the sun went down.

She turned one way and then another under her blankets, seeking sleep. She had to get up very early in the morning and needed some rest. After a while she flopped onto her back and admitted defeat. Eventually she would fall asleep, and maybe she was trying too hard to relax and causing the opposite to happen instead.

Sighing, she let her thoughts go where they may. Mack, Rand, her financial dilemma and what she'd learned of the Kincaid family today went around and around in her mind.

The ranch was plowed out now—even the long driveway to the road. Rand had put a couple of men to work shoveling out the vehicles on the ranch, so everyone was mobile again. Mack had gone to bed unhappy, because Rand had told him the school bus went by the ranch at 6:20 in the morning and he was to be out at the road in time to wave it down. "Unless you'd like me or your sister to drive you to town and enroll you in school," Rand had said firmly. "It's your choice."

Mack had chosen to go by himself. Suzanne knew his pride would not permit him to be enrolled as though he were a child. Her heart had gone out to Mack, as it always did when he was truly downcast. However surly he could get at times, however sassy-mouthed or downright rude, she loved him and never failed to feel any emotional pain *he* felt.

But the bottom line was that Mack listened to Rand, a small miracle if she'd ever witnessed one. She knew her brother would not have agreed to going to school at all if it had been her telling him to catch that early bus. Not only did Mack want to stay and work on the ranch bad enough to do something he abhorred, he respected Rand.

Well, so did she, Suzanne thought. She not only respected him, she was in love with him. "Damn," she mumbled with an agonized groan. She never should have made love with Rand. What had come over her to do such a thing? And why had it seemed logical at the time and totally illogical now? She had never acted so heedlessly before, and she knew in her soul that she was going to pay for that rash, impulsive behavior for a long, long time.

Rand, too, was finding sleep elusive. As tired as his body was from a long day of hard work, his mind would not shut down. For one thing, he couldn't stop thinking of Suzanne in bed just next door to his own room. Maybe what bothered him most were the powerful feelings he was developing for her. He shied from the word *love* because of all the heartache he'd suffered over Sherry. He didn't think he could live through something like that again, and he was not going to put himself in that position with a woman ever again.

Of course, Suzanne and Sherry were miles apart in personality. Suzanne automatically put others before herself, proof of which was in her concerns for her brother. With Sherry it had been me, me, me, and to hell with everyone else. Rand knew that now, and deep down he was glad that Sherry had dumped him. But the pain of those agonizing weeks was easily recallable, and he knew it would influence him for the rest of his life.

Still, he was lonely, and he knew that only a wife, a helpmate, a partner in all things, was what he wanted. Not a girlfriend for a night or even a month—they were easy enough to find—but a woman to stand by his side through thick and thin, someone to talk to without reservation, and to plan the future with. Someone to laugh with, to make love with, to be happy with.

Suzanne fit the bill perfectly. She was brighter than most, as pretty as any man could hope for, considerate, even-tempered and sexy as sin in bed. And she was fun. He could kid around and laugh with her. Why couldn't she admit that she felt the same about him? He knew she liked him, he *sensed* her liking, and she'd proved her physical attraction to him in her very own bed. What was stopping her from taking that final step and agreeing to marry him?

Lying there in the darkness of his room, he wondered if she was sleeping. Who knew if there would be an opportunity for them to talk tomorrow? They had talked today, mostly about the Kincaids, but once the plows came, the whole place had exploded into a beehive of activity and there'd been no further chance of private conversation.

That was all he wanted, he told himself, a few minutes alone with her, one more chance to plead his case. Although he wouldn't like hearing it, even a sound explanation as to why she thought marriage was wrong for them would be better than he had now.

His heart beat faster at the thought of going to her room. Of sitting on the edge of her bed and the two of them talking in the dark. She might object, she might refuse to talk, she might get angry, but what if she did none of those things? What if she was still awake, as he was, and thinking thoughts similar to his own? Worrying about doing the right thing, worrying about her and Mack's future?

I want to be a part of her and Mack's future, dammit! And there has to be a way to make her understand what it would mean to all three of us.

Throwing back the covers, Rand got up and pulled on his jeans. Barefoot and shirtless, he quietly opened his door, just as quietly closed it behind him and tiptoed the short distance to Suzanne's. Cocking his head to listen, he rapped lightly.

Suzanne heard the soft brushing of knuckles on her door and instantly knew who was out there. Her heart leapt into her throat. She hugged the covers tighter to her chest. If she let Rand in, no telling what would happen. If she didn't, he would probably come in anyway, and no telling what would happen. He was nothing if not persistent, and maybe it was exciting to be pursued so diligently. Certainly no other man had ever wanted her as much as Rand seemed to.

And yet, any further intimacy between them would only intensify the feelings she already had for him. She should not open herself to more heartache by being nice to him when they should both be sleeping.

She slipped out of bed and found the doorknob in the dark, which she turned and then pulled the door open. Her voice was not particularly friendly. "What do you want, Rand?"

Because of the night-light in the hall, he could see her quite clearly. She was wearing baggy pajamas, her hair was disarrayed and she looked as young as her kid brother.

"Can we talk?" Rand asked.

"At this hour? No, I don't think so. Good night." She tried to close the door, but he pushed on it harder than she did and it opened wider.

"Suz, please. Talk is all I want, I swear it."

"That's well and good, but it's late."

"It's not that late. You couldn't have been asleep or you wouldn't have heard my knock. Let me come in, please?"

"What do you want to talk about?" The fact that he was pretty much dressed, other than his feet, was a point in his favor, although she still didn't want him in her room, since she didn't trust either of them not to misbehave.

"Don't ask me that while I'm standing in the hall."

He sounded so plaintively desperate, very much like Mack did when the boy was pining for some unattainable thing, and Suzanne's innate kindness kicked in. She sighed hopelessly, fearing that she was on the verge of digging herself a deeper hole.

Still, she must at least attempt to maintain the upper hand. "If I let you come in, will you keep your distance? Can you promise that?"

"I can and I do."

"Come in, then. Pull the chair over to the bed, if you want. I'm getting under the covers again. I'm cold."

Darting to the bed, she jumped back under the blankets. Rand shut the door, which also shut out the hall light.

"I can't see anything," he said. "Is it okay if I turn on the light?"

"I don't want the light on. Just wait a minute. Your eyes will adjust." Now why wouldn't she let him turn on the light? Suzanne frowned about it. Wasn't it safer talking in bright light than in the dark?

But maybe they would be both more honest if they couldn't see each other's faces, and it could be honesty that she needed from Rand. Not that she thought him a liar. For a fact, he seemed to be one of the most straightforward, aboveboard people she'd ever met. But she still didn't know why he had felt the need to advertise for a wife, did she? Not his deep down private reason, she didn't. Yes, she knew it had something to do with a relationship gone sour, but why would one bad experience turn a man off love for the rest of his days? Her own experience was worse than his—at least he hadn't been married and then tossed aside like an old shoe—and she'd fallen in love again. Against her better judgment, of course, but it had still happened.

She heard him fumbling around in the dark for the chair, and then a bump and a "Dammit!"

"What's wrong?" She sat up.

"I ran into the dresser."

"Oh, turn on the damned light," she said with some disgust, and lay down again.

"No, we're going to do this your way," he said, bending over to rub his barked shin. "Did you move the chair? I thought it was next to the bathroom door."

"Never touched it. Where are you?"

He was feeling around again, and felt the foot of the bed against his legs. "Guess I'm by the bed."

"Well, the chair's not over here. Go in the other direction."

Rand was getting tired of this silly game. She didn't want the light on? Fine, but he wasn't going to play blindman's buff any longer. He followed the configuration of the bed with his hands until he stubbed his toe on the nightstand.

"Ouch! This whole room is a damned booby trap."

"You're right next to me! Rand, go and get that chair."

"I'm going to sit on the edge of the bed. If you don't want me touching you, move over."

Annoyed, Suzanne left her nice warm spot and slid over to the middle of the bed. It jiggled from Rand's weight when he sat down, but finally they were both settled.

After several moments of silence she said, "You're not talking."

"I'm figuring out the best way to start."

"Let me start. I heard you saying something to the men about George during dinner. Did you talk to him today?"

"I called him, yes."

"Is he all right?"

"Sounded like it. He's taking therapy treatments for his back."

"Did you tell him I was doing some of his work?"

"Sure did."

"And how did he take it? I mean, did it upset him?"

"Heck, no. Why would it? He'd been worrying about the payroll and was glad to hear you'd taken care of it. He said to call him if you had any questions about the books."

Suzanne sighed softly. "I knew he was a nice man. You told him I'm only helping out temporarily, of course."

"I…don't remember. Probably did."

"I hope you did. I wouldn't want him worrying about my taking his job."

"I'm sure it never entered his mind. His doctor wants him to stay in town after he's released from the hospital, so he can continue treatment. I told him to stay for as long as it takes. You know, I wouldn't have been able to be that generous if you weren't here, and I'm sure George knows it."

"Well, you certainly couldn't have told him to come back to work with a bad back and a broken leg!"

"You're right, but your being here and seeing to the record-keeping made it easy to be generous."

"Did you talk to Handy, too?"

"I don't know how to reach Handy. He left here in such a rush, he never gave me a phone number or the address of where he'd be staying in Seattle."

"Maybe he didn't know."

"It's possible, but I think what's more likely is that he

didn't think about it. Handy's sort of excitable, and he drove out of here like a bat out of hell." Rand's bare feet were getting icy. "Would you mind if I put my feet under the covers? I'm not wearing any socks or shoes."

"You're cold?"

"It's not exactly warm in here. Guess I could go turn up the furnace."

Suzanne took a quiet breath. Again he'd spoken with that little-boy quality in his voice, and she was definitely susceptible to it.

"But then everyone sleeping upstairs would get too warm," she said. "Put your feet under the blankets." Put all of you under the blankets! She'd been participating in casual, completely impersonal conversation, but there was nothing casual or impersonal about the feelings he was arousing within her, just because he was sitting on her bed.

She suddenly felt like bawling. Her own body was betraying her, and it wasn't fair!

The bed quivered and shook as he maneuvered his feet off the floor and under the blankets. "There, that's a lot better," he said. "Thanks."

"Do…do you think the men upstairs can hear when this bed moves?" she asked.

"Can you hear their beds? I'm sure they turn over at night. It's bound to make some noise. Ever hear it?"

"No," she said in an uneven little whisper. "It's just that I wouldn't want them thinking…"

"Thinking what, Suzanne?"

"You know."

"That you and I are making love?"

"Must you say it?"

"Must you pretend we don't want each other right now?" Rand returned, speaking low.

"You didn't come in here to talk at all, did you?"

Rand changed positions so fast, Suzanne didn't know where he was until she felt him leaning over her. "Listen to me. I *did* come in here to talk, but you affect me so much my mind seems to go blank when I'm alone with you. And you know something else, I think I do the same thing to you. Am I wrong?"

She gulped and whispered, "No."

"Thank you for that. I do admire honesty."

"So do I, Rand."

"We're a lot alike, Suz." Slowly he lowered himself on top of her. The blankets were between them, but the feel of her under him, warm and alive, and the scent of her, had him moving his mouth over her face. "I want you in my life, Suz."

"I know you want me, but—"

"In my life," he repeated, emphasizing each syllable. He was too cautious to add *as my wife,* though he was thinking it. But he felt that he was making some real progress and he didn't want her doing another turnabout and kicking him out of her room, which he knew could happen if he started talking about marriage again. "Oh, Suz," he groaned, "do you have any idea what you do to me?"

"Some" was all she got out before his lips covered hers. A sob welled in her throat. Had she let him in for this? Had he known this would happen when she'd agreed to "talk"? Achingly sweet desire held her prisoner. She felt both hot and cold—how could that be? He entered her mouth, and she heard a moan of pleasure deep in his throat and felt his body tense.

His tongue tasted of toothpaste, and it moved over her teeth and mated with hers. The heat of his arousal seared her through the blankets. His breathing was erratic and loud.

But so was her own. She could hold back or pretend no longer.

"Get undressed," she whispered hoarsely. Her hands slid down his back and impatiently plucked at his undershirt.

Rand shifted away from her and yanked the undershirt

over his head. It took about three seconds to shed his jeans and briefs, and when he crawled under the covers he discovered that she had torn off her pajamas in the same brief span of time.

He wrapped himself around her and absorbed the heat of her skin. Nothing had ever felt so delicious to him. She was satin and silk, everything beautiful in the world, and he touched her with awe, with wonder, with…could it be love?

He quickly buried the word deep in his psyche. He didn't even want to think it, and he would never say it aloud, not to anyone. It meant nothing. The only things that had meaning between a man and woman were an overwhelming need for each other at night and a genuine liking for each other during the day. They had both. They were a perfect match. He *would* convince Suzanne of that, he was certain of it.

But not now. Right now all he wanted to do was hold her, kiss her creamy throat, her full sultry lips and her small perfect breasts. All he could concentrate on was caressing her incredible body, making love to her until she was moaning and completely his, and then taking her all the way to the finish line.

This is sheer madness, Suzanne thought, but knowing she was playing with fire only seemed to triple her excitement. Rand's body was hard, lean, muscular, sinewy and totally male. She couldn't touch it enough, explore it enough. His kisses were magical, chasing common sense and sensibility clear out of the room. Beneath the covers, the temperature was getting steamy. She was lost, she finally admitted weakly, totally and completely lost, and it was the most incredible sensation she had ever felt.

Hungrily she sought his mouth again. It was so dark she couldn't make out his features, but she knew his face as well as her own. Within the devouring kiss her fingertips traced the contours of strong chin and high cheekbones, and finally twined into his hair.

Rand's hand skimmed down her body. She knew where it was going and parted her legs in throbbing anticipation. His touch was gentle but knowledgeable and it was only seconds before she couldn't lie still. Tearing her mouth from his to suck in a badly needed breath of air, she gasped his name.

"Rand, oh, Rand."

It was the plea he'd been waiting to hear; he needn't hold himself in check any longer. Rising up, he fit his hips between her thighs. When he slid into her, her long, moaning sigh confirmed her readiness.

"Suz," he whispered raggedly as he began moving within her. Her hips rose and fell with his. His mind clouded over as pleasure saturated his system. Gentle thrusts gradually evolved to a hard, driving rhythm, and each time he plunged into her, she cried out, softly at first, then louder and louder.

He felt her fingernails dig into his back. Her head moved back and forth on the pillow. He recognized the signs, she was getting very close to the end. His chest swelled with self-satisfaction. He had never taken his own pleasure without first seeing to his lady's. Any man that did robbed himself of the greatest pleasure of all and was a damned fool.

He would never be a fool with Suzanne, not in bed, not out of it. She was one very special woman, and he would always treat her with the highest regard.

He kissed her with all the emotion he was feeling, and Suzanne, as far gone as she was, recognized the difference between this kiss and the others they had exchanged. She had no time to think about it, however, for she was nearly to the peak of the mountain and about to go over.

So was Rand. Writhing and rocking together, they reached the pinnacle at almost the same moment. It was so strong and beautiful for Suzanne that tears filled her eyes and dripped down her temples. Rand roared her name, and she chokingly whispered his. He collapsed upon her and breathed heavily in her ear, and she closed her eyes and strove to catch her own breath.

Minutes ticked by and neither moved. Suzanne's thoughts began to coalesce. She should regret another misstep and didn't. Someone should commit her for what could only be another bout of temporary insanity.

She sighed and was surprised to hear a chuckle from Rand. "I bet we woke up everyone upstairs," he said.

Her heart nearly stopped. "Oh, my God, do you really think so?" Mack was up there. What if he had heard them? He would never forgive her, or respect her again, and she already had enough trouble with his lack of regard for anything she said to him.

Rand raised his head and brushed his mouth against her cheek. "Honey, I was only teasing. No one heard us."

"Did...did the bed make noise?" She had worried about the bed creaking before they'd made love and then had completely forgotten it. That made a lot of sense, she thought disgustedly.

"Some, but you made more." Rand moved in the bed and curled himself around her.

"Me! What did I do?"

"You don't remember?"

Embarrassment struck without mercy as memories of her torrid cries suddenly flooded her brain. "Oh, no," she groaned.

"Don't you dare be sorry," Rand said with a gentle shake of her body. "You're a passionate woman and people with passion have to express it."

Her mouth turned down wryly. "Well, I must admit, I've never been accused of being passionate before."

"You're kidding."

"Believe me, I'm not."

"Then I must bring out your best side."

"You bring out something, I can't deny that. But whether or not it's my best side is a debatable point."

"All right, let's debate it."

"I didn't mean that you and I should—"

"I'll play prosecuting attorney. Ms. Paxton, is it your misguided belief that a man prefers a woman to lie beneath him and make no sound?"

"Rand, you're embarrassing me."

He laughed and hugged her. He would like to lie with her every night, to be able to laugh with her and to hug her close every night for the rest of his life.

But she already knew that, and things were so good between them right now he was afraid to mention marriage on the chance it would ruin Suzanne's mood. There's time, he told himself. There's plenty of time. Don't rush her again.

A gust of wind hitting the building startled Suzanne. "I hope that doesn't mean another storm," she said anxiously.

"It's a chinook," he told her. "Been expecting it. I had the radio on earlier, and the weather forecaster said it was coming."

"What in the world is a chinook?" Suzanne asked, mystified over a term she'd never heard before.

"It's a warm wind off the coast. We get them every so often in the winter and spring. Melts the snow so fast sometimes that the area has some flooding to contend with. We're lucky out here, though. Our only flooding since I've been here has been a little overrun from the creeks. No damage done."

He was getting sleepy, and he snuggled closer to Suzanne and closed his eyes. She knew she should tell him to go back to his own room, but he felt so good wrapped around her that she couldn't bring herself to break the spell.

Yawning, she settled deeper into his arms. "Good night," she murmured drowsily.

"Night, sweetheart."

She thought of only one thing before sleep took her. While

they'd been making love, she had almost said, "I love you," several times.

How would Rand have reacted to hearing that?

Thirteen

It was 2:00 a.m. A man in dark clothes cautiously tiptoed down the stairs in his stocking feet, carrying his boots close to his chest. He didn't know why Rand had pulled the men off guard duty tonight, but he wasn't going to pass up this opportunity.

Noiselessly he made his way to the laundry room. There was so much in his favor right now it was hard to keep from laughing out loud. George gone, Handy gone, no one sleeping on this end of the first floor, a wind that would blow away any sound he might make. It was fate, that's what it was, he thought while pulling on his boots. About time, too. Things had been quiet on the ranch too long. Harding was apt to get complacent. The man grinned and let himself out through the laundry room door.

The warm wind hit him full in the face. He breathed it in and grinned again. Even the weather was on his side.

Peering around he searched the dark shadows of the compound, even though he knew no one else was up. But he took pride in his vigilance; it was the reason no one had discovered who had been keeping the ranch in an uproar. He couldn't prevent a quiet but gleeful chuckle. Tonight—this morning, actually—the ranch would experience a *real* uproar!

He knew how to move quietly, and how to keep himself in the shadows. It was strictly instinctual, as he'd never had any formal training in the fine art of sneaking around in the dark. He always felt an adrenaline rush before one of his capers, but he managed to function around it, to keep his excitement under control, until it was over. Then he would sit back—if only symbolically—let the excitement roll and wait for someone to discover what was sometimes a grisly mess. He didn't like butchering cattle in the dark, but running across a mutilated animal scared the hell out of the other men and had proved to be one of his most effective tactics. It was so funny to hear grown men speculate about ghosts and little green people from outer space that he could hardly stop himself from laughing in their faces.

Tonight, though, would be the ultimate thrill. He was going to blow up the equipment shed. His plan was firmly fixed in his mind, down to the smallest detail. Pandemonium would break loose after the explosion. He would be as shocked as everyone else. Losing thousands of dollars of heavy equipment and a good metal building would be a financial setback for the ranch, but no one would be physically injured. He drew the line at that, and the man who was paying him to wreak havoc with this ranch knew it.

Away from the bunkhouse he walked faster. The warm wind was smoothing out tracks and ruts in the snow, and melting it down to slush in spots. If the chinook blew for days there wouldn't be any snow at all. He was glad. When the snow had been unblemished he hadn't dared to go to the big house because of footprints. Tonight it didn't matter. He'd noticed today how someone had ridden a horse all around the house, and there was no way anyone would be able to separate his boot prints from so many other tracks.

He made a wide circle and approached the house from its hind side. That put it between him and the bunkhouse, and he had all the freedom he wanted to move freely. Quickly, eagerly, he walked up to the side door. At once he saw the large white rectangle plastered against the varnished door. He could tell it had something written on it, but it was too dark to read what it was.

Cursing under his breath, he pulled the small flashlight he had known he would need once he was inside the house, and at the equipment shed later, from his jacket pocket. Glancing around nervously—he hadn't planned to turn on the light outdoors—he put it close to the sign and switched it on. It took a minute because he wasn't a fast reader, but he finally got to Rand's signature.

Rage began in his midsection and radiated outwardly from there. He turned off the flashlight and tried the knob. The door was locked! Harding had found the dynamite and written him this insulting, degrading message. It was a kick in the teeth he hadn't anticipated, and he stood there and cursed for a good five minutes. He'd been hearing and smelling that explosion for days, and now there wasn't going to be one!

He had to do something to get back at Rand, the low-life bastard. Prancing around, running the show, ordering everyone to work their butts off. He hated Rand Harding. He would have made a hell of a lot better foreman than Rand was.

Grinding his teeth in the most abiding fury of his life, he struck out across the field toward the sheds. He'd do something to scare the bejabbers out of everyone on the place, he had to for his own peace of mind. In fact, maybe he'd do *more* than one thing.

Yeah, that was the ticket. His snort of laughter sounded mean and vengeful.

It was precisely how he felt.

* * *

Rand was sound asleep one second and wide-awake the next. If a noise had awakened him, he couldn't remember it. But there was an uneasiness in his system that wouldn't let him relax and go back to sleep. Maybe a dream had disturbed his slumber, he mused. But he couldn't remember that, either.

He lay in Suzanne's bed, aware of her warmth next to him, alert and listening. Other than the wind outside, Suzanne's quiet breathing and his own heartbeat, there was nothing to hear.

He was getting too jumpy, he decided, feeling some of the tension leave his body. Small wonder, though, he thought next with a wry twist of his lips. Anyone with half a brain would get jumpy over the things that had happened on this ranch.

Thing was, he felt responsible. No matter how many times Sterling assured him that the incidents weren't his fault, he couldn't shuck his innate sense of responsibility. It was too much a part of who he was, the kind of man he was. He hated calling Sterling and Wendell with reports of dead animals and fires. At least the call to Sterling about having found and disposed of that case of dynamite had been gratifying; so few were these days.

He realized that he was second-guessing every decision he made when he started worrying about having pulled the night guards. His confidence was taking a beating; he wasn't positive of anything anymore, and he didn't like the feeling.

Turning his head on the pillow, he studied Suzanne's form in the dark. Maybe his waning confidence in his ability to do his job was carrying over into his private life, he thought with a frown of uncertainty. Maybe Suzanne sensed that in him. Maybe it was the reason she couldn't or wouldn't commit herself to him. What woman would want a man who had very little faith in himself?

It was a disturbing thought and Rand tried to shake it by

bringing to mind what he *did* have faith in. There was very little about cattle ranching he didn't know. He took his job seriously and worked hard. He was a damned good foreman, and if it weren't for some loony causing trouble on the ranch, it would be running as smoothly as any cattle operation in the country.

He grinned humorlessly. Telling himself how great he really was an abysmal waste of time. If he was smart enough to figure out who was behind the sabotage, and why he was doing it, then he'd have cause to pat himself on the back.

Suzanne stirred, snuggled against him and flung an arm across his waist. His response was instantaneous, and he drew her into his arms.

"Are you awake?" she murmured drowsily.

"No, are you?" he teased.

"No. I'm asleep and dreaming a man is in my bed."

He skimmed a hand down her belly to nestle between her legs. "Are you dreaming he's touching you like this?"

"I think so."

He kissed the soft underside of her jaw. "Is he kissing you like this?"

"I'm afraid I'm more focused on what he's doing below my belt," she said breathlessly.

Rand chuckled softly. "Like that, do you?"

Her voice was no more than a husky, sensual whisper. "I hope he does it for a very long time."

"He will, I guarantee it."

She snuggled even closer. "Good. I like this dream."

At 4:30 a.m. Rand slipped out of Suzanne's bed, felt around in the dark for his clothes and tiptoed from her room to his carrying them.

Suzanne heard the quiet closing of her door, opened her eyes and checked the clock. The ranch came awake at five, it was time for her to get up and start breakfast. Groaning, she pulled the pillow over her head. She hadn't gotten enough sleep; she was still tired.

But then a smile toyed with her lips. Tired or not, she would not trade last night for anything, especially not for an undisturbed eight hours of sleep. Tossing the pillow aside, she reached for the bedside lamp, turned it on and got out of bed. She'd been taking her shower after breakfast, but this morning she needed one before she even entered the kitchen.

Switching on the faucets in the shower stall, she caught sight of herself in the bathroom mirror. There was a glow about her that she'd never seen before. It was in her eyes, which appeared larger and more luminous than normal, and in the almost mysterious curvature of her lips. She had been well and thoroughly loved last night, and it showed.

"Goodness," she murmured. She must watch herself today or every person on the place would figure out what had occurred last night.

Her expression changed suddenly, becoming sad and wistful. As exciting as last night had been, it hadn't been wise, not wise at all. Giving everything she was to a man who didn't love her, and never would, was a witless act. She never should have come to Montana. Mack might never realize the extent of the damage he had caused, but it would haunt her into eternity.

Sighing soulfully, she stepped into the shower stall.

Deep down Suzanne wasn't completely sold on Mack starting school in Whitehorn. When George and Handy got back, she would be out of a job again, hopefully with a nice paycheck in her purse, but unemployed all the same. She couldn't imagine Mack liking school here any better than he had in Baltimore, but anything was possible, and if he happened to like school even a tenth as much as he did the ranch, she would never get him to go home with her. Not without taking legal measures, which would probably cost more than what she was making, and they would both be back at square one.

She should hate Rand for that damned ad, which was more or less how she had felt when she got here. But now she couldn't even work up a good solid dislike for him, not when her insides melted and oozed together at the mere sight of him. When he came into the kitchen after breakfast, they just stood there and looked silly, smiling at each other.

"How are you this morning?" he asked, as though he hadn't made love to her throughout the night. The men were bringing in their dishes, and he was doing his best to sound normal.

"Very well, thank you," Suzanne replied. Mack walked in, and her eyes widened. He was shiny clean and his hair was neatly brushed. "Good morning, Mack."

"Morning," he said sullenly.

"See you later," Rand said, and left them alone.

Suzanne's attention was fully on her brother. "You look very nice," she told him with a cheerful smile.

Mack flopped down on a counter stool without appearing to notice his sister's smile or her compliment. "Rand said to hang around the bunkhouse till it's time to catch the bus. I don't *want* to hang around the bunkhouse. I don't *want* to catch the stupid bus. Only dorks ride school buses."

"I told you I would drive you to school for your first day."

"Oh, yeah, as though one day would help. Why do I have to go to school, anyway?" he whined.

"Because fourteen-year-old kids *belong* in school!" She was losing her ambiguity about Mack starting school in Whitehorn, and even found herself hoping that the teachers in the high school, and the principal, were strict disciplinarians. The school Mack attended in Baltimore was huge, with overcrowded classrooms and overworked teachers. They tried. Given the sheer numbers they were dealing with, they tried very hard, but it simply wasn't possible to single out students for special attention. Suzanne had often wished for the money to send Mack to a private institution. Maybe a small town school would work as well.

"If I was gonna be a teacher or something like that, I'd need some more school, but I'm gonna work on a ranch." After a pause he added, "I'm gonna work on this ranch."

"Rand wants you to go to school," Suzanne said.

"He doesn't know everything."

"Oh, really? Does he know how you feel about his intelligence? Why don't you go find him right now and tell him? I'm sure he would enjoy hearing what you think of him."

"I didn't say anything wrong. Why do you always make such a big deal out of everything?"

"Oh, Mack," Suzanne said on a weary-sounding sigh. "Don't you realize I'm on your team? You and I are all each of us has. There are no other Paxtons. Doesn't that mean anything to you?" She saw the smear of red in his cheeks, the embarrassed realization that he was behaving like a jerk. It was these moments when she loved him most, when she felt protective of him.

"I would never knowingly do anything to hurt you," she said quietly. "I want to be your friend, as well as your sister. Talk to me, Mack. If you can't talk to me as a sister, do it as a friend."

His cheeks were still flaming, and he couldn't quite meet her eyes. "I wanna be a cowboy. It's what I've always wanted."

"Did Mom and Dad know?" she asked gently.

"No."

"But you talked to them, didn't you?"

"Not about that." Mack got off the stool. "I gotta go."

Suzanne glanced at her watch. "You're right. Have fun today, Mack. Talk to your classmates. Make some friends."

"Yeah, right," he drawled sarcastically.

Suzanne watched out the dining room window as he trudged down the muddy driveway toward the road. Her heart ached for him. He had so much to learn about life, and he fought so hard against learning anything.

Except for what he had here, or thought he had.

When he was out of sight, she sighed heavily, returned to the kitchen and dove into the mess. But her thoughts remained with Mack while she worked, and she no longer had to speculate on his reaction to being legally forced to go back to Baltimore, should she decide to take that route.

She knew, without the slightest doubt, that he wouldn't stay.

J.D. had called Rand over to the main storage shed. "Take a look at this," J.D. said, leading Rand inside. Freeway went in, too.

Rand gaped at the pile of twisted, broken, melted metal that had once been six brand-new rolls of barbed wire.

"Looks like someone used a welding torch on it," J.D. said.

Rand glanced around; the portable welder was nowhere in sight. "And I'll bet the portable is clean and back in the toolshed where we keep it." He slammed a fist into his other palm. "Damn, will he never stop!"

J.D. was studying the heap of ruined wire. "What point do you suppose he was trying to make with this trick?"

"It's just another scare tactic. He's probably hoping the men will think a lightning bolt appeared out of a clear sky, maybe thrown by a flying saucer, and honed in on this barbed wire. The sad thing is that some of them might." Rand shook his head disgustedly. "I'm glad you're the one who found this. I'd appreciate your not mentioning it to the other men."

"They're in and out of this shed all the time, Rand. Tell you what. I'll stay behind today and get this mess loaded on a truck and hauled to the dump."

"Can you handle it alone? It's not six rolls anymore, it's one big lump of heavy metal."

"I'll get it out of here if I have to cut it up in little pieces."

Rand was thinking. "Did you happen to hear anything in the night? Someone moving around?"

"You know, Freeway woke me up around two." Freeway's head came up at his name. "I petted him for a minute and told him to go back to sleep, which I did myself. Maybe he was trying to tell me something."

"Bet he was."

"Doesn't Daisy ever bark when someone's wandering around at night?"

"The only times I've heard Daisy bark is when Freeway tries to go into the barn. No, she's not a watchdog."

J.D. snorted out a laugh. "Two dogs on the place and each of them would hold a flashlight for a burglar. Fine pair of mutts they are."

"Lovable but useless," Rand agreed. "Well, I'd better get going. I'm taking the crew to check the water level in the creeks and ponds. The snow is melting so fast in this warm wind, we could have some flooding."

"Doesn't look to me like this ranch has had any problems with flooding in the past," J.D. said casually.

"It hasn't that I know of, but I'd rather play it safe than sorry. See you later." He stopped at the door of the shed. "J.D., I'm going to have Suzanne make some sandwiches and pack a lunch to take with us. That way, we'll be gone most of the day. Should give you all the time you need to haul that wire away."

J.D. nodded. "Good plan."

Gritting his teeth during the walk to the bunkhouse, Rand paused to alter his expression before going in. He still didn't want Suzanne knowing about the maniac running wild on the ranch. All it would do was scare her, and he didn't want her scared. She had enough on her mind without worrying about that, too.

He walked into the kitchen just as she was sliding a huge sheet cake into one of the ovens. "Chocolate, I hope?" he said.

She shut the oven door, set the timer and smiled. "Is there any other kind?"

"Your favorite, too?"

"I'm a nut for chocolate cake."

He looked at her pretty face. There was a joy within him just from seeing her, from being with her. "I'm a nut for you, Suz."

She laughed. "Maybe you're just a nut, period." It was said fondly but lightly, as she didn't want this evolving into a conversation about marriage. There were moments when she felt she could marry Rand—for Mack's sake, for instance—but most of the time she couldn't see herself settling for second best. In all honesty she wasn't sure she wanted to ever get married again, even under the best of circumstances, which certainly wasn't the case with her and Rand.

Rand loved kidding around with Suzanne, and he would like to forget work today and spend it with her. But the men were saddling their horses and waiting for his direction. Actually, he needed to get a move on, before one or more of them came looking for him and wandered into the storage shed.

"I'd like to take lunch with us today," he told Suzanne. "Will you help me make some sandwiches?"

"Of course." Suzanne immediately went to the immense bread box. "Any particular kinds of sandwiches?" she asked.

"Anything will do."

Suzanne pulled out leftover roast beef, chicken, a brick of cheese, some lettuce and an array of condiments from the refrigerator. Rand helped, and in about ten minutes they had made close to three dozen sandwiches.

"What will you all drink?" Suzanne inquired. "How about a couple of thermos jugs of lemonade? There's a huge can of mix in the pantry, and it would take only a minute to make."

"Sounds good. I'll bag these sandwiches while you do that."

"You're pretty good in a kitchen," Suzanne told him while stirring the lemonade with an eye on how deftly he was bagging the sandwiches.

Rand grinned. "Comes from being a bachelor all my life, I guess."

Suzanne smiled weakly. He would grasp the seriousness of marriage so much better if he had experienced it, she felt, and his quip about bachelorhood reminded her of that simple but crucial fact.

"Guess so," she murmured.

Rand gathered everything up. "We'll be back in time for supper. Don't work too hard." He started out, then stopped. "There should be a mail delivery today. Normally it arrives before noon. If you feel like it, drive down to the mailbox and pick it up. The driveway is muddy, so take my rig. The keys are in it."

Suzanne nodded. "Okay."

After Rand left she started worrying about the daily charge on her rental car. It wasn't a large sum, but every dollar counted. Thinking about how tired she was of scrimping and watching every penny, she felt her good mood being overcome by a surge of despondency. Fearing it was going to get worse because of being alone all day, she hurriedly put away the perishables still on the counter and then ran to her bedroom for those old boots and her coat. A breath of fresh air just might jolt her out of the doldrums.

Then, remembering the cake in the oven, she took off her coat and dawdled in the kitchen, impatiently, until the timer buzzed.

* * *

Rand passed the canvas bags of food to some of the men. "We're taking lunch with us today," he announced, automatically making a head count of the crew. "Where's Dale?"

Someone spoke up. "He went looking for J.D."

Rand groaned inwardly. If Dale had gone looking for J.D., he'd probably found him. "I'll be right back," he said, and started away. Sure enough, when he entered the storage shed, there was Dale with J.D.

"Holy smokes, Rand," Dale exclaimed. "What d'ya think happened to that wire?"

"Someone torched it," Rand said sharply. "Dale, I told the crew to saddle the horses and wait for me. Why aren't you with them?"

"My horse is ready. I was just wondering where J.D. was."

Rand swallowed his temper. The way Dale had been shadowing J.D., he should have foreseen this happening.

But Dale had stayed throughout the many incidents on the ranch, he reminded himself. And he had never, to Rand's knowledge, laid the blame on little green men. He might not be overly bright about some things, but he was smart enough to recognize the work of a demented human.

"All right," Rand said. "Since you're here, you might as well stay and help J.D. haul that wire to the dump. And, Dale, I don't want the other men hearing one word about it, understand? Not one word. If it gets around I'll know where it came from."

"They won't hear it from me, Rand, I swear it."

Behind Dale's back, J.D. shook his head and looked disgusted. Rand caught the grimace on J.D.'s face and understood what was going through his mind. He didn't like Dale Carson, he avoided him whenever he could, and now he had to work with him all day.

"J.D.," Rand said. "This okay with you?" Losing J.D. over

something like this would be the height of stupidity. He'd rather lose Dale than J.D. Hell, he'd rather lose any two men in his crew. J.D. had an instinct about this ranch. He seemed to know what was over every hill and behind every bush. He was the best cowhand Rand had ever worked with, and he would do just about anything to keep J.D. happy.

J.D. raised his hat, brushed down his silvery hair with a gloved hand and set the hat back on his head. "Yes," he said brusquely. "It's okay." He looked at Dale. "But we're going to do this my way, understand?"

Rand backed out of the shed. It was in J.D.'s hands now, and he would deal with Dale in his own way. Rand always tried to stay away from clashing personalities among the men, but he couldn't blame J.D. for his attitude toward Dale. If Dale was a little brighter, he would know that asking too many questions and all but gluing himself to the back of someone would make that person dislike him.

In all honesty, Rand didn't know if Dale trailed after J.D. because he admired or resented him. In any case, he had made a pest of himself since the day J.D. came to the ranch. Maybe working alone together today would better the two men's relationship, Rand hoped as he approached the rest of his crew.

"Okay, mount up," he said. "We're going to inspect every creek and pond on the place today."

Suzanne walked along in the bright sunshine. In spite of the mud, the day was gorgeous. She looked at the Kincaid house, but only from a distance, and she went inside the barn to take a look at Daisy's puppies. They were fat little balls of fur and adorable, and since Daisy seemed friendly enough, Suzanne sat down in the straw and played with the pups.

Going outside again, she began another meandering stroll. The sound of voices coming from one of the sheds startled her so much, she nearly ran for the bunkhouse.

"You flaming coward," she muttered to herself, and forced herself to walk to the shed and peer into it. "J.D.!" she exclaimed. "And Dale. I thought everyone went with Rand."

J.D. straightened up. "Hello, Suzanne. Dale and I stayed behind to clean out this shed."

Suzanne's gaze fell on the twisted mass of wire. "What's that?"

"Just some old barbed wire," J.D. said quickly, before Dale could put in his two cents. "We're going to be hauling a load of junk to the dump."

"You'll be here for lunch, then."

"If you don't mind."

"Of course I don't mind. I'm just surprised, that's all. Will you be in at the usual time?"

"Yes," J.D. said.

"Well, fine. I'll let you get back to work now. It's such a great day I've been doing some walking. See you at noon." She left the shed feeling better because she wasn't alone in the compound. Some pioneer she was, she thought with a laugh, afraid to be alone in the country.

But it was so different here than anyplace she'd been. Different but very beautiful. The chinook was still blowing, but without the force of last night. The air felt warm on her face and hands, and the scenery was breathtaking. In one direction was a tall stand of evergreens—either pines or firs, she wasn't sure. In another, the fields seemed to go on forever. There were still patches of snow, especially against the buildings where the drifts had piled up six and seven feet deep, and rivulets of water ran wherever there was a slope.

Her oversize boots were getting heavy with mud, but she wasn't ready to go back inside and so she set off down the driveway. She'd only gone a short distance when she spotted a huge animal in the brush alongside the driveway, a cow.

Or was it a bull? Much of the animal's bulk was concealed by leafless underbrush and she could only speculate on its gender.

She stopped in her tracks and watched the cow or bull or whatever it was watching her. Its hide was an unusual color, a pinkish tan, and it had an enormous head. After a few moments of primal terror, she told herself to stop being so damned cowardly. That animal would not be loose if he was dangerous. She set out again, sending the animal cautious glances until she rounded a curve and he was out of sight.

In the very next heartbeat she heard a car. Someone was coming! The thought of company was rather exciting and she waited at the side of the roadway with an expectant smile.

A mud-spattered black pickup truck appeared. It slowed down and stopped next to her, and a young woman with long blond hair rolled down the window. "Hi, you must be Suzanne. I'm Janie Carson."

"Janie! You said you might drive out here. I'm glad you did." Suzanne hadn't realized how lonesome she was for female companionship until now. "Come to the bunkhouse and we'll have a cup of coffee or something. It will be great talking to a woman for a change."

"Sounds great," Janie replied. She opened the passenger side door and invited Suzanne inside.

"Thanks." Suzanne hurried around the front of the truck and climbed into the passenger seat. "Isn't this a fabulous day?"

"One of our better ones, that's for sure." She sent Suzanne a glance. "You must be half-crazy from that storm. No one expected it to be nearly as bad as it was, you know. It took everyone by surprise." Janie pulled up next to Suzanne's rental car and turned off the engine.

"It was bad, but it's over," Suzanne said. "The men seem very glad it is. Come on, let's go in. It will take me only a minute to frost a chocolate cake I baked this morning. We'll have a piece of cake with our coffee. Oh, I hope you like chocolate."

"Love it," Janie said with a laugh.

They got out and went into the bunkhouse.

Fourteen

"*You're* twenty-four? *I'm* twenty-four," Janie exclaimed with a delighted clap of her hands. "Imagine that!"

Suzanne liked Janie Carson. While the coffee brewed and she made icing for the cake, Janie chatted on as though they were old friends.

"I'm a waitress. I went to college for two years, hoping to become a teacher," Janie said with a sigh. "But I finally had to admit that I couldn't handle working and going to school at the same time. I quit college, came back to Whitehorn and found my present job."

For a moment she was silent, then her countenance brightened. She was really very pretty, Suzanne thought, fresh and wholesome looking with her bright blue eyes and pale hair. "Dale and I were raised on a ranch, you know. Our folks had a real nice little ranch not too far from town. I don't know the details of what took place—I was just fourteen at the time—but Dad got into some kind of financial bind and we lost our home."

"Oh, I'm so sorry," Suzanne said sympathetically.

"Thank you. I won't say it didn't bother me, 'cause it did. I was even embarrassed to face my friends at school. I got over that, of course, but being forced off our ranch is still a bad memory."

"I'm sure it is. Janie, do you still want to be a teacher?"

"Yes, but there's just no way to do it."

"What about a student loan?" Suzanne began spreading icing over the large sheet cake.

"I will never go into debt for any reason," Janie declared adamantly. "Debt is what caused us to lose our ranch. Suzanne, why are you doing the baking? Where's Handy?"

"Handy is in Seattle. His sister fell ill."

"Oh, that's too bad. I didn't know he had a sister."

"Apparently he does." Suzanne looked up and smiled. "The cake and coffee are ready. I'll—"

A roaring bellow from outside had both women jumping and running to a window.

"Oh, my God, it's Pinky!" Janie cried.

Suzanne got a sickly feeling in her stomach. It was the huge animal she'd seen in the brush and walked right past, and he was standing very close to her and Rand's vehicles.

"Uh, I take it he shouldn't be out there?" she said to Janie.

"No way! Jeremiah Kincaid raised the meanest, orneriest bulls in the county, and Pinky was the worst. Dale told me that Pinky was kept locked in a specially built steel corral, 'cause there wasn't a wooden one ever made that could hold him. I wonder how he got out. Oh, look, he's pawing the ground and snorting. That means he's going to charge something. Can you see what it is?"

"Not from this window." Suzanne had an awful feeling in the pit of her stomach. Dale and J.D. were working in that shed, and one of them might have come outside. She had to warn them! Dashing to the dining room door with Janie hot on her heels, she yanked it open and saw Dale loading a chunk of metal onto the back of a truck. "Dale!" she shouted.

"Is Dale out there?" Janie wormed her way past Suzanne and shrieked, "Dale, get out of sight!"

The wonderful warm wind playfully took her words in the opposite direction, and Dale couldn't make out what she was saying. Recognizing his sister and grinning because she was here, he started walking toward the bunkhouse.

"No, no!" Janie screeched. "Go back! Go back!"

"What?" Dale continued to plod to the bunkhouse.

J.D. heard the commotion and stepped out of the shed. He saw Pinky coming around the corner of the bunkhouse, and *he* started yelling. "Dale, get under cover!"

Dale turned his head to see what J.D. was hollering about, and in the next instant heard the pounding of Pinky's hooves. Instead of running, Dale froze.

J.D. sized up the situation real fast. Dale had left his saddled horse in the corral, Pinky was racing toward the stunned young man, and Suzanne and another woman were watching with horrified expressions from the door of the bunkhouse. It was up to him to do something! Freeway apparently thought it was up to *him,* because he took off after the bull, barking, snarling and snapping.

Racing for the corral, J.D. hopped the fence and leapt into the saddle on the horse. Backing the startled animal up as far as it could go in the corral, J.D. kicked him in the ribs. The horse leapt forward in a dead run and J.D. took him over the corral fence. It wasn't a good trick to teach a horse, J.D. knew, but a man's life was at stake.

Dale finally started to run, but it was too late. Pinky ran right over the top of him, gashing his right thigh on one of his horns. Blood spurted through Dale's pant leg. Dale took one look and passed out. Janie kept screaming, Suzanne wondered if she wasn't going to faint, and J.D. came pounding into the picture on that horse. And all the while, Freeway kept barking and throwing a fit. She had never seen anything even close to what she was looking at now, and she began to shake so hard it was a wonder she was able to stay on her feet.

Pinky turned around to come at Dale again. Snorting, drooling and pawing the ground, the enormous animal prepared itself for another charge.

"Dale, Dale, get up!" Janie screamed.

Suzanne took her hand. "He's unconscious, Janie. He can't get up."

Janie was frantic. "He's going to be killed!" She spotted J.D. riding hell-for-leather. "Who's that?"

"J. D. Cade. He and Dale were working together today. That dog out there belongs to him."

J.D. rode right up to Pinky, screeched his horse to a halt and kicked the bull right between the eyes with the heel of his boot. For a second Pinky looked dazed, but then he came back to roaring, enraged life and started after J.D. and the horse.

"I'm going to draw him away from here," J.D. yelled to the women. "Can the two of you pull Dale into the building?"

"Yes, yes!" Janie shrieked. "Go! Get out of here! He's almost on you!"

The horse took a sudden leap forward and Pinky was right behind him, with Freeway right behind him. The foursome— J.D., the horse he was riding, the enraged bull and Freeway— raced through the compound and into the open fields.

Suzanne and Janie ran outside. They didn't take the time to try to bring Dale to or to examine his wound, they each grabbed a boot and began dragging him along the muddy ground to the bunkhouse. Panting and gasping, they finally got him inside and the door closed.

Janie was in tears as she knelt beside her brother. "Dale, oh, Dale, please be all right."

Suzanne went to the kitchen for a pair of scissors and returned to first yank off Dale's right boot and then to slit his pant leg from its hem to the wound.

Blood pumped from the terrible gash in a steady, frightening rhythm. "I think it's an artery," she said, trying with all her might to speak normally for Janie's sake. "Call for an ambulance, Janie." Both women ran from the dining room, Janie to the phone, Suzanne to get something with which to make a tourniquet.

In the kitchen she grabbed a dish towel and ripped it in half. Rushing back to Dale, she flipped the cloth around and around until she had a strong length of fabric, which she looped around Dale's leg just above the wound. She tied it securely, though not too tightly, and almost at once the bleeding slowed.

Greatly relieved, she returned to the kitchen and made an ice pack with the other half of the towel. She was applying it to Dale's forehead when J. D. walked in.

"How's he doing?" J.D. asked.

Dale began moaning. "He's just coming to," Suzanne replied. "I put a tourniquet on his leg, and it seems to be working. I think that monster severed an artery. J.D., how did he get loose? Janie said Pinky was confined in a steel corral."

"I don't know how he got loose," J.D. said. "He's still running wild, but he's a good mile from the compound, so—"

Janie rushed in, interrupting J.D. "The ambulance is on its way!" She knelt on the other side of her brother and took his hand. "Dale, can you hear me?"

Dale's eyes fluttered open. "I—I'm okay." He tried to get up.

"No, you are not," Suzanne said, firmly pushing him back to the floor. "We've called an ambulance, and it's on its way. Please lie still."

Janie looked up at J.D. with tears in her eyes. "You saved his life," she whispered emotionally. "I'm Janie, Dale's sister. I'll never be able to thank you enough."

"I don't need any thanks," J.D. said in that gruff, impersonal way of his.

Janie blinked at him, then wiped the tears from her face. Suzanne was watching, and she witnessed the precise moment when Janie Carson saw J. D. Cade as a man. Even while holding her brother's hand and being genuinely upset over his accident, Janie suddenly became very feminine.

It flashed through Suzanne's mind that J.D. was not a man for a sweet girl like Janie to get a crush on. He was a loner, and a lot older than Janie. True, he was attractive, tall and lean, and maybe Janie was drawn to the strong, silent type. Regardless, Suzanne felt that J. D. Cade and Janie Carson were opposites, and that any relationship between them would end badly.

But there was hero worship in Janie's blue eyes, and Suzanne heaved an inner sigh.

"J.D.," she said, all but praying that he wasn't being taken in by teary blue eyes and a pretty face. "You were saying that you left Pinky about a mile from the compound?"

"Yes. When Rand and the crew get back, we'll drive him back into his pen." She was holding the makeshift ice pack to Dale's forehead, and he was restless, moving his head, making it difficult.

"Please, Dale," she said. "Try to lie still."

It was as though he hadn't heard her. He seemed focused on saying something to his sister.

"I...didn't know he'd...come after me," he mumbled thickly.

"Of course you didn't," Janie said soothingly.

"A steel pen," Suzanne said musingly. "How on earth did Pinky get out of a steel pen?"

"Hard to say without inspecting it," J.D. said. "You know, I think I'm going to finish my work in the shed, then ride out and take a look at it. It might need some repairs." He started for the door. "Are you going to be okay here alone with Dale?" he asked Suzanne.

She nodded. "I think I'm doing all that can be done, J.D. Go on with your work."

"All right, if you're sure."

She tried to smile. "I'm sure."

He stood there thinking, then made his decision. "Don't bother making lunch for me, Suzanne. I won't be in."

"Whatever you say, J.D.," she murmured.

Janie let go of her brother's hand and jumped to her feet to corner J.D. at the door. She stuck out her hand. "Please, you must let me thank you, at least with a handshake."

"If you want," J.D. said, and took her hand.

Oh, Janie, don't be so obvious, Suzanne thought. Not that a thank-you and a handshake were out of line, but it was Janie's giddy expression and the flirtatious lilt in her voice that J.D. would have to be brain dead to miss.

She didn't have to worry. She could see J.D. was fully aware of Janie Carson's adulation, and from the light in his eyes she guessed it amused him. But he was nothing more than nice to Miss Carson and clearly unmoved by her charms. He shook her hand for a moment and dropped it.

"See you later," he said to Suzanne. Out the door he went.

Janie returned to kneel beside Dale and Suzanne. "J.D.'s wonderful, isn't he?"

"He was very courageous and quick-thinking today, if that's what you mean."

"Oh, yes, that's exactly what I mean. But he's also very handsome, don't you think?"

"J.D.'s good-looking, yes." Dale was attempting to get up again. "Janie, help me hold him down. If he moves around too much, he's going to lose more blood."

"Be still, Dale," Janie said sharply.

To Suzanne's surprise, Dale quieted. "He listens to you."

"We're very close," Janie said with unmistakable pride. "We're only a year apart in age, you know. Dale's twenty-three."

Suzanne thought of herself and Mack, and what she wouldn't give to be as close to her own brother as Janie was to Dale.

"That gash in his leg looks terrible," Janie whispered.

"It needs stitches," Suzanne said calmly, wondering if that ambulance would ever arrive. She applied pressure to the wound with the ice pack, which slowed the bleeding even more. Privately she believed that Dale was going to need surgery to close that artery. External stitching was not going to be the only medical procedure he was going to have to undergo.

"He's going to be all right, though, don't you think?" Janie asked anxiously.

"He'll be fine, Janie. Probably laid up for a while, but he's young and healthy," Suzanne said reassuringly. Janie seemed to relax.

"Tell me about J.D.," she said.

"I don't know anything to tell."

"You must know something. Was he working here when you got here?"

"I...couldn't say for certain. Probably."

"He's not married, is he?"

The payroll records came to Suzanne's mind. "I just remembered something. He *was* working here when I arrived, and he's not married."

Janie's face lit up. "I knew it!"

It was funny how much older Suzanne felt than Janie when they were exactly the same age. It made her feel even older to think about it. Janie's life was no bed of roses, either, and yet she had maintained a much more youthful outlook than Suzanne had. It made Suzanne wonder if *she* didn't take things too seriously.

In the next instant she sighed. How could she not take an empty wallet, no security whatsoever, no permanent job and a troublesome brother like Mack seriously?

The distant wail of a siren broke her train of thought. "It must be the ambulance," she said to Janie. Thank God! Her hands were aching from holding the ice pack, there was blood and mud smeared all over the floor and on herself, and she was truly concerned about Dale's loss of blood. It would be a tremendous relief to turn him over to people with medical training. She had done the best she knew how, but was it enough?

The ambulance arrived and Janie ran outside to direct them through the right door of the building. A young man and woman came in and took over. Suzanne weakly sank onto a chair to watch. Their competence and efficiency was gratifying.

"Who applied this tourniquet?" the young woman asked.

"I did," Suzanne said.

"Good job. You probably saved his life."

Janie came over, took Suzanne's hand and squeezed it. "Oh, Suzanne, thank you. I wouldn't have known what to do. Dale and I both owe you and J.D. everything. I'll never forget what you did today, never."

Suzanne continued to sit there even after everyone had gone. She had never been so shaken in her life, and she'd gotten through it on instinct alone. Maybe she functioned best in a crisis, some people did.

If only she could deal with her own problems as well as she had with Dale's.

Heavyhearted, she finally forced herself off the chair. She would clean the floor, then herself.

She was glad that she didn't have to make lunch for anyone today. She honestly didn't have the strength.

Mack was carrying an armload of mail when he walked in that afternoon.

"Oh, the mail!" Suzanne exclaimed. "I forgot all about it." She looked closely at her brother as he dropped his load on the kitchen counter. "How was it?" She didn't have to say the word *school,* Mack knew what she meant.

"It was okay," he said nonchalantly.

Suzanne wasn't sure she should believe her own ears. "You didn't hate it?" she asked cautiously.

"It's different. The kids are real friendly. And guess what? The coach asked me if I wanted to play on any of the teams. Football season is over, but they're still playing basketball and getting started on baseball and track."

"You haven't…I mean, are you interested?" Mack had always poked fun at the jocks in his school in Baltimore.

"Might be," he said. "It's different here, sis. Anyone can be on a team. At home you had to be a top athlete to get into sports. Coach said anyone can play any game he wants in this high school."

"Yes, that is different," Suzanne said slowly. She had never, not once, heard Mack say anything positive about school. This conversation was suspiciously close to positive and she was having trouble digesting that fact.

"There's only one hitch. Good grades." Mack made a face.

Suzanne rushed to encourage him. "You're smart, Mack. You've always had the ability to pull good grades."

"Yeah, but who cared?"

"I did. Don't I count?"

She was shocked when Mack laughed. When had she last heard a real laugh from him, one that wasn't heavily tinged with sarcasm?

"Guess you do count," he said. "I'm gonna change clothes now and go find Rand."

"I don't think you'll find him, Mack. He and the other men—"

"I spotted 'em way off, heading in when I got here," Mack said, bounding away.

Suzanne heard him taking the stairs two and three at a time.

His boyish enthusiasm brought tears to her eyes. This was the brother she loved, and if Montana, this ranch or that wise and wonderful coach at the high school had brought about the change in him, God bless them all.

The pile of mail caught her eye, and she haphazardly stacked it in her arms and carried it to the office, where she dumped it on Rand's desk. He had asked her to pick up the mail, not to open it, and even if he had requested she open and sort it, she didn't have time to do it now. With the men on their way in, probably ravenously hungry after such a meager lunch, she had to see to their dinner.

Returning to the kitchen, she checked the twelve-pound beef roast in the oven, then set to work peeling a small mountain of potatoes. It was a mindless task and her thoughts rambled. Mack was happier today than he'd been since their parents' deaths. But what about her? He had every right to happiness, but didn't she, as well?

Her breath suddenly caught in her throat, and she stopped with a potato in one hand and the peeler in the other. Was it going to come down to Mack's happiness or hers? Oh, God, she was frightened, she thought with a barrage of fearful emotions. Falling in love was scary enough when the man you loved held the same strong feelings for you. When he didn't…?

In a hopeless gesture she let her head drop forward, almost putting her chin on her chest. What was she going to do? Dear Lord, *what* was she going to do?

Mack had been mistaken. He'd spotted some of the crew on horseback, all right, but they hadn't been heading for the compound, they'd been looking for Pinky. Once J.D. had gotten rid of that heap of ruined wire, he'd ridden out to Pinky's pen and saw the gate swinging on its hinges. After inspecting the heavy-duty latch and deciding that someone had deliberately set the fierce, perpetually angry bull loose, he'd gone to find Rand. He had caught up with the crew near Goose Creek.

Rand had seen him and Freeway coming and told the men to keep following the creek; he and J.D. would catch up with them.

"What's wrong?" Rand called as J.D. got closer.

J.D. rode up to Rand and Jack and reined in his horse. "Pinky's loose. He gored Dale before I could draw his attention. I let him chase me for about a mile, then outmaneuvered him and rode back to the compound to check on Dale. Suzanne and Dale's sister had the situation under control."

"Is he badly hurt?"

"He's got a rip in his thigh, but I've seen worse. He'll be all right. The thing is, Rand, I rode out to check Pinky's pen, and there's nothing wrong with the gate latch. Someone let him out."

Rand's lips tightened. "The same someone who destroyed that barbed wire last night."

J.D. nodded, his expression grim. "I'm sure of it."

"And Dale could have been killed. My God, Suzanne might have been killed! This is going too far, *way* too far. No one's been injured before, this guy is getting violent. I swear, J.D., when I find out who's behind these rotten stunts, I'm going to tear him limb from limb. He's going to think an atom bomb hit him."

"And if you want some help, you've got mine. Hell, Rand, either one of those women could have run into that bull."

Just the thought of Suzanne or Janie Carson facing a charging bull made Rand feel queasy. "Where'd you leave him?"

"Near the middle pond."

"Okay, let's get the men and go round him up." Turning Jack's head, Rand began riding.

J.D. rode beside him. Freeway trailed behind. "I don't usually have trouble with animals, but Pinky's one for the books," he said. "If this was my ranch, I'd get rid of him."

"If *I* owned this place, so would I," Rand said grimly. "Believe me, J.D., so would I."

Pinky was nowhere near the middle pond when the crew got there. Rand's anger was going deeper by the minute. "Spread out," he told the men. "We've got to find him before dark. And be careful. He'll charge a horse as fast as he would a man on foot."

"And he *is* fast," J.D. put in. "Moves like greased lightning."

"How'd he get loose?" one of the newer men asked, sounding nervous.

"We don't know," Rand said. He studied the faces of the men looking at him. At least one of them knew he was lying, he thought, but which one? Then he realized that even the older hands looked uneasy over the possibility of tangling with Pinky. Any second now someone was apt to start talking about a ghost having unlatched the gate of the bull's pen. Someone would do it for sure when they saw that the latch was undamaged, or figured out that Pinky hadn't simply butted his way through the steel fencing.

"Come on, let's go," Rand said brusquely. He would deal with nonsensical speculation—it was bound to happen—about ghosts and little green men *after* they got Pinky penned up again.

Mack hung on the corral fence and wondered why in heck Rand and the other men hadn't arrived yet. He kept eyeing a handsome black gelding in the corral that he'd heard the men call Joe. He thought it was a dumb name for a horse, and if Joe belonged to him, he'd call him Ebony, or Midnight. Yeah, Midnight was a cool name.

"Come on, Midnight, come over here and let me pet your nose," he crooned.

The horse trotted over to the fence, surprising Mack. "Well, ain't you a friendly fellow?" Mack stood on the first rail and stroked the gelding's head. "I'll bet you'd let me ride you, wouldn't you?"

The horse's head bobbed up and down, as though he was agreeing. Mack giggled like the boy he was. "Man, I wish old Kip could see me now." He'd been meaning to write to Kip, but until today he'd been working with the men and coming in too tired to do anything except eat and go to bed.

Today he wasn't tired at all, and he wanted to ride a horse more than he'd ever wanted anything. Rand had promised to teach him how to ride when he had time, but what was so complicated about it? Seemed to Mack you just got on and let the horse do the work.

Looking around to make sure no one was watching, he slipped between the rails. He felt a foot taller inside the corral, as tall as Rand and J.D., and he just knew that Midnight would let him get on his back.

He coaxed the horse to stand lengthwise along the fence, climbed onto the first rail and then, hanging on to Joe's mane, threw his right leg over the animal's back. Joe calmly side-stepped and Mack landed face-first in the mud.

He came up sputtering. "Jeez…jeez…what'd you do that for?"

He was muddy from head to foot and felt like a moron. Suzanne would ask how he'd gotten so muddy, and he'd have to come up with a lie, because he sure wasn't going to tell her the truth.

Going into the barn, he found a towel and wiped the mud off his face. Remembering Daisy and her pups, he tried to forget what Midnight had done to him and went to sit with the dogs. At least they were friendly.

The mud gradually dried on his clothes.

It was long after dark when Suzanne heard the men coming in. Dinner had been ready for hours. She'd kept it warm but knew it couldn't possibly be as good as it would have been two hours ago.

Carrying his boots, Rand walked into the kitchen. Suzanne was seated at the counter, nursing a cup of tea. He couldn't read her expression, maybe because she wore none. There was a blankness to her face that disturbed him.

"Hi," he said cautiously. "Are you all right? I heard you had quite an experience today."

"J.D. told you," she said dully. "Do you want to know something, Rand? I walked right past Pinky only a few minutes before he charged Dale."

Rand felt himself go pale. "You were outside."

"Taking a walk. Janie Carson arrived and we came inside for cake and coffee. Have you figured out how that brute got out of his pen?"

He didn't know what to tell her. Scaring her more than she already was went against his grain. On the other hand, he might have been wrong about keeping the truth from her. He'd thought her only danger had come from the dynamite, and he'd been wrong about that.

He made his decision. "Someone deliberately opened the gate on Pinky's pen," he said quietly.

She stared. It took a moment to assimilate what he'd told her. "Why would anyone do that? From what Janie said, it's common knowledge that Pinky is a dangerous animal."

"He is."

"And yet someone turned him loose. I don't understand."

"Neither do I." He paused for the briefest of moments, praying she wouldn't ask questions. He could tell her part of the truth, but not all of it. "I'm going to go get cleaned up for supper."

He walked past her, then on impulse turned around and came back to stand behind her. "I'm sorry," he said softly, and leaned forward to press a kiss to her hair.

He felt a shiver go through her and knew it was because of him, because they affected each other so strongly. His emotions suddenly churned. Losing Suzanne would be like losing the sun. She had brought something into his life that he hadn't let himself hope for. He was a different man than the one who had met her at the door that first snowy night. He…loved her.

Facing his feelings was a shock. He needed time to think. "See you in a few," he said, then left.

Suzanne bit down on her bottom lip painfully hard. There were no answers for her dilemma, none at all.

Fifteen

When it had grown dark and spooky in the barn and the men still weren't back, Mack had crept into the bunkhouse through the laundry room door, hurriedly undressed down to his underwear and tossed all of his clothes, jacket included, into a washer. Skirting the kitchen to avoid Suzanne, he had tiptoed up the stairs, taken a shower and put on clean jeans and shirt.

He'd stayed in his room until the men started coming upstairs, then decided to stay where he was a little longer, until they went down for supper.

He was totally mortified over his first attempt to get on a horse, but even abject humiliation couldn't daunt his determination to learn to ride. What he needed to do, he knew, was to talk one of the men into giving him some instructions, preferably Rand or J.D. Mack couldn't decide which man he admired most. They were both so cool.

Lying on his bed he thought it through from all angles. J.D. was on this floor, Rand was harder to get to. He would talk to J.D.

He could hear showers running and men moving around getting cleaned up for the evening meal. Leaving his room, he heard some of them talking.

"That latch didn't open by itself," one of them said.

"Nope, sure didn't," another voice agreed.

"And since no one with a lick of sense would turn Pinky out, how'd the latch get opened?"

The conversation didn't interest Mack in the least. He didn't know who Pinky was, or what latch the men were discussing, nor did he care to know. He was focused on one thing, talking to J.D. about a lesson in horsemanship. Going to the door of J.D.'s room, he knocked.

"It's open," J.D. called.

Mack turned the knob, pushed the door open and grinned nervously. "Uh, hi, J.D."

J.D. was buttoning his clean shirt. "Hello, Mack."

"Uh, could I ask you something?"

"Go ahead." J.D. began tucking the tail of his shirt into his jeans.

"I—I want to learn to ride a horse. Everyone's always so busy around here, but…" His voice trailed off.

"It's a working ranch, Mack. A cowhand's work is never done."

Mack nodded and gulped. "I know, but…" Again he stopped.

One corner of J.D.'s mouth turned up in a knowing smile. "You want some pointers, right? Well, how about tomorrow morning before you head off for school? Would that be soon enough?"

"Tomorrow? Really? Gosh, J.D., that would be great!" Mack started backing out of the room. "Thanks, J.D., thanks a lot."

J.D.'s grin broadened. Mack could be a pain in the neck with his constant questions, but teenage curiosity didn't make him a bad kid in J.D.'s eyes. He did wonder at times what had brought the Paxtons to the ranch, but he would never ask. He didn't stick his nose into other people's business because he didn't want them prying into his.

Whatever, he'd have Mack riding in no time, probably in one lesson.

Mack excitedly leapt down the stairs, two at a time, and ran into the kitchen. "Suzanne, guess what? J.D. is gonna give me a riding lesson tomorrow morning."

Suzanne felt as though her heart had just slipped down to her knees. Her smile was as genuine as she could make it, but if Mack hadn't been so rambunctiously thrilled he would have seen the sadness in his sister's eyes.

"That's wonderful," she said, and turned back to the stove. "Dinner will be on the table in five minutes."

"Great! I'm starving."

Rand looked at the pile of mail on his desk with outright disgust. Opening mail was not how he wanted to spend the next few hours.

But it had to be done. Accepting his fate, he sat down and reached for the topmost envelope. It was a power bill, and he set it aside. The next several items were advertisements, which he tossed into the wastebasket. He made a stack of the trade journals, and continued slitting envelopes until he came to one from the company that sold dynamite.

In it were two sheets of paper, copies of the delivery receipts for those two cases of dynamite. Frowning, he studied the signatures, both of which were supposed to be his. They were so much alike it took a few minutes to decide which one was genuine and which was the forgery. The creep he was dealing with was a lot more clever than he'd given him credit for, he thought with a burning knot of anger developing in his gut. Wasn't that great news.

Jerking a drawer open, he dropped in the copies. He would show them to Reed Austin, the next time he saw him.

He couldn't get rid of the anger as he worked his way through the pile. Bills went in one stack, trash went into the wastebasket, and all the while he was simmering inside.

Then he stopped cold. In his hand was the letter Suzanne had told him she'd written to him before coming to Montana to find her brother.

He took an uneasy breath. The storm had delayed his receiving this, and a lot had happened since Suzanne had written it. He had terribly mixed emotions about reading it. Something told him to tear it up and not read it, but his curiosity was more powerful than that nagging little voice in his head, and he slit the envelope quickly, before he could change his mind. Shaking out the letter, he unfolded it and began reading.

Mr. Harding,
First of all, I did not answer your ad, my teenage brother did. Secondly, I don't know whose photo…

Rand continued reading to the very end. Humiliation seared him as he reread, "I am not now nor ever could be interested in an advertisement such as yours… As for your letter, I can only say that I have never read such drivel in my life. If you're lonesome, it's your own doing. I could not care less."

Laying the letter down, he leaned back in his chair, feeling as weak as a newborn babe. *Drivel. If you're lonesome, it's your own doing. I could not care less. Please do not contact me again…if you do I will turn this whole ridiculous matter over to the police.* The cruel words went around and around in his head. My God, he thought in abject misery, how could he have put himself into such an embarrassing position? How could he even face Suzanne again after reading her letter? Her opinion of a man advertising for a wife couldn't be any lower.

Hearing footsteps in the hall, he grabbed the letter and its envelope and shoved them into a drawer. He was flipping through one of the trade journals when Suzanne walked in.

"Would you like some help with the mail?" she asked. "I wasn't sure you wanted me to open it, and I didn't have time today, anyway. But I'd be glad to help you with it now."

"Not necessary." He didn't raise his eyes and look at her. "I'm almost through. Oh, some bills came in. You can write checks for them tomorrow. Just leave them on my desk and I'll sign them when I can."

"All right." She had never heard that distant tone in Rand's voice before, and it was very strange that he wasn't looking at her. "Is anything wrong?" she asked.

"Nope, not a thing." *Nothing other than having made a horse's ass out of yourself, and then having fallen in love when you swore on your life you never would again.*

Suzanne kept standing there, mystified and puzzled. Only a few hours ago Rand had tenderly pressed a kiss to her hair, and now he wouldn't even look at her. Her gaze fell on the mail, on the neat stacks he'd made of what he had already opened.

It hit her then—her letter! It had finally come, he had read it and was hurt by it!

But that was so silly. They hadn't even met when she'd written that letter. She hadn't known him at all, and had written of her disgust to a stranger she was positive she would *never* meet.

In fact, she could hardly remember what she had written. Surely it couldn't be as bad as Rand seemed to be taking it.

"Rand," she began, uncertain of how to get past this. "Why won't you look at me?"

He swiveled his chair around and looked her directly in the eye. "You think I got a problem with looking at you? No way, sweetheart." *No woman was going to break his heart again, especially not one who had threatened to call the police if he contacted her again. He didn't need Suzanne; he didn't need* anyone. That ad had caused enough trouble; it wasn't going to cause any more.

Suzanne's mouth was dry as desert dust. His sarcasm was undeserved. He had started this nightmare, if he cared to remember, not her. How dare he act as though she were at fault here?

She lifted her chin. "I'll take care of the bills in the morning. Good night." She walked out.

Rand stared at the empty doorway for a while, then turned back to the desk. He felt like a complete fool, and when he found that he could no longer concentrate on the mail, he put his head in his hands and groaned. What in God's name had possessed him to put that ad in that damned magazine?

He wouldn't tell Suzanne to pack up her brother and leave, but she would get the message sooner or later. They were through. He couldn't face her day after day knowing how she really felt about him.

Then he remembered their lovemaking and groaned again. Miserable, frustrated and angry, he shoved his chair away from the desk, got up and strode stiffly to his bedroom.

He didn't even look at Suzanne's door as he passed it. There were too many unnerving memories connected to that room, and he didn't want to think about them.

But think about them, he did, far into the night. Cursing did no good, punching his pillow, either. He was bleary-eyed exhausted and still couldn't sleep.

In her room, Suzanne wept quietly into her pillow. She hated herself for crying over Rand's withdrawal. She hadn't been going to marry him, had she? No. Then why was she crying now because he so obviously no longer wanted to marry her?

She had to get away from here. She would tell Mack in the morning. She was no longer worried that Rand would let him stay on the ranch if she didn't. He would be only too happy to be rid of both of the Paxtons.

Well, maybe she would be happy to be rid of him, too.

Her sobs increased. She wouldn't be happy about it at all. Why was she lying to herself?

Her emotions became more ragged the longer she lay there and wept. One minute she hated Rand, the next she loved him. One minute she couldn't wait to get away from this hideous place, the next she thought of its beauty, and how accustomed she had become to cooking huge meals and working in the office.

Around midnight she thought of facing Rand in the morning and got sick to her stomach. Why should she put herself through that? She and Mack could leave tonight. She knew which room was his, and she could go upstairs right now and wake him up. He wouldn't like it, he would probably revert back to his old, surly self, but when she explained…

She was suddenly bitter and furious. This whole awful thing was Mack's fault, and why should she worry about how he might take being dragged out of a deep sleep? She was going home! To hell with Rand Harding.

Wearing a robe over her pajamas and slippers on her feet, she dashed from her room, down the hall and up the stairs. Counting doors, she stopped at Mack's, drew a big breath and walked into his room. Without a by-your-leave, she snapped on the ceiling light. Mack never budged.

Hurrying over to the bed, she shook Mack by the shoulder. "Mack?" she whispered. "Mack, wake up."

"Wha-what's going on?" Mack came to partial alertness.

"Keep your voice down. I don't want to wake the men. We're leaving. Get up and pack your things."

Blinking at the light, Mack sat up. "What d'ya mean we're leaving?"

"We're going home."

"Back to Baltimore?"

"That's home, isn't it? Now, hurry." She started for the door.

"I'm not going anywhere!" Mack shouted.

Suzanne rushed back to the bed. "For Pete's sake, keep your voice down! Do you think I want to wake the whole bunkhouse?" She sat next to her brother. "Mack, we *have* to leave. Rand doesn't want us here."

"Who said?"

"He did."

Mack looked stunned. "He came right out and said it?"

"Not in so many words, but his meaning was very clear."

Mack lay down again. "I ain't going."

Suzanne's lips thinned. "Do you think I'm lying? When have I ever lied to you?"

"I thought you and Rand were getting along," Mack said with a sulky expression.

"Well, we weren't, and he made it very obvious to me tonight that we've overstayed our welcome. Will you please get up and get packed?"

"I got clothes in the washer."

"Wet clothes? Mack, dammit…" Suzanne calmed herself. "All right, I'll put them in the dryer. You get busy packing the rest of your things. I'll be in my room. Come down there, very quietly, please, when you're ready." Rising, she started for the door again.

"J.D. was gonna give me a riding lesson in the morning."

Suzanne turned around. "I know, and I'm sorry about that. Mack, I'm going to promise you something. After I find a job and get back on my feet financially, I'll see that you get your riding lessons. There's a very good stable on Westwood Road, and I've heard they have some lovely riding trails."

Mack didn't answer. Sighing, Suzanne said, "Please get dressed and packed right away. I'd like to leave as soon as possible." Quietly slipping out of his room, she made her way back down the stairs and to the laundry room. It took only a few moments to transfer the wet clothing from washer to dryer, which she turned on, winced at the sound, prayed no one would hear it and then sped to her own room.

Her hands were shaking when she took her two pieces of luggage from the small closet and brought them to the bed. In fact, the trembling was rampant throughout her entire body, not just in her hands.

She gritted her teeth and told herself that she was doing the right thing, the only thing she could do. The thought of even seeing Rand again, let alone acting as though everything was all right between them for everyone else's benefit, was unbearable. He would be greatly relieved in the morning when he discovered they were gone, and she would be relieved to be gone. Mack was the only one who would have regrets, and he would get over them. Eventually.

She couldn't worry about Mack's regrets, anyway. She was leaving without a paycheck, which wouldn't have been princely, in any case, but still would have been more than she had in her purse at the moment.

"To hell with it," she muttered. She wouldn't ask Rand for that money if life itself depended on it.

Taking off her robe, she folded it and laid it in the suitcase. It irritated her that they could be ready to leave in fifteen minutes if it weren't for Mack's clothes in the dryer. If money wasn't so tight, she would go without them. But jackets and jeans were costly, and she was going to have to watch every penny.

A wave of nausea struck her, and she sat on the edge of the bed. It's only nerves, she thought while rubbing her tummy. Only the worse case of bad nerves she'd ever had. Why was she letting herself fall apart like this? Rand wasn't her first disappointment, after all. And perhaps that letter arriving when it did was opportune. She'd been so worried about saying no to Rand when he mentioned marriage again, and now she wouldn't have to.

Thirty minutes later she was dressed, packed and impatiently waiting for Mack. She was certain she'd made no noise and wasn't concerned that Rand, sleeping right next door, might have heard her. It occurred to her, however, that Mack might come stomping down the hall instead of being extraquiet, as she had asked.

Besides, it was possible that he was in the laundry room waiting for his clothes to finish drying.

Putting on her coat, she slung her purse over her shoulder and stealthily opened the door. Picking up her two suitcases, she set them down in the hall to slowly, soundlessly shut the door again. To make absolutely sure no one would hear her, she took off her pumps, shoved one in each pocket of her coat, took up her luggage again and traversed the hall in her hosiery.

The laundry room light was on. Good, she thought, she'd been right about Mack being in there. But when she reached the doorway, the room was empty.

Well, *she* hadn't left the light on, she thought with intense aggravation. Couldn't Mack ever do anything right? If he'd come down to check his clothes in the dryer, or even to take them back upstairs to stuff in his backpack, why hadn't he turned off the light?

She snapped it off, detoured to the kitchen to set down her luggage and then perched on a stool to wait for Mack. After five minutes she wondered what on earth was taking him so long. After another five minutes, her annoyance had doubled.

"Darn you, Mack," she whispered. "What are you doing up there?"

Okay, she'd give him a few more minutes, she thought. But only a few. Then she would brave the stairs again and find out for herself what was taking so long.

Another five minutes dwindled by, and then five more, only because she didn't want this trip to start out bad, with Mack accusing her of being on his back about everything he did.

But then she couldn't twiddle her thumbs one more

second, and she tiptoed to the stairs and silently ascended to the second floor. Again she counted doors to make sure she got Mack's room. It was a hallway of doors, and it would be very easy to walk into the wrong room.

It wasn't the wrong room, but it was dark. Mack, dammit, you went back to sleep! Quickly she stepped inside, closed the door and switched on the light. The bed was in total disarray and Mack wasn't in it! She stood there dumbfounded. If he wasn't here and he wasn't in the laundry room, where was he?

And then she knew. He wasn't going with her. He'd run away again!

Her knees buckled and she grabbed hold of the dresser to keep from sinking to the floor. Running away *to* Montana was a far cry from running away *in* Montana. He knew nothing about the wilderness, nothing about camping; he would die out there!

No, calm down. You can't be right. He's hiding somewhere, he wouldn't leave the compound all alone.

She knew there were unused bedrooms up here, she just didn't know which doors to open. And he could have gone to the barn, or one of the storage sheds. There were many places in which to hide outside. Her mind raced, searching for some sign of what she should do next.

Nothing came to her, nothing that made sense. Anger and fear collided in her system, bringing on another bout of nausea. This time it lingered while the reality of her situation tore at her flesh. She had no choice, none at all.

No, that wasn't true, she did have a choice. She could either wake Rand up now and tell him Mack was gone, or she could wait and do it in the morning.

Suzanne nearly hyperventilated at that notion. She could *not* wait until morning! If Mack wasn't just hiding on her, if he had actually left the compound, he could be miles away by then!

Scrambling into her shoes, she ran from the room and

down the stairs, forgetting completely about the sleeping men. Without stopping to knock she rushed into Rand's room.

"Mack's gone," she gasped. "He's gone!"

Sixteen

Rand hadn't been asleep very long and couldn't immediately come awake. "What in hell's going on?" he said, sounding grumpy over being disturbed.

Suzanne flipped the wall switch and the ceiling light came on. "Mack's gone. You...you have to help me. I don't know where to look for him, what to do..." She was literally wringing her hands.

He put a hand up to shield his eyes from the light. "Suzanne?" His foggy mind wondered why she was wearing her coat...and what was it she was saying about Mack? He sat up, put his feet on the floor and shook his head in an attempt to come to. "What time is it?"

Suzanne couldn't contain her anxiety. She swept over to Rand and knelt in front of him. "Rand, listen to me. Mack is gone."

"What do you mean, he's gone? Gone where?"

"He...I..." Oh, God, now she had to confess that she'd

been planning to leave and had awakened Mack, and the whole ball of wax.

Rand was becoming more alert, and taking in her coat again, as well as her hose and pumps. "Why are you dressed like that in the middle of the night?"

"Every minute we talk, Mack could be getting farther from the ranch," she said sharply. "I need your help. I need *somebody's* help. I don't know in which direction to start looking for him!" She grabbed his arm in desperation. "Are you grasping what I'm saying?"

He was…finally. Parts of it, anyway, the part about Mack being gone, and the fearful panic in Suzanne's voice. He took her by the shoulders. "How long has he been gone?"

"Um…let me think. About thirty minutes, maybe a little longer. I'm not real sure because…"

Rand cut in. "Then he can't have gone far. Let me get into some clothes." Suzanne stumbled to her feet. "You don't have to leave, I'm wearing underwear."

She sighed. Would it matter if he weren't? She'd seen, touched and kissed almost every inch of his body, just as he'd done to her. Modesty at this point seemed gratuitous.

Still, she turned away and was facing the door when J.D. appeared, wearing jeans, an unbuttoned shirt and socks.

"Sorry," he said when he saw Suzanne, turning to go.

"J.D.?" Rand was in his jeans and buttoning his shirt. "Come on in."

"This isn't what you think," Suzanne said.

J.D. nodded at her, accepting her comment without question, then looked at Rand. "Freeway woke me. I heard someone running down the stairs and figured I'd better check it out."

"That was me," Suzanne said. "I was looking for Mack. He's gone, J.D." She wiped at the tears that were beginning to blur her vision.

J.D. cocked an eyebrow. "Are you saying he left the ranch?"

"I don't know what I'm saying. All I know is that he's not in his room or in the laundry room."

The two men looked at each other and said almost simultaneously, "The laundry room?"

"It's a long story," she said dully.

"Make it a short one," Rand said with chilling abruptness.

His tone reminded Suzanne of why she'd been planning to leave at this late hour. Her tears vanished as she sent him a defiant look. "I woke Mack and told him we were going home. I told him to pack his things, and he said he had clothes in the washer. That's why I thought he might be in the laundry room when he wasn't in his bedroom."

Rand gaped at her. "You were going to leave in the middle of the night? For God's sake, why?"

If J.D. hadn't been there, she would have told him why. Instead, she said, stiffly, "I really don't feel like talking about it right now." She turned to J.D. "Do you think it's possible that he's merely hiding in the barn, or someplace like that? He didn't say he wouldn't go home with me, but I...I know he loves this place."

"Well, he's not very old and it's awfully dark out there. He probably didn't go very far, Suzanne," J.D. assured her. "Rand, I'm going upstairs to get my boots and jacket. I'll give you a hand in looking for him."

"Thanks, J.D., appreciate it."

After J.D. had gone, Rand sat on the bed to yank on his own boots. Suzanne was pacing back and forth. He could see she was worried sick, and he couldn't tell her she had no cause to worry. It was possible that Mack was merely staying out of sight in one of the outbuildings, hoping his sister would leave without him, but Rand didn't think so. Mack wasn't stupid, and he would know that Suzanne would roust the whole bunkhouse, if necessary, to find him. No, Mack wasn't hanging around the compound. This could be serious.

"Did he take any food with him?" Rand asked.

Suzanne's eyes widened, and she ran out of the room and down the hall. Rand got up from the bed, grabbed his jacket and gloves and followed.

She was frantically opening cabinets when he caught up with her in the kitchen. "I can't tell," she wailed. "What would he take? Canned goods? There's so much of it that it's impossible to know if any is missing."

"How about bread?"

She checked the huge bread box, and her shoulders slumped. "There might have been another loaf, but I really can't remember."

Rand ardently hoped that the boy had taken *something* to eat with him, but he couldn't pass that concern on to Suzanne. She had no idea what Mack could encounter out there, and he wasn't going to enlighten her.

J.D. came in, carrying two flashlights. "Did he take some food with him?" he asked.

"I'm sure he did," Rand said for Suzanne's benefit. Behind her back, he shrugged at J.D. and mouthed, "Can't tell."

"I checked the empty bedrooms upstairs," J.D. said with a nod at Rand, indicating that he'd gotten his message. "Figured that was the place to start."

"Okay, let's go check the outbuildings." J.D. handed him one of the flashlights, and out they went.

Suzanne sank onto one of the counter stools, put her face in her hands and wept. She had wondered if Mack ever did anything right many times, but now she was wondering that about herself. Pity for both of them nearly choked her, then she thought of their parents' untimely deaths and sobbed even harder. She had taken Mack home with her after the double funeral, but had she shown him, unequivocally, that she wanted him in her home, that she loved him? He'd been only twelve, a lost little boy, and she and Les had been fighting. Obviously Mack had never felt as though he could talk to her about his innermost feelings, or he would have told her about his dream of becoming a cowboy.

Maybe he'd tried, she thought sadly. Maybe he'd tried and she'd been too swamped with adult problems to listen to a boy's dreams.

But her problems had never been imaginary, she thought in defense of how she had related to Mack. The divorce had been very real and very traumatic. She'd finally been getting over it when she lost her job.

Sighing, she got up for a tissue to dry her eyes and blow her nose. She had felt sorry for herself long enough. She could at least put on a pot of coffee. J.D. and Rand might appreciate a cup of hot coffee when they came in. In her heart she was positive that Mack hadn't left the compound, and that they would have him with them when they returned to the bunkhouse.

Her brain wasn't that sure, but in this case she preferred listening to her heart. After preparing the coffeepot, she went to her room and changed from her traveling clothes into jeans, a sweater and her loafers.

Rand and J.D. met at the main corral. "He's not in the barn," J.D. said. "Freeway sniffed out every corner." The mangy dog woofed and wagged his tail, as though saying, "Aren't I a clever helper?"

"The other buildings, either," Rand said. "I had a feeling he wouldn't be."

"He's just a kid, and a city kid at that. I can't believe he would go very far. Rand, it's black as pitch in the woods, but I can't see him taking off across the open fields. Even a city kid would know we'd find him easy enough in the fields."

"Not in the dark, we wouldn't. That gives him till dawn to get wherever he's going."

"Rand, he wouldn't head for Granite Mountain, would he?" There was disquietude in J.D.'s voice.

Rand shifted his weight uneasily. "I sure hope not." He looked up at the sky, brilliant with stars. "It's cold at night. Even colder on the mountain. Too bad we lost the chinook." He shone the flashlight on his wristwatch. "It's another three hours to dawn."

"Rand, what's the problem between Mack and his sister?" J.D. asked quietly. "It has to be pretty serious for the boy to run off like this."

Rand's lips stretched tightly across his teeth. "It's my fault, J.D., the whole damned thing." He couldn't say more, couldn't explain, and was glad that J.D. wasn't the type of man to pry. Actually, it surprised him that J.D. had brought it up at all.

"Well, I've got to give Suzanne the bad news sooner or later. Might as well go in and get it over with," Rand said. "She's probably half-crazy with worry by now."

They started walking to the bunkhouse with Freeway on their heels. "She's going to be even more worried when you tell her Mack's not in the compound," J.D. said.

"Yes, but it might help when I tell her the whole crew is going to go looking for him at first light."

"Might," J.D. agreed.

They went in through the laundry room door. "I smell coffee," J.D. said.

"She must have made a pot."

Suzanne heard them coming, and was waiting, expectant and tight as a drum, when they walked into the kitchen. Mack wasn't with them. Her hand rose to splay at her throat. There was fear in her eyes. "You didn't find him."

"No." Rand suffered an emotional ache in his chest.

Whatever she thought of him, he was in love with her. It wasn't comforting knowledge. He didn't want to spend the next year trying to forget her, as he had with Sherry.

He kept his voice curt and impersonal, when he would have preferred a consoling tone. But he had taken enough risks with Suzanne. She had been planning to leave without so much as a simple goodbye, sneaking out in the night so she wouldn't *have* to say goodbye. He wasn't sure he would ever be able get over that, even if he did manage to forget the rest of it.

He filled two mugs with coffee and handed one to J.D. His words were spoken to Suzanne. "We'll start looking for him beyond the compound at first light. The whole crew."

"But…but he could be miles away by then."

Rand took a swallow of coffee. "We could ride right past him in the dark, Suzanne. It's only sensible to begin the search in daylight."

"Yes," she said unevenly. "I see what you mean. It's just that…" She stopped herself. Insisting they start the search in the dark only proved that she was as out of her element here as Mack was. But that was what frightened her so. To her knowledge, and she was sure it was accurate, he had never spent one entire night outside by himself. Oh, he had stayed out late in Baltimore—much too late for a boy his age—but the city wasn't strange to him. Montana was.

She thought of the ranch's isolation, of the miles and miles of unpopulated country surrounding them all, and shivered. How would Rand and the men even know in which direction to start looking? The woods, the fields, the mountains, where would they start?

"J.D., you may as well go back to bed for a few hours," Rand said.

J.D. set his mug on the counter. He was nothing if not tactful, and it looked to him as though Rand would like to talk to Suzanne alone.

"Think I'll do that," he said. "See you both later."

Suzanne managed a weak smile. She felt Rand's eyes on her, and her own swung around to meet them. "You should lie down, too," he told her. His gaze dropped to the mug in his hand. Looking at her hurt.

She knew that standing, sitting or lying down, she would get no rest. Rand must know it, too, so his suggestion had to have been motivated by a wish to be alone. Away from her.

She swallowed the lump in her throat and started to leave, but she had to know something first.

"Do you think you'll find him?" she asked tremulously.

He sucked in a long breath. He *knew* they would find him, but in what condition? How was he dressed? Did he have food with him, water? A blanket?

"Yes," he said firmly. "We'll find him."

"Thank you for that," she whispered, and left him alone.

She'd been positive she wouldn't rest when stretching out on her bed in her clothes, but she realized that she had dozed off when someone knocked on her door and she awakened with a start.

Jumping up, she ran to open it. It was Rand.

"We're leaving now. It's just starting to get light."

"But no one had breakfast! I should have—"

"We managed just fine." She looked so forlorn he couldn't stop himself from touching her. It was a simple caress, just a gentle brushing of his fingertips against her cheek, but the second he did it he rued the impulse and drew his hand back. "Try not to worry too much," he said gruffly, and turned on his heel and hastened down the hall.

She leaned against the doorjamb and watched his tall, rugged body vanish into the dining room. She loved him. She would never love anyone so much again. How had all of this happened? Why had it happened?

Tears dribbled down her face as she listened to men's voices without being able to make out their words. Then a door slammed and everything was quiet. They had gone.

She stumbled back to the bed and curled into a ball of pure misery.

It was going to be the longest day of her life.

Rand divided the men into groups of three, except for J.D. and himself. Rand figured that he and J.D. could cover twice the ground of the other men, and do it in half the time, to boot.

Before the groups of men and horses separated, Rand, seated on Jack, gave a little speech. "You might think that Mack deserves a swift kick in the seat of his jeans for running off like this, but I'm damned worried about the boy and so should you be. He's been out for most of the night. We lost the chinook and the temperature got down to freezing again. We all know it was colder than that in the mountains, and if Mack made it that far, he could be suffering from frostbite or hypothermia.

"We're going to have some help. I called Deputy Austin and he's going to bring out anyone he can round up to give us a hand. I want Mack found before tonight. Give it your best shot."

He had already issued instructions on which group would search where, so he didn't repeat himself on that. But he did on the signals. "Again, if you find him and he's all right, fire one round. If you find him and he's *not* okay, fire three. That's it, let's get going."

Rand, J.D. and Freeway headed for Granite Mountain.

Suzanne was stunned by the arrival of a dozen vehicles pulling horse trailers around eight that morning. Men and women piled out of their rigs and began unloading horses. One man separated himself from the crowd and trudged to the bunkhouse. Suzanne hurriedly opened the door.

"Hello," she said, uncertainty written all over her face.

"Hello, ma'am. I'm Deputy Reed Austin. You must be Suzanne, Mack Paxton's sister."

"Yes. What…what is everyone doing out here?"

"These folks volunteered to help find your brother, Suzanne, and if they aren't enough, more will show up."

"But…that's wonderful," she said in amazement. "I really must thank them."

"Go ahead," Reed said. "They'd all like to meet you."

"They would?" More cars were arriving; the yard was beginning to look like a parking lot.

"I'm going to unload my own horse," Reed told her. "Just walk up to anyone you want to talk to, Suzanne. Everyone here is friendly and concerned about both you and your brother."

"Thank you, I will." She hadn't known Rand had asked for additional help in looking for Mack. It made his disappearance more ominous and at the same time increased her hope. She was a bundle of raw nerves, but passing on her gratitude to these good people was a must.

She walked among them, shaking hands, murmuring her thanks, listening to and accepting their upbeat comments. However many times she heard, "We'll find Mack, Suzanne, don't you worry none," though, however much hope these people tried to impart, she noticed a cast of worry in their own eyes that nearly negated their smiles.

A woman rushed up and took Suzanne's hands. She was middle-aged, had bleached blond hair and wore enormous purple earrings. She began talking before Suzanne could even say hello.

"I'm Lily Mae Wheeler. I won't be joining the search party, but I had to drive out here and see you for myself. My, this must be such a strain for you to bear. I heard your brother is only fourteen, and that the two of you were caught out here in the storm. There were others like you, you know. The motels and restaurants in Whitehorn did a thriving business during the blizzard. Oh my, yes, it wasn't all bad. They went on their way once the roads were plowed, of course.

"But you and your brother stayed, and isn't that curious? Of course, I did hear about poor George's accident, and that you've been doing the bookkeeping for the ranch in his absence. If he's not lying in that hospital bed, worried to tears about his job, I'll be eternally surprised. You're much prettier than George Davenport, and how could Rand Harding not notice? Not that Rand is a womanizer, you understand. I've been trying real hard to remember if he's done more than take a woman to a movie, and I can't put him and anyone in the area together. Strange, if you ask me.

"Goodness, you must be in shock over your brother wandering off. Why on earth would he do that? Let me tell you something, Suzanne, this country can be very dangerous. There are people who've been lost for weeks, and there've been some who've died in the mountains. It's no place for a youngster, I can tell you. I would never—"

"Lily Mae!"

Suzanne had been almost hypnotized by the steady stream of words coming out of Lily Mae's mouth. She'd never heard anyone talk so fast or so long without a breath. And the things she was saying! Had she no tact whatsoever?

"Winona," Lily Mae acknowledged with a sniff.

"Hello, Suzanne, I'm Winona Cobb." A round little woman, with gray hair but of an indeterminate age, disengaged Suzanne's hands from Lily Mae's and took them in her own. "Don't you pay one bit of attention to anything Lily Mae said."

"Well, really!" Lily Mae exclaimed, obviously put out. "What did I say that was so terrible?"

"You know what you said, and if you say it again I'm

going to put a hex on you." When Lily Mae only glared at her, Winona let go of Suzanne's hands, closed her eyes and raised her fingertips to her temples.

Suzanne had never met two such peculiar women in her life. Winona was older than Lily Mae, Suzanne felt, but how much older would only be a guess. Under Winona's purple parka Suzanne spotted strange jewelry strung around the woman's neck—silken cords and leather strips attached to smooth polished stones, crystals and feathers. Goodness, she thought, did Winona actually believe she was putting a hex on Lily Mae Wheeler?

Apparently Lily Mae believed it, because she pursed her lips and scurried away like a mouse into its hole. Winona opened her eyes. "Is she gone?"

Suzanne nodded. Winona patted her arm. "Don't look so scared, honey. Lily Mae's got a tongue that just won't quit, but she's harmless enough."

Winona's expression sobered. "That's enough about Lily Mae. The reason I'm here is to tell you something. Give me your hand."

Suzanne didn't know whether to give Winona her hand or to run. Her eyes darted past the rotund little woman. Men and women were mounting their horses, preparing to leave. She spotted Reed, who was doing something to the saddle on his horse, and he beckoned her over.

"Would you excuse me for a moment?" she asked Winona, relieved to have an excuse to get away from her.

Winona smiled. "Of course. But I must tell you what I know. I'll wait here."

Suzanne hurried over to Reed. "That woman…" she began nervously.

"Is psychic," Reed said. "Maybe you don't believe in that sort of thing, but most of the people around here have faith in Winona's visions."

"She told that other woman, Lily Mae, that she would put a hex on her if she didn't shut up."

Reed laughed. "I've never heard of Winona putting a hex on anyone before. She was probably kidding."

"Lily Mae didn't think so. Reed, Winona said she came out here to tell me something. If she tells me something about Mack, should I believe her?"

"I wouldn't discount it, Suzanne." He swung up into the saddle. "I saw you talking to her and could tell you were uncomfortable. Don't be. That's what I called you over here to tell you." He touched the brim of his hat. "We'll be going now."

Tears suddenly sprang into Suzanne's eyes. "I will never be able to thank all of you enough."

"Finding your brother will be all the thanks we need." He rode away to join the others on horseback.

Suzanne waved them off, then turned to see Winona watching her. Was it possible that she was a true psychic? If so, what had she come out here to tell her? Suzanne drew in a long, uneasy breath and walked back to her.

"Reed advised you to listen to me, didn't he?" Winona said.

"Yes, he did."

"Take my hand, Suzanne."

Suzanne laid her hand in Winona's, and was startled when Winona closed her eyes. Winona's eyelids fluttered and her facial muscles went slack. Suzanne had never seen anyone go into a trance. Was she watching one now? Shivers raced up and down Suzanne's spine. Oddly, she no longer felt like running away from this woman. There was a connection between them, something almost spiritual bonding them.

Winona began speaking. "I see a young deer. There's something blue on his back, a bag of some kind. He's darting this way and that. He's very frightened. He's cold, and hungry. The bag on his back is getting heavy, but he dare not shake it loose."

"Mack's blue backpack!" Suzanne exclaimed.

"Hush," Winona murmured. "My vision has broadened, as it did early this morning. There are other deer, many of them, and they have come for the young one. But they are milling, confused and sniffing the air. Two bucks enter a grove of trees." She said no more for several minutes, then she opened her eyes and looked deeply into Suzanne's. "Your brother will be found by two men."

"Today?"

Winona shut her eyes again, and Suzanne held her breath until the stout little woman opened them again.

"It's all very close. I would have to say yes."

"Would...would you like to come in for coffee?" Suzanne asked. She hadn't been aware of it, but even Lily Mae had gone. Other than Winona and herself, there wasn't a person in sight. She didn't want to let Winona go. She might come up with another vision and even pinpoint Mack's location.

Winona patted her hand and released it. "Thank you, but no. There's nothing more I can tell you, Suzanne, and I must go home and feed my pets."

"Yes, of course," Suzanne murmured. Her mind was focused on Winona's vision, and she would like to ask questions about it. How she could be so positive that the young deer represented Mack, for one.

"Come and visit me sometime," Winona said as she began waddling to her car.

"Thank you, but I won't be here very much longer. As soon as they find Mack..." She suddenly ran out of energy, and her voice simply failed her. *If* they found Mack, she reminded herself. She wanted to believe Winona's prediction in the worst way, and maybe some part of herself did believe it, but the pragmatic side of herself, the one that only believed what she saw with her own eyes, remained doubtful.

To her surprise Winona chuckled. "Oh, you'll be here, my

dear. Believe me, you'll be here. Goodbye for now, Suzanne." She hefted herself into her car, started the engine and drove away.

It's your fault, all of it. Rand relentlessly beat himself up as he rode his horse, Jack, around granite boulders and into brushy copses on the mountain. *That ad, that miserable damned ad, started everything, and you put it in that magazine. If Mack dies, or we find him seriously injured, it's your doing.*

In the bunkhouse, cooking like a fiend to keep herself from complete insanity, Suzanne was doing the same thing. *You pushed Mack too far. You know he loves it here, and you knew in your heart that he wouldn't leave without some show of rebellion. Why didn't you wait until morning and tell him the truth, rather than just saying that Rand didn't want us here? Mack adores Rand...and J.D. He looks up to them, and he's never looked up to any other man except Dad. How could you do what you did to your own brother? It's your fault he ran away...your fault...your fault...*

"Rand, over here!"

J.D.'s shout echoed and reverberated off the canyon walls. Rand's heart skipped a beat. "What've you got?"

"A cold, hungry young man!" J.D. yelled.

Rand nudged Jack into a faster walk. "Is he okay?"

Mack himself answered. "I'm okay, Rand."

"Thank you, God," Rand breathed. He took his rifle from its sheath and fired one shot into the air.

The sun was almost down, Suzanne saw with a distraught sensation. She had been on the ranch long enough to know that once it descended behind that one hill of trees, darkness would soon follow.

And they weren't back. No one was. The kitchen was full of food—two whole baked hams, bowls of potato and macaroni salad, an enormous platter of fried chicken, three apple pies, three pumpkin pies, three chocolate pies, two kinds of cookies—and there was no one to eat it.

She felt drained. She had spent her highly strung energy on cooking, merely to keep from going mad, and there was none left in her limp body. The sound of a car on the driveway didn't even cause a reaction, other than a rather disinterested curiosity. Changing windows, she watched the approach of a modest gray sedan.

There were so many vehicles and horse trailers in the yard that the driver was unable to get close to the bunkhouse. Listlessly, Suzanne watched the car finally squeeze into a narrow opening between two pickup trucks. For a few seconds her view was cut off, but then she saw a woman rounding the back of the nearest truck and walking to the building. She was carrying a black leather bag that looked to Suzanne like a medical bag, the kind that doctors carried.

Even that didn't whet Suzanne's curiosity, although she couldn't imagine why a medical person would be dropping in, today of all days. The closer the woman got, the better Suzanne was able to see her. She was attractive in a quiet way, around thirty, Suzanne estimated, and bore a serious expression.

Suzanne let her knock on the door before opening it. Her "Yes?" wasn't the most hospitable thing she'd ever said to a visitor, but her spirits were so low it was all she could manage.

"I'm Dr. Hall, Carey Hall. Are you Suzanne Paxton?"

"Yes, I am."

"Obviously they haven't returned yet. Suzanne, Reed Austin used his cellular phone to call the sheriff's department. They, in turn, called me. Your brother has been found and… Suzanne!"

She had crumpled to the floor in a dead faint.

* * *

"Please, everyone," Dr. Hall said firmly. "I'd like to be alone with my patient."

Mack's tiny bedroom was overflowing, and he was embarrassed to be the center of so much attention. A little pleased, as well, but still embarrassed. Suzanne was sitting on his bed, holding his hand and, he could tell, trying not to cry. Rand and J.D. kept grinning at him. Dr. Hall—Mack wasn't thrilled about a lady doctor—had been waiting to do her job, and even Freeway sat there with a grin on his homely face, obviously very proud of himself. It was his magnificent nose, after all, that had sniffed out Mack's hiding place. He had barked at J.D., calling him to the spot, which had been a very clever thing for a dog to do.

Carey took Suzanne's arm and urged her up from the bed. "I feel certain he's fine, Suzanne, but let's make sure with an examination."

"You'll find me when you're through?" Suzanne asked anxiously.

"Absolutely."

Rand watched as Dr. Hall turned Suzanne over to J.D. Dark emotions swirled within him, guilt, regret, self-incrimination. He owed Suzanne a whopping apology; she would hear it at the first opportunity. She had looked at him, of course, more than once. When they'd gotten back and brought Mack in, she had even hugged him.

But she'd also hugged J.D.

The three of them started downstairs. "Sounds like a party to me," J.D. said. When Rand had seen all the food in the kitchen, he had invited everyone who had participated in the search to come in and eat. No one had refused. They had taken care of their horses, then filed into the bunkhouse.

It did indeed sound like a party, Suzanne had to agree. Laughter, conversation, comments on the day, pride in their good works, it all drifted up the stairs to engulf her. Still a little light-headed, it seemed more than she could face. So many people, so much noise. She would like to sit in some quiet corner and wait for Dr. Hall's diagnosis.

And then give her heartfelt apologies to Rand. She would not attempt to sneak away again. Even if Mack was given a clean bill of health by Dr. Hall, Suzanne swore an oath that she would not leave this ranch until she had talked to Rand alone.

But she could not appear ungrateful to these kind, generous and friendly people, and so she waded into the melee in the dining room and kitchen, smiled, chatted and tried to force food into her mouth despite her rebellious stomach.

After about thirty minutes she saw Dr. Hall on the sidelines, obviously looking for her. "Excuse me," she said to the couple with whom she'd been talking. "I see Dr. Hall. She must be through with her examination of Mack."

"Let us know how he's doing," they called after her.

"I will." Suzanne wound through the crowd to Dr. Hall's side. "How is he?" she asked at once.

"Let's go someplace quiet," Carey said. "I fully understand everyone's euphoria, but this is a madhouse."

Suzanne took her to the office and shut the door. "Please sit down."

They each sat at a desk. Noticing Suzanne's wary expression, Carey rushed to ease her concern. "Physically, he's fine, Suzanne. I saw no sign of frostbite or hypothermia. He's very tired, probably already asleep by now, but I'm sure he'll be his normal self tomorrow."

"I hear a 'but' in your voice, Doctor," Suzanne said quietly.

"Well, he's so…unhappy. Suzanne, I'm a pediatrician and normally work with much younger children. But any physician would sense Mack's state of mind. Do you have any idea of what's bothering him? Why he felt the need to run away?"

"Yes, I know exactly why he did it. I know why he's unhappy and I know what to do about it."

Dr. Hall nodded. "I'm very glad to hear that. Is there anything more you would like me to do?"

"No. Thank you for driving out here." She smiled. "I honestly didn't know that doctors made house calls in Montana."

Dr. Hall smiled and got to her feet. "Not all of them do."

Suzanne rose. "Please have something to eat before you go."

"Thank you, I will." On her way out, Carey shut the door.

Alone in the blessed silence, Suzanne sat down again. She rubbed her throbbing temples with her fingertips, sent one more prayer of thanks heavenward for Mack's safe return and then closed her eyes. It was over, or most of it, at least. Until she talked to Rand, it wouldn't be completely over.

As though on cue, the door opened and Rand stood there. "Is it all right if I come in?"

Suzanne slowly got up. "Please do. I've something to say…"

"So do I." He closed the door.

They stood there looking at each other, neither of them comfortable, each of them determined to do what was right.

"So, who goes first?" Rand finally said.

"It doesn't matter. You can be first, if you want."

"Ladies first."

"No, really, you…" She lost her voice. Her knuckles rose to press against her mouth. She hadn't known she would get so emotional over an apology.

Rand decided that since she was having trouble saying her piece, he would say his. He opened his mouth, and to his dying day he would swear that what he'd intended saying was "I'm sorry for everything." But what he heard from his very own lips was "Suz, I love you so damned much, and you're breaking my heart."

She gasped, she paled, she trembled, and then she got hold

of herself and threw herself at him with such force that Rand nearly lost his balance. Teetering, he managed to put his arms around her and keep them both on their feet at the same time.

He let her cry her eyes out against his chest. He held her, blinked at the tears in his own eyes and finally thought of something to say besides, "I love you."

"I'm such a fool," he whispered with his lips in her hair.

"You?" She tilted her head to see his face. "I'm the fool, not you. Oh, Rand, will you ever be able to forgive me?"

"I have to ask you the same thing. Suz, I caused so much trouble with that stupid damned ad."

"It was no worse than the way I judged you for it. So neither of us is perfect. Does that mean we shouldn't be happy?"

He tenderly brushed strands of hair from her tearstained cheek. "Are you saying you're happy because I'm in love with you?"

"I'm happy because we love each other. I was going to apologize and then ask you if Mack could stay on the ranch. This is so much better."

"I would have said yes, you know."

"I suspected that. I'd hoped for that. I've made a lot of mistakes with Mack. Trying to force him away from here was the worst." Sobbing again, she slid her arms up around his neck and draped herself all over him. He felt so good, and she loved him so much that she couldn't seem to get close enough.

"Hey," Rand said gently, although he was becoming uncomfortably aroused from this emotional embrace. "Mack and I are friends. We'll make it, Suz, the three of us will make it."

She was beyond holding anything back. He loved her, she loved him and she sincerely believed there was only one logical conclusion to their relationship. Sniffling, she leaned back against his arms and again looked into his eyes.

"Rand Harding, will you marry me?"

He didn't immediately answer, and her heart nearly stopped beating. But then she watched a slow, wonderful, loving smile develop on his lips, and he nodded his head. "Yes, Suzanne Paxton, I will marry you."

Epilogue

Dear Kip,

I been meaning to write you a letter since I got here, but there's always something going on. To tell you the truth, I don't know where to begin.

Okay, I'll start with Suzanne. She and Rand Harding are getting married! Told you answering Rand's ad would work. He's not a lonesome cowboy anymore, believe me.

Suzanne's doing the bookkeeping for the ranch. The old guy who did it before had an accident. Don't know all the details, but after he got out of the hospital he rented a room in town so he could take some kind of special treatments. Anyhow, he met a rich widow lady and they're moving to Tucson, Arizona. Old George did pretty good for himself. Suzanne did the cooking, too, for a while, but the cook came back to work and now she only works in the office.

I got some real good friends, Kip. J. D. Cade is one of them. He's like a supercowboy, and he's teaching me how to ride and rope. I would've been glad if Suzanne and J.D. had liked each other, almost as glad that Suzanne and Rand did, but that didn't pan out. J.D. seems pretty steamed up over a lady doctor, Dr. Carey Hall. They met when she came out to the ranch to check someone over who'd done something stupid and gotten everyone all worried and upset about him. Don't know if J.D. and the doc have done any dating, but I know he likes her.

Guess what? There's some really eerie things happening on this ranch, and no one knows who's causing them. Some of the guys think the ranch is haunted, but I laugh at them when they say that. Rand doesn't laugh when they quit their jobs, though. I'm sort of glad he doesn't have a full crew, though, because he pays me to work after school and on weekends.

By the way, I don't hate school here. Coach let me join the track team, and guess what? I'm the fastest runner on the team. You probably won't believe that, but I swear it's the truth.

Kip, you've never seen anyplace like Montana. It's so beautiful you can hardly believe your eyes. At least it is around here. Might be ugly as a toad down the road a ways, but right here it's like you see in the movies. We got mountains, we got prairies, we got rivers and creeks and ponds, and Whitehorn, the nearest town, isn't so bad, either. That's where I go to school. Suzanne would drive me if I wanted her to, but I prefer taking the bus. Out here it's cool to ride the bus. (You probably won't believe that, either.)

Guess what? Rand talks to me. I mean he talks to me like I'm his age, or something. He told me why he put the ad in that magazine, and I know he won't care if I tell you. He had a girlfriend a long time ago and she dumped him. But he was lonely, see, and I know how that feels. He told me he wanted to meet a nice woman, but he didn't want to romance her. He thought that ad would get him a wife without any soppy romance.

But you know something? Him and Suzanne are so soppy around each other I have to leave the room. It makes Rand laugh every time it happens, and he told me that someday I'll be just as soppy over a girl. Fat chance. All I want to do is ride the range, like they do in the movies.

He told me something else, too. He's been saving his money for a long time, and when he gets enough saved up, he's going to buy his own ranch. He said it wasn't just going to be his ranch, it was going to be Suzanne's and mine, too. Won't that be something?

Well, guess that's all the news on this end. Write and tell me what's going on in Baltimore. (As if I care.) So long for now, pardner. (That's how they say goodbye around here.) Your friend,
Mack Paxton

Mack read his letter over and declared it "excellent." After stuffing it into an envelope with Kip's name and address on it, he put a stamp on the envelope, stuck it in his shirt pocket and left the bunkhouse. Whistling as he walked, he brought the letter down to the mailbox.

If there was another kid as happy as he was, he sure would like to meet him.

With a sudden burst of joyous energy, he took off running and ran all the way back to the bunkhouse without even breaking a sweat.

He was, after all, the fastest runner on the high school track team.

Proudly he walked into the bunkhouse to see what Handy was cooking up for supper.

Handy, too, had become a friend. Life was great.

Just great.

* * * * *

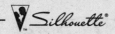

Silhouette®

SPECIAL EDITION

FROM *USA TODAY* BESTSELLING AUTHOR
CHRISTINE RIMMER

BRAVO FAMILY TIES

A BRIDE FOR
JERICHO BRAVO

Marnie Jones had long ago buried her wild-child
impulses and opted to be "safe," romantically
speaking. But one look at born rebel Jericho Bravo
and she began to wonder if her thrill-seeking side
was about to be revived. Because if ever there was
a man worth taking a chance on, there he was,
right within her grasp....

*Available in March
wherever books are sold.*

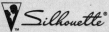

HARLEQUIN
Ambassadors

Want to share your passion for reading Harlequin® Books?

Become a Harlequin Ambassador!

Harlequin Ambassadors are a group
of passionate and well-connected readers
who are willing to share their joy of reading
Harlequin® books with family and friends.

You'll be sent all the tools you need to spark
great conversation, including free books!

All we ask is that you share the romance
with your friends and family!

You'll also be invited to have a say in
new book ideas and exchange opinions
with women just like you!

To see if you qualify* to be
a Harlequin Ambassador, please visit
www.HarlequinAmbassadors.com.

*Please note that not everyone who applies to be a Harlequin Ambassador will
qualify. For more information please visit www.HarlequinAmbassadors.com.

Thank you for your participation.

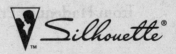